THUNDERING HOOVES

Spirit of the West

by Steven W. Krull

ISBN 13:979-8-9860766-5-2

Cover design by: Steven W. Krull
Printed in the United States of America

DISCLAIMERS

THUNDERING HOOVES is a work of fiction. Names, characters, business, events and incidents in the storyline are the products of the author's imagination. Any resemblance to actual persons, living or dead, or actual events is purely coincidental.

The account surrounding the horses themselves however, is a matter of historical record. And although the names of the horses and some of the stories about them have been fictionalized, the places and political decisions regarding them are well documented and have been loosely adhered to in the storyline. Supporting documentation can be found in the Epilogue and Acknowledgments sections of this publication.

Generative Artificial Intelligence (Generative AI) was not used in the writing of this work, or in the photography of the horses.

CONTENTS

THUNDERING HOOVES   1
DISCLAIMERS   3
CONTENTS   4
INTRODUCTION   5
ABOUT THE COVER   8
Chapter One   10
Chapter Two   20
Chapter Three   32
Chapter Four   47
Chapter Five   62
Chapter Six   75
Chapter Seven   92
Chapter Eight   102
Chapter Nine   116
Chapter Ten   124
Chapter Eleven   139
Chapter Twelve   157
Chapter Thirteen   175
Chapter Fourteen   200
EPILOGUE   213
ACKNOWLEDGMENTS   216
ABOUT THE AUTHOR   217
BOOKS BY THIS AUTHOR   218

INTRODUCTION

For thousands of years, the vast expanse of western Colorado has remained virtually unchanged, wild and untouched. Upon discovering North America, Europeans arrived in the New world with their horses and pack burros and pushed westward. A few of those animals escaped or were abandoned to fend for themselves, and a number of them found their way to the desolate countryside of Colorado's western slopes where they roamed free for centuries. The wild horses of Spanish origin were called mestengo or the English version mustang, meaning, having no master. The mustangs enjoyed complete freedom on the landscape until cattlemen and sheepherders arrived to compete with them for the land.

Horses first arrived in North America with early explorers in the 1500s. A few of these managed to escape and began to form wild herds on the outskirts of civilization. As European settlers pushed west, so did the horse population. By the late 1800s, wild horses now known as mustangs roamed the western landscape in great thundering herds. Native Americans prized these majestic animals and captured many for their own use. The mustang became an iconic symbol of the wild west but as time passed, reverence for the animal began to fade. According to *Americas Mustang* on the web, in the early 1900s the pet food industry eyed wild horses as a cheap source of protein for inclusion in their products. That is where real trouble began for the horses as they were mercilessly rounded up and slaughtered for their meat byproducts. The cruel methods of that industry also resulted in the first efforts at protecting the iconic animals, and in 1859 the *Wild Horse Annie Act* was the first law passed to provide for humane treatment for the horses with no home.

Eventually the wild equids found themselves in direct competition with cattle for resources on federal lands, and began to be regarded as a nuisance by the ranchers. As more and more cattle were turned loose on public land, scarce grazing resources became insufficient to support both wild horses and livestock. Ranchers turned to the government for an answer to the problem, and in 1971 the *Wild Free-Roaming Horses and Burros Act* was signed into law to allow for helicopter roundups to limit their numbers. They were then confined in government run corrals to make the horses available for adoption. It is illegal to purchase the horses for slaughter, but there is little oversight to assure that it does not happen. The horses are often shipped to other countries where there are no longs against their slaughter.

Rapid expansion into the American west during the 20th century resulted in frequent mistreatment of wild horses until the *Wild Free-Roaming Horses and Burros Act* was signed into law in 1971, preventing the harassment or killing of the iconic symbols of the Old West. The new law allowed for the confining of mustangs in herd management areas and some of Colorado's western slope horses were eventually confined in the Sand Wash Basin management area. In 1982, the Bureau of Land Management officially set aside the Sand Wash Herd Management Area for the mustangs.

Ranchers in the 2020's demand even more public land for grazing their livestock, and helicopter roundups are the preferred method for removal of the mustangs by the government. The government has little regard for the safety of the animals in the roundups, and many are injured or run to death in each action. Many young horses are left orphaned with little chance of survival on the harsh high desert environment, that is if they manage to survive the cruel roundups.

The previous novel in this series, *Spirit of the Wolf* left off with main characters Caleb and Lacy working to protect Yellowstone National Park's wolf population. In this installment, Caleb gets a tip about the plight of the wild horses and considers an offer to come and write a story on them. Also, voters in Colorado consider a ballot measure that requires Colorado Parks and Wildlife to begin rebuilding the extinct Colorado wolf population. Caleb becomes interested in being involved in that effort, while his friend Lacey wants to expand her sports clothing line into the larger Denver fashion market.

The two consider the move to Colorado, and Caleb starts his work with wild horses and eventually the new wolf pack. This historical fiction novel, loosely based on the life of the famous Sand Wash Basin stallion Picasso, documents the mistreatment of mustangs while also highlighting problems Colorado's wolves will face as their range expands across the state. Throughout the story, the main characters will face danger and many harrowing encounters as they continue the exciting adventures of the previous book, *Spirit of the Wolf.*

Astro and Ukraine

ABOUT THE COVER

The cover of this book was a project three years in the making. I first became interested in the mustangs of the Sand Wash Basin when reports of the massive 2021 helicopter gather hit the Denver news outlets. Many were overjoyed when it was reported that the Colorado governor had been able to convince the BLM to scale back their plans, but unfortunately I later discovered that only 100 additional animals of the 784 to be removed were allowed to remain. A total of 684 were taken, leaving only a fraction of the original herd. I was still writing *Spirit of the Wolf* at the time, but vowed to use my main characters to write a sequel including the wild horses.

A buddy of mine and I had gone to Rocky Mountain National Park to photograph the elk rut in 2022, and were going to cross over to the west side on our last day to visit the Sand Wash Basin. However a late autumn snowstorm hit Trail Ridge Road, so we were forced to abandon our plans. In 2023 we went to Yellowstone National Park, and were going to venture into the Sand Wash on our way back through Colorado. However when we arrived, the area was so vast, and the dirt road so intimidating, that we just sat at the entrance contemplating the risk of a pass through the rugged terrain, and eventually decided against a drive to the interior.

This year I finally acquired a Jeep with tires rugged enough to handle the rocks and wash outs. In late summer I finally made the trip and was fortunate to photograph a pair of wild horses on my first foray into the park. I was happy with the pictures I was able to capture the first day, but was eager to explore more of the area in hopes of a larger cache of images from which to choose the final cover design.

Thunderstorms rumbled into the area that night threatening my plans for the next day, but the morning sun quickly dried the roads so I could continue. At the north end of the management area, I came across a number of bands making their way to a watering hole, eventually capturing the image of the two white mustangs that I chose for the cover.

The semi translucent rendition of the horse and blonde cowgirl represent a poignant moment from a scene at the Sand Wash Basin during a visit by Caleb and Angie And the black helicopter of course depicts the terrifying machines used by the BLM to brutally herd the mustangs into the holding pens.

All of the horse pictures used in this book are photographs captured by myself, of actual mustangs living in the Sand Wash Basin at the time of my visit.

Evening Star and Jude Jophiel

Chapter One

It was a cold and starry late spring night in the Colorado Sand Wash Basin, and Winter Storm had been growing inside his mother Morning Mist for nearly a year. The time for his birth was at hand, and Morning Mist had already picked out a quiet and comfortable place to bring him into the world. Morning Mist laid down in the soft dirt, and a few minutes later Winter Storm gazed into his mother's eyes for the first time. A couple hours later he struggled to his feet, and was soon ready to join the rest of the herd.

Winter Storm stared in wonder at the sky as he followed his mother. The heavenly bodies dotting the expanse overhead shown brightly upon his arid high elevation Colorado range. The galaxy viewed from this pristine environment appeared as a solid splash of illuminated milk, lighting the way for mother and son. Nickering sounds coming from the herd grew louder as the two approached. Winter Storm knew nothing about what he was about to experience, but new sounds and scents filled him with excitement anyway. In his eagerness to meet his new friends, the young horse began to jump and buck a little as he stretched his untested legs.

Morning Mist and Winter Storm were immediately welcomed into the herd by the other mares and his father Lightning Bolt, the herd's patriarch. Soon the faint light of dawn began to glow behind the rugged desert terrain to the east, alerting the herd to arise and begin feeding on spring foliage. Winter Storm instinctively searched for his mother's milk. He didn't know it, but he would need to quickly grow strong and swift. The life of a mustang on the western range is not an easy one, and all the more difficult for a diminutive foal.

As the first rays of sunshine illuminated his world, Winter Storm discovered he wasn't the only youngster in the band. He soon met Dusky, another foal born that season just a few days ahead of himself. He and Dusky quickly made friends and spent many hours each day, romping and bucking on the vast open desert. However adventurous as they were, the two never strayed far from their parents. Even though wolves and mountain lions are scarce in the desert landscape of western Colorado, coyotes are plentiful and sure to be on the hunt. To an adult horse a coyote is nothing to be concerned with but to a nearly helpless foal, the little canines are a serious threat.

Winter Storm's first weeks on the range were uneventful. Dirt roads soggy with snow melt are difficult to negotiate for the wheels of human visitors to the Sand Wash Basin, and welcome spring rains had produced plenty of nutritious green grass. For the time being, the desert was mustang paradise.

The herd meandered slowly toward Coffeepot Springs on the north end of the reserve, enjoying succulent spring grasses along the way. Winter Storm led his family of mares, foals and yearlings to the shores of the spring, where they would rest and graze until forced to move on.

Far north of the Colorado Sand Wash Basin, Caleb was enjoying a beautiful spring morning in Bozeman, Montana. Sunlight was streaming through the windows and warming his shoulders as he took his first sip of coffee. He soon heard the familiar sound of a second cup being poured, and knew that Lacey would soon be joining him on the loveseat. He enjoyed watching the back lit form of her perfect body as sunlight illuminated her night gown as she walked between him and the big window. For a moment his thoughts drifted back to their beginning in the Bay Area of California, where he had helped her get started as a model in the fashion industry. More than once they had awakened to the California sunshine on a similar loveseat in his photography studio, after a long night of shooting her pictures.

"Good morning hon," she said.

Caleb replied, "It is a pretty one isn't it!"

She sat down beside him and the two watched as the city slowly came to life. The owner of the coffee shop across the street a few doors down was out in front sweeping the sidewalk in preparation for the onslaught of businessmen and women stopping by for their morning jolt of caffeine.

"What do you think, should we go over and grab some breakfast at the coffee shop?" Caleb asked.

"I would love to but my new girl called in sick. I'm going to have to go in and run the store."

After becoming a successful runway model in the fashion industry, Lacey had opened a line of sportswear that she marketed online. In addition to her thriving online business, she operated a small storefront in downtown Bozeman to showcase her newest designs.

She asked, "What are you up to today?"

"I don't know, I might go down to Yellowstone to shoot some pictures. I heard the last few days there has been a grizzly bear hanging around right after sunrise in the Lamar Valley."

"Sounds like more fun than I'm going to have."

Lacey took the last swallow of her morning coffee and went back into the bedroom to dress for a day at work.

Caleb poured himself another cup of coffee, and walked over to power up the computer. He sat down with the fresh cup to wait for Lacey to finish getting dressed. His gear was in the closet and he didn't want to get in her way while she was preparing for work.

She soon stepped back into the living room and Caleb met her at the door. After a quick embrace, the two bade each other goodbye and Caleb closed the door behind her. Before he could gather his thoughts, he heard the familiar plink of a text message coming in. It was his friend Angie saying good morning. Angie was the first person Caleb had gotten to know upon moving to Bozeman a few years before, while Lacey was off to London taking the fashion world by storm.

Angie previously worked at a local microbrewery that Caleb had visited soon after his arrival in town. Caleb had moved to the mountains to be closer to the wildlife he wanted to photograph and as fate would have it, Angie was the leader of the local wildlife advocacy association. The two became close, forming a strong bond as they worked tirelessly to save the wolf population from slaughter as their endangered status wavered from one political administration to the next. Eventually though, Angie received an offer from friends in Denver to apprentice as a real estate agent in the exploding Colorado home sales market. However the two had stayed in touch by text message over the years, infrequently catching up on each other's progress.

"It's been awhile!" Caleb texted.

"I know, time is just flying!"

"How's the real estate business?"

"It's steady, enough sales to make a living anyway! How are the wolves holding up under the new administration?"

"Well it didn't take the Republicans long to start grumbling about getting the wolves off the endangered list, but so far there hasn't been any serious legal effort to actually do it," answered Caleb.

"That's good, you know we are having our own wildlife problems here in Colorado. We have herd of wild mustangs living out on the western slopes on government land, and the feds are itching to eradicate of most of them. It's causing a real outrage among horse lovers who know that they will be placed in pens indefinitely while awaiting adoption. We also know that some of them will eventually be sold to slaughter by those who adopt them. You should come down and do a story about them! Maybe you could even write a book like you did with *Spirit of the Wolf*."

"Maybe I will! That sounds like a good project for summer, during the tourist season in Yellowstone."

"Right, Memorial weekend is only a couple weeks away now," she added.

"So what have you been up to besides selling houses?"

"Not much, but I've been staying in touch with the wildlife groups in my spare time. Denver is so big, and the traffic is so bad it's hard logistically to get people together for a physical meeting."

"You don't have any wolves in Colorado do you?"

"No, but we have mountain lions and bears. There are plenty of people who want to kill them off too."

"Well I need to run," said Angie. "I have a 9:00 showing to get ready for."

"Okay, well it was great hearing from you!"

"Yeah, let me know if you are going to come down and see the horses. I might be able to get away for a day or two!"

"I'll do that," answered Caleb.

He pulled his camera bag out of the closet and headed out the door. He briefly considered breakfast at the cafe, but was in a hurry to get on the road. Gardiner was only a little more than an hour away, and just outside the Yellowstone Park entrance. There was also a rustic cafe in Gardiner where he liked to stop for breakfast before entering the park. He wondered if his favorite server Michelle would be there. He had also met Michelle when he first arrived in Montana years before. At the time she was working at the cafe to save up money for college. He wondered if she had graduated yet, and hoped she might be home for the summer.

Michelle recognized him instantly as he came through the door, and rushed to greet him with a hug.

"Caleb, how are you?"

"I'm good, how are you?"

"Great, I got my masters this year so I guess I'm going to be a working person from now on!"

"That's great news! What was your major again?"

"Wildlife biology, I want to work with the animals in the park."

"That's awesome Michelle! Do you have a job lined up?"

"Nothing for sure yet but I've been talking to the park service, and they are sure they can find a spot for me. For now I'm just working here. Gotta eat you know!"

"That is a fact!"

"Speaking of eating, what are you going to have today?" Michelle asked.

"I think I'll just have a short stack of pancakes and a cup of coffee."

"You just take your coffee black right?"

Caleb answered, "You have a good memory!"

"Coming right up."

The cafe wasn't busy, so Michelle sat down when she brought out his order.

Michelle asked, "What are you up to on this beautiful morning?"

"Oh, not much. I'm just heading down to the park to get some pictures for my weekly article in the Gazette. I'm hoping to see this years crop of baby animals out enjoying the sunshine. I'd especially like to see some grizzly cubs."

Michelle exclaimed, "Cool, I heard Scruffy and her two cubs were hanging around Tower Junction lately."

"I heard that too and I'm hoping to see them yet this morning. If not, I might hike in a ways to see if I can spot the Lamar Pack. They are supposed to have some new pups."

"Yup, I heard they've been around too."

Caleb finished his breakfast and drove to the park entrance where he flashed his season pass.

Caleb asked the ranger, "Any wildlife news for me this morning?"

"There have been bear and wolf sightings in the mornings east of Tower Junction."

"That's what I heard too. You all have a great day!" Caleb told the rangers.

"You too sir, stay safe!"

"I will, thanks."

Tower Junction is another half hour from the entrance at Gardiner, so he settled in for a long drive over the curvy mountain approach to the Lamar Valley. By the time he drove into the first clearings of the valley, the sun was already higher in the sky than he had planned. As expected, it wasn't long before he saw the first gathering of bison down by the river. There were a few tourists parked along the side of the road, but Caleb wasn't interested in bison. They were always there, and if he needed bison pictures for his story he could capture those images any time he wanted.

He soon spotted a bunch of cars and photographers with big white lenses about a half mile ahead. He knew that meant there were likely bears or wolves somewhere nearby. A parking place at the front of the line would be unlikely, so he looked for the nearest safe pullout that wouldn't get him in trouble with the rangers. He grabbed his pack and his carbon fiber tripod, and began the quarter mile hike down to the action. As he neared the front of the line, he asked a couple of other photographers about the reason for all the excitement.

Caleb was lugging his 400 millimeter telephoto lens at the time, his preferred glass for long distance shooting. He also packed his 1.4 and 2x teleconverters if he needed the extra reach. He found an empty spot as he neared the scene and set up his tripod. As he peered through the powerful lens, Scruff just happened to look his way. The glare of a grizzly bear through a long lens is unnerving, but Caleb was used to that optical effect by this time in his long career.

After getting a good capture of mama bear, he turned his attention to the cubs. They were sound asleep, using mother bear as a pillow to shield them from the hard ground. He knew if he waited long enough the little ones would begin to stir. After about a half an hour of waiting and fiddling with camera settings, mama bear stood up and the little ones burst into action. Much to his surprise, Scruff led her young ones down to the river for another drink. Caleb quickly packed up his tripod with the camera still attached, and moved to a high knoll where he could get a better view.

He watched and snapped pictures while the young ones frolicked in the water. Suddenly the big female stood on her hind legs and sniffed the southerly breeze. Caleb heard her grunt as she quickly herded her cubs across the stream. He assumed she had caught wind of another grizzly and wanted nothing to do with an encounter with a cranky boar. She paid no attention to the crowd of people lining the road, and passed right through them to the open range on the north side. She was well aware that a boar would not approach the line of photographers, and she and her cubs would find safety behind them. Before they would stop for the night, she and her offspring would put miles between her and the threat that a male bear posed to her youngsters.

She and her little ones disappeared into the high country to the north, and Caleb packed up his gear and walked back to the truck. He could see wolves along the tree line to the south, but they were far too distant for compelling images. It was too early to quit for the day, so he got in his truck and drove east toward Cooke City. It was a long stretch along the Lamar River and he hoped to see more wildlife drama to add to his images that day.

The drive was fruitful and soon he had enough pictures for his weekly column in the Gazette. Also he wanted to be back in time to greet Lacey after a long day at her sportswear boutique.

As Lacey came through the door, Caleb asked "How was your day?"

"It was okay, a little slow but not too bad."

"It should pick up pretty soon when the tourists return," Caleb replied.

"I hope so. I hope I'm not being limited too much by the small Montana market. Have you ever wondered if maybe we should consider leaving this place someday?"

Caleb asked, "What do you have in mind?"

"Denver is a much bigger market and the winters aren't nearly as bad. The ski industry would keep my sales up year round there."

"Funny you should mention that. Angie texted me this morning and thinks I should come down to Colorado to do a story on the wild horses. Of course the horses are a few hours from Denver, but we could easily drive over for a look around."

"She's a real estate agent now isn't she?"

"Yup, and I guess she's doing pretty well too."

"Perhaps you should make the trip this summer, and maybe run over to Denver to see what she might be able to offer us."

"Yeah, that sounds like a good idea, I'll look into it."

After a few moments of silence Caleb asked, "Did you eat today?"

"No, I got busy and kind of blew off lunch. All I had all day was a couple of snacks."

"Want to hit the Alpine Tap for a burger or something?"

Lacey responded, "That sounds really good!"

"It's pretty nice out. Maybe should we just walk up there."

"Sure!" Lacey answered.

The Alpine Tap microbrewery was only a few blocks from their apartment, and it was a beautiful calm spring afternoon for a walk in Bozeman.

Caleb and Lacey walked along in silence, each lost in their own thoughts. Lacey with her glamorous modeling background, was daydreaming about a more cosmopolitan life in Denver. Meanwhile Caleb pondered adding wild horses to his wildlife photography repertoire.

Soon they were at the Tap and Joanie was there to greet them. She had just returned from college and was already working to save up money for her senior year. Joanie was a slender and pretty young woman with long brown hair and an outgoing personality, perfect for her position as bartender at the restaurant.

Joanie saw them at the door and exclaimed, "How are you guys? Come on in!"

Lacey answered, "We're doing well, how was your school year?"

"Doing all right I guess. School was great, but I'm glad to be done with the semester and free for the summer. What can I get you today?"

"I think we'll each have a burger," responded Lacey.

"It will be about 20 minutes for your orders."

"Have you ever been to Denver?" Caleb asked Lacey.

"No, have you?"

"No, but I once had a layover in the airport on my way back from the Gulf. It looked like a beautiful place from the air."

"Is the city itself very mountainous?" Lacey asked.

"Not really, it appears to be mostly flat until you get to the foothills anyway. The high mountains aren't too far west of the city and they look pretty rugged, much like Montana. They say the climate there is relatively mild, not too hot in the summer because of the elevation, and not too cold in the winter due to the Chinooks."

"What are Chinooks?"

"They say that the air warms as it cascades down from mountains. I guess it gets cold sometimes but when the wind changes and the warm breeze blows back in, you could have a 60 degree day in the middle of January."

"That sounds perfect!"

Soon Joanie was back with their orders saying, "Here you go, do you need any ketchup or extra seasonings?"

Caleb asked, "Could I get some steak sauce?"

"No problem. Have you gotten any good pictures lately?"

"I was just at the park today, and I got some great shots of Scruff and her two cubs."

"I need to get down there and see her," responded Joanie.

"She's been hanging around Crystal Creek at the junction with the Lamar River. Today she crossed the highway and went up toward Slough Creek. I think she must have smelled a male bear, because she stood up and looked toward the south before quickly herding her cubs across the road past the photographers in a pretty big hurry. Hopefully she'll come back down to the Lamar, otherwise you might have to go up to the campground road to find them. The photographers will tell you where she is when you get there."

"Cool, although I don't have a day off for a while now."

Caleb and Lacey drifted off into their own thoughts about faraway Colorado as they ate in silence. Lacey dreamed of new fashions she might offer, while Caleb wondered what life would be like without easy access to Yellowstone. He also wondered what it would be like to photograph wild horses. He had never seen a mustang in the wild and was intrigued by the prospect.

Chapter Two

It was Friday before the big Memorial Weekend rush of tourists into Yellowstone Park. Caleb put the finishing touches on his weekly wildlife article for the Gazette, and hit the transmit button. Lacey had already gone to work and he didn't have anything big planned for the rest of the day, other than avoiding the holiday crowd in the park.

With no other big ideas in mind, Caleb succumbed to the inevitable morning hunger pangs. He grabbed his phone and walked across the street for a quick breakfast. He was happy to see Brooke working behind the counter as he made his way to the order desk. Brooke was a bubbly and energetic young brunette from the high school, filling in for the summer to save for college. Had he seen Colin on duty today, he probably would have turned back around and left. Brooke was always quick to take his order, and generally appreciative of her customers. Colin was always busy on his phone and seemed annoyed whenever he had to look up from his screen.

"Hi Caleb, black coffee as usual?" Brooke asked.

"That sounds good, and how about one of your big cinnamon rolls?"

"You got it, and would you like it heated up a little?"

"A few seconds would be nice."

Caleb left Brooke a nice tip as she poured out a cup of steaming hot dark roast and handed it to him. He took the cup and sat down at his favorite table in the front corner by the window. The coffee shop had Wi-Fi, and Caleb enjoyed sipping his morning brew while checking his stock photo accounts along with the day's news. Brooke soon brought over his pastry and sat down with him, since he was her first customer of the day.

She asked, "So what are you up to today?"

"Oh, I don't know yet. I was concentrating on getting my article published and haven't really thought about the rest of the day. I know one thing for sure, I don't want to get caught in the holiday traffic in the park!"

"Yeah, summers are such a mess. But at least I make good tips!"

Caleb smiled and said, "I hope you make a fortune this summer!"

She just smiled and said, "Thanks."

Another customer came in and Brooke stood up to greet them. Caleb sipped his coffee and stared out the window. His mind once again drifted off to Colorado as he tried to imagine wild horses running free in the high mountain desert. He wondered, "*Would it would be possible to camp out among them, or would they flee at the first sign of a human?*" He also thought of Angie as his thoughts drifted back to their camping trip in Yellowstone years ago, when she first told him of her opportunity in Denver. At that very moment he decided he would make the trip to Colorado and see the mustangs for himself.

He wondered if Angie would be able to join him on the high plains of western Colorado, and sent her a text, "Hey Angie, how are you today? You won't believe this! Right out of the blue Lacey asked me if we might consider leaving Bozeman and moving out to Denver. I told her about the horses and she thinks I should make the trip, maybe even hop over to the city and check out the prospects for buying a house in Colorado."

There was no immediate answer, and after a few minutes Caleb said goodbye to Brooke and walked outside. It occurred to him that if he was going on a road trip, it might be a good idea to get his truck serviced. He had nothing else pressing to do, and It was only a few blocks to the nearest quick lube garage. He checked his truck in and paid for the full lube before walking down the hall into the lobby. At that moment he heard the plink of a text message arriving on this phone. A quick glance at the screen revealed a message from Angie.

"Sorry I didn't get right back to you Caleb! I was out on I25 and didn't want to take my eyes off the road."

"No, I don't blame you. Actually I can't even imagine driving in that mess."

"So you're going to come and visit Colorado!"

"Yeah, I want to do the story on the horses like you said, and I also want to come and check out Denver as a possibility for relocating. I can't imagine living in a big city like that again though. When I left California, I swore I'd never live in the city again."

Angie answered, "Well, the Denver area covers a lot of territory. You don't have to actually live right in the city to have access to the metro area. In fact you could live anywhere along the Front Range and still have access to all Denver has to offer. My house is out in the southeast suburbs near a little horse town called Franktown. It's a small town out in the country, but I can be in the city in about a half hour."

"That sounds like my kind of place," mused Caleb.

"I like it, but it's growing really fast. In just the few years that I've been here, there are subdivisions shooting up all around. The traffic is getting bad too, however there is still some nice open space between here and Colorado Springs. I think you might like it out here in ranch country near where I live."

Caleb asked, "So do you think you would be able to meet me at the Sand Wash to spend a few days with the horses?"

"I do have some time off. Would the middle of June work with your plans?"

"I think I can arrange a trip in June. Why don't you figure out exactly when you can get off work, and I'll make my plans around your schedule."

"Okay, I'll check with the office today and see what I can work out."

"Cool, I'm looking forward to hearing what you find out."

The minutes had flown by talking to Angie, and Caleb was surprised to hear his name called so soon. The work on his truck was already done, and he walked to the counter to pay the bill.

"Well sir, your truck is in good shape. We didn't find any issues and you are good to go!"

"Awesome, that's good news. I'm going to be making a road trip to Colorado next month, so it's good to know she's ready for the miles."

Caleb had nothing else to do, so he drove over to Lacey's sportswear boutique to tell her the news.

"Hey Caleb, what brings you in here today?" Lacey asked.

"Oh, I don't know. I just got done getting my oil changed and I don't have anything else planned yet. I texted Angie and she said she'd be happy to show us around the Denver area!"

"That's awesome Caleb, do you really think we can pull it off?"

"Well I don't know. I think I'll run over to Denver after I get done with the horse research, and check around a little bit if that's okay with you."

"That sounds great Caleb! I wish I could go with you but until I get some people hired to run this place, it looks like I'm stuck here."

"Okay, well I guess I'll get the trip set up then."

It was the middle of the day by that time, and Caleb wondered what to do with the rest of his day. He knew it was too late for a long hike, but Sypes Canyon was only a couple miles north of Bozeman and was known for great views and wildlife. He thought a nice hike would be a great way to clear his mind for the major life change ahead. He pulled into the trailhead parking and found a good spot not too far from the trail. He threw on his camera backpack with all the equipment he might find useful. He had filters, a long lens, a wide angle for the grand vistas and of course the trusty digital camera that he had acquired a couple seasons before. He had upgraded his equipment not too long after that fateful winter in which Luna the alpha she wolf and her mate were killed just outside Yellowstone. Ironically, the death of the wolves is what inspired him to write the book *Spirit of the Wolf*, the royalties from which now sustained his enviable outdoor lifestyle.

Finally he grabbed his sunglasses and trekking pole, and began the long hike to the 8,000 foot high turnaround point. About a mile in on the section next to Sypes Creek, Caleb thought he spotted a large black animal slowly traveling along the edge of the water. He carefully picked his footsteps as he made his way out of the trees and down toward the creek, all the while watching for the animal that he was hoping to photograph.

Finally there it was, a black bear wading out into the stream for a cool swim and a drink. Caleb quietly raised his camera and selected a focus point that would pinpoint the bear's eye while also taking in the view of the stream to the south. Caleb was still a good fifty yards from the massive beast, a reasonably safe distance for photography. He didn't want to startle the bear so he made sure to make just enough noise to alert the animal to his presence, but not enough to cause it to flee.

The bear heard the minor disturbance and looked Caleb's direction. He hit the focus button, making sure the bear's eye was sharp as he snapped the picture. The great beast heard the slap of the camera's mirror and stared with calm curiosity. The big animal eventually decided that the photographer wasn't an immediate threat, and went back to gulping down water. He continued to capture images until the bear was satisfied with his drink, and ambled across the stream and into the woods on the other side. Caleb was amazed at his unexpected midday encounter, and sat down on a rock in the shade to review his bounty of images. He was delighted to discover that he had captured the scene perfectly, and would have plenty to upload for sale on his online portfolio.

Just as he was ready to continue ahead with his hike, he heard the sound of a text message arriving. It was Angie, already writing back with new information about their upcoming adventure.

"Hey Caleb, how are you?"

"Great, I just got some awesome pictures of a black bear down by Sypes Creek!"

"That's awesome Caleb, I hope they turn out spectacularly! So hey, can you make the trip down to the Sand Wash next week? I checked with the office and they said I was free to take my time off right after the holiday weekend."

"I don't see why not. I brought it up to Lacey and she thought it would be a great idea. She wanted to come, but she's having trouble keeping help in the store and can't make it."

"Well, when do you think you can be there? Is it a long drive?"

"I don't know, but I can shoot down to West Yellowstone and through Jackson. South of there are a couple of government campgrounds along 189 where I could camp out for free. From there it looks like I could easily make it down to Craig and the Sand Wash the next day. I don't see any reason why we couldn't camp right in the Sand Wash boundaries if we want to avoid an expensive pay site. Should we meet in Craig and caravan out to the mustang management area together?"

"That all sounds like a good plan. I figure it will take me about five hours to get there from the south metro area."

Caleb replied, "I think it will also take me about that long to get there from the campground in Wyoming. I'm sure I'll be leaving Wyoming early, but I'll want to stop for breakfast somewhere and Rock Springs looks like a likely spot for that. Should we plan on hitting Craig by about one in the afternoon?"

"That will work for me. Maybe we can get a good meal in town before we head out. Do you still have the camper topper on your truck?"

"Yes, we can sleep in there like we did in Yellowstone that time."

"Okay then, I don't need to worry about bringing a tent or anything."

"Nope, just bring your sleeping bag and a comfortable mattress. I still don't have padding on the floor."

"Okay then, Craig around 1:00 it is!"

"Perfect, we can stay in touch throughout the day and then find a restaurant to meet at when we get to Craig."

Angie replied, "I can't wait!"

"Hopefully we will get some good pictures of the horses by the weekend, and then I'll plan on coming into Denver to check out the Front Range."

"Sounds good, you can stay with me down in Franktown if you want to."

"That sounds perfect Angie. Is that sort of your area for selling houses?"

"It's my primary district, although I can go anywhere if need arises."

"Okay, I'll try not to be too much of a bother while I'm there."

"I'm sure you will be no bother. I'm looking forward to seeing you again!"

"I know right? I miss you too," responded Caleb.

"Okay, I'm sure we'll be in touch over the weekend to finalize our plans."

"For sure, In the meantime I'm going to head back to my apartment to process these bear pictures!"

"Okay, talk to you soon."

Caleb was surprised by the speed at which his Colorado plans were coming together, perhaps maybe even some kind of heavenly sign. Suddenly he had no interest in finishing the climb to the turnaround point, and just began the short one mile walk back to the parking lot. He was eager to fill Lacey in on the new developments, and sent her a message as he strode along the trail.

"Hey Lace, what time are you closing up shop today?"

"I'm going to try to be closed and out the door by 7:00," she wrote back.

"Why don't you meet me at the Tap for dinner. I have some news about Colorado!"

"Oh, that sounds exciting!"

"Yeah, kind of! I'll tell you all about it in a couple hours."

Caleb made it to the Tap well before Lacey, and was greeted by the always effervescent Joanie.

"Hi Caleb, how are you today? Are you alone or will Lacey be joining you?"

"She'll be here in a couple hours after she closes the shop for the day."

Joanie quipped, "Well you can keep me company then!"

"Works for me!"

Joanie asked, "Anything new today?"

"As a matter of fact, there is! Looks like I'm going out to Colorado next week to do a story on the wild horses of the Sand Wash Basin mustang refuge."

"Wow, that sounds like a blast!"

"Yeah, it should be. Lacey already knows I was thinking of going, but I'm going to spring it on her tonight that it's going to be next week."

"Okay, I won't blurt it out the second she arrives then," Joanie laughed.

"What can I get you this beautiful spring afternoon?"

Caleb answered, "I guess I'll start with a pint of the dark."

"You got it!"

Caleb sipped his beer and looked up the Sand Wash Basin on his phone to do a little research, while he chatted with Joanie and waited for Lacey.

"So what's the story going to be about?"

"I'm not sure yet. My friend Angie lives out in the Denver area, and she says that a lot of people are upset about how the government is treating the wild horses."

"What are they doing to them?"

"I'm not completely sure. I guess they have a habit of rounding them up with helicopters and auctioning them off. Apparently it's pretty inhumane the way they do it. A lot of horses get hurt and have to be put down, and some die of heat exhaustion. She wants me to do a story, maybe write another book."

"Well that sounds like a noble cause," responded Joanie.

The time passed by quickly as he chatted with Joanie, and Lacey soon walked through the front door and sat down with Caleb.

Joanie exclaimed, "Hi Lacey, how are you doing this evening?"

"I'm doing okay, just glad to be out of the store for the night."

"What can I get you?"

"I'll have what Caleb is having."

"Okay, another one of our famous dark brews on the way!"

"Okay Caleb, what's the big news?" Lacey asked.

"Well I talked to Angie and she can get next week off to come over and see the horses, and then show me around the south Denver area afterwards."

"Next week you said?"

"Yup, coming up quick!"

"Yeah, that just leaves us the weekend to get you ready to go."

"You don't mind if I take off for Colorado next week?"

"The sooner you scope the place out, the sooner we can move!"

Joanie asked Lacey, "Are you moving to Denver?"

Lacey answered, "We are thinking about it. Business at the store isn't near what I had envisioned, and Denver is a much bigger market."

"I'm going to miss you guys if you move!"

Lacey answered, "We will miss you too. I really like all the people I've met here in Montana!"

Caleb spent the weekend preparing for the big trip. The camp stove needed propane, flashlights needed batteries and of course the cooler needed stocked with enough food for a few days in the primitive Sand Wash Basin. With so much preparation required, the hours prior to the trip were a blur and all of a sudden the day of departure was upon them.

He had trouble sleeping the night before the trip and was awake well before dawn. It was going to be a long day of driving and he wanted to get on the road as soon as possible. Lacey heard him rustling around and startled Caleb, who didn't hear her walk into the room. Her modeling training years before had taught her to move smoothly and silently, and he often likened her to a ghost.

"You scared the crap out of me!"

"Sorry, I should remember to make an announcement before I sneak up behind you," she smiled coyly. "What time are you leaving?"

"I reckon as soon as I get ready. I have to make it at least all the way through the park to Jackson, and then I'll see where I'm at. I'd like to make it to Warren Bridge before stopping for the night."

"Where's Warren Bridge?"

"It's down close to Pinedale, between Jackson and Rock Springs."

"Oh okay, whatever. Never been there."

Caleb took a load of camping gear out to the truck and then came back for his camera equipment. Lacey had tears in her eyes as she wrapped her arms around him.
"I'm going to miss you!"

"I won't be gone any longer than some of my camping trips down in the park. I'll be back before you know it!"

"I know, it just seems so far this time."

"Yeah, it does seem like a pretty major road trip doesn't it? Well I guess that's it, I'm ready to hit the road."

Lacey hugged him again, and told him to "Do good!"

Caleb carried his camera gear down to the truck and loaded it in the passenger seat where he could access it quickly should the need arise. He fired up the engine and looked back at the apartment one last time. Lacey was standing at the window waving, so he got out and waved back. She smiled and blew him a kiss, and he climbed back into the driver's seat and headed south out of town toward West Yellowstone. The trip to the little resort town in Idaho at the west entrance to the park only took about an hour and a half, and soon Caleb was getting out his national park season pass for entry into Yellowstone National Park.

By then the sun was rising, and the beautiful mountains inside the park were coming into view. However he had no plans to visit any of the park's major attractions, as his focus was set upon reaching Colorado. Before long, Yellowstone Lake was behind him and Jackson Lake was drawing near.

By then Caleb's legs were starting to cramp, and he decided to take a break for lunch in the town of Jackson. He pulled out his phone while he ate a burger at a local restaurant along the main drag through town and checked his messages. Lacey had sent him a text asking how the trip was going, so he sent back that he was already in Jackson having lunch. He also fired off a message to Angie to let her know he was actually on his way.

"Just wanted to let you know that I'm on the road!"

"That's good news Caleb. I'm just finishing up some last minute details before I take off tomorrow!"

Eventually Caleb was at Warren Bridge, where he crossed over the river and found a quiet little spot down by the water about a mile in. As he rested in his sleeping bag in the topper, he enjoyed listening to the Green River gurgling past. The soothing sound of flowing water sent him immediately into a blissful sleep. He snoozed soundly until morning when a ray of bright sunshine in his eyes brought him back to consciousness. He immediately regretted not filling his thermos with coffee the night before, but resolved to drag himself out of his sleeping bag anyway. Rock Springs was just a couple of hours away and he could get fresh coffee and a bite to eat there.

As he neared the small towns dotting I80 and his phone began detecting a signal, he heard the chimes of new messages hitting his phone. Lacey had sent him a good morning message the moment she awoke in Bozeman, and he had a message from Angie that she was already on her way to Craig. He felt both excited and nervous to see her again. He had strong feelings for her a few years ago before she had left Montana for Denver, for her real estate career opportunity.

He pulled off to the side and sent them both a message saying he would be in Rock Springs by 8:00, followed by another message to Angie that he was looking forward to seeing her again. Caleb could tell from the strength of the phone signal that he was on the outskirts of a major town, which could only be Rock Springs. Getting his coffee thermos filled was foremost on his mind, and soon in the distance he could see a lighted billboard indicating a truck stop. *"Perfect,"* he thought. *"Food, coffee and gas all in one stop."*

He pulled into a truck stop and was glad to see a buffet of hot foods near the counter, including some pretty good looking breakfast burritos. As he went about the business of preparing for the next leg of his journey, his thoughts turned to Angie and his goal of photographing wild horses. He was suddenly eager to get back on the road, and he cut his respite short.

With fresh coffee in his thermos and the radio cranked, Caleb was soon barreling down the interstate. The town of Creston on I80 marked the junction with the highway that went south to Craig, so he set a GPS alert just in case he was too engrossed in the road to notice the turnoff. He didn't want to end up fifty miles down the highway in the wrong direction. Colorado doesn't have that many roads winding through the back country, so a mistake like that could be costly.

Chapter Three

Creston was already in Caleb's rear view mirror, and Craig was yet a couple hours away when he spotted a big raptor perched on a power pole. "*Hawk*," he thought to himself. He'd been on the road without respite since Rock Springs, so he decided to take a break and try to capture an image of the majestic feathered predator. He hadn't seen a car since the turnoff, but wisely searched for a safe pullout anyway. He would have to walk back a quarter of a mile to see the bird, but this was a good opportunity to stretch stiff legs and get his heart pumping anyway.

As he neared the great raptor, it became apparent that it was not just a common red-tailed hawk. It was something much bigger with brown and gold plumage, motionless and utterly unafraid. He wondered if it was a golden eagle, or perhaps maybe a juvenile bald eagle. There was no white at all in it's feathers so Caleb surmised it must be a golden eagle. He had yet to capture a good image of that species, and excitement mounted as he drew near the great raptor. As he peered through his lens, the massive bird stared intensely with no sign of abandoning his perch.

The eagle continued it's menacing stare as Caleb reached the optimal distance, a range of about 25 yards with the light behind him. The sun in the east was still low in the sky, and power lines running perpendicular to the sunlight placed the raptor in perfect golden hour illumination. Caleb snapped a few images of the bird glaring down at him and then waited. He hoped the eagle would see or hear it's prey rustling around in the vast prairie to the west, giving him the opportunity for a flight shot with the massive bird's wings spread wide.

Finally the eagle began looking about furtively and preening his feathers. Caleb had photographed enough raptors to recognize the signs of an impending launch, and prepared himself for the action. After a few moments of fluffing it's wings and tending to breast feathers, the eagle flew directly toward the camera with the blazing blue Colorado sky in the background. Caleb maintained focus lock as the bird passed by, while firing as many shots as possible at ten frames per second. When it was all done, he had captured some of the best eagle pictures of his life.

He climbed back into his truck and thumbed through a few of the images to check the results on the LCD screen, and was not disappointed. There were images of the eagle with wings up, down and spread out wide. He used the zoom function to look for the all important sharply focused eyeball, and was delighted to see that many of the pictures displayed catch lights. Catch lights are the reflection of the sun in the eyes, and an important effect in depicting vibrant life in a bird or animal.

Eventually satisfied, he turned off the camera and placed it in the backseat. The eagle was well worth the stop, but he didn't want to spend so much time that he missed his planned meeting time with Angie. There was no phone signal in the Colorado hinterlands and it would be impossible to alert her that he was running behind. He fired up the truck and after a quick look back at the vast expanse of empty road behind, he safely maneuvered the truck back onto the highway.

The town of Baggs is about halfway between Creston and Craig, and Caleb hoped to obtain a signal there. He had been on the road about 45 minutes since the turnoff from I80, and knew he had to be getting close. Soon he noticed his phone acquiring a faint signal, indicating the nearness of a town. When he had three bars he pulled over and checked his messages.

No messages had arrived since Rock Springs, so he took the action of sending one himself.

"Hey Angie, I'm almost to Baggs, which is probably a half hour to 45 minutes from Craig."

Once he was sure the message had been delivered, he turned back out onto the road and began the home stretch to Craig. Soon he heard the plink of a message arriving and took a quick peek. He didn't want to take his eyes off the road too long, but the short glance revealed the word, "Steamboat." Steamboat Springs was about the same distance from Craig as Baggs, and Caleb was glad their plans were steadily coming together.

As he rolled into the middle of Craig, he spotted a local cafe and pulled into the parking lot.

"I'm in Craig now, where are you?" Caleb texted.

"I just passed through Hayden, so I guess maybe 10 or 15 more minutes."

"There's a little cafe on your left in the middle of town right on your way. Look for my black truck in the parking lot. I'll go in and get us a table."

She answered ,"Okay, be right there."

The waitress greeted Caleb at the door and asked, "Table for one?"

"Two, my friend Angie will be joining me in a few minutes."

"Okay, can I get you something to drink while you wait?"

"Sure, how about a nice cold local microbrew? I'm not sure what Angie will be having."

"You got it Cowboy," she replied, probably referring to his khaki safari hat which reminded him of the one the great Ansel Adams always wore.

Caleb glanced out the window every few seconds hoping to see Angie pull in. Soon he spotted a blue SUV pull in beside his truck, and waited with bated breath for her to step out. He watched as a tall slender blonde strode toward the restaurant, and Caleb thought to himself "*She hasn't changed a bit!*"

The waitress met her and said, "You must be Angie! There is a gentleman waiting for you right over here."

Angie looked over and locked eyes with Caleb, who stood and walked toward her. The two met and locked in a long embrace, as old friends might.

"I didn't think I'd ever see you again," Caleb exclaimed.

"I know, at first I thought I'd return to Bozeman someday but how time flies!"

Eventually they pried themselves apart and sat down.

The waitress asked, "Can I get you a drink?"

Angie answered, "I'll have what he's having."

"Okay, another dark ale coming right up!"

"How was your trip?" Caleb asked.

"Once I cleared downtown Denver it went fairly smoothly. I took I70 out to Berthoud Pass and then highway 40 on over to Steamboat. There's still a lot of snow up there!"

"I've so missed seeing your face," said Caleb as he gazed into her blue eyes.

"I've missed you too. I tried not to think about it, especially when Lacey came back from London. I figured you were too busy to be thinking about me."

"I never forget my friends, especially the ones that have gone out of their way to help me."

"We did have some good times didn't we," responded Angie.

Caleb asked, "So what's the deal with these horses?"

"Well, the government has set a number of horses that they believe can live on the refuge. If their numbers exceed what the government feels is sustainable, they round some of them up and auction them off. The problem is they also allow ranchers to graze livestock there, and consequently a lot of people are really angry about the roundups. Even on land designated as horse management area, the mustangs get only twenty percent of the land while livestock are allowed eighty percent. Then when the land is overgrazed they declare an emergency to remove the horses. By declaring it an emergency, the government can circumvent the *National Environmental Policy Act*, which requires public input. Congress is being asked to intervene, but so far nothing has been done to close the loophole."

After enjoying a couple beers and eating a good meal Caleb said, "Well, should we get out to the Sand Wash and get our campsite set up?"

"Let's go, I can't wait to see the place!"

"Maybe we should both set the GPS on our phones for the Sand Wash, just in case we get separated or lost."

"Good idea," replied Angie.

Soon Caleb was westbound on highway 40 with Angie close behind. He wasn't positive where the Sand Wash horse management area started exactly, so he watched hopefully across the barren countryside for wild horses. Without so much as a glimpse of a mustang, the turnoff from the main highway onto 318 appeared and Caleb took a right turn and looked back for Angie. She had indeed made the turn and they both proceeded toward the refuge. So far there were no horses to be seen, just sheep and cattle quietly grazing a few yards from the road. Caleb watched as the destination grew near on his phone's GPS indicator.

Finally they were upon the primitive federally owned land, and they pulled in to take a look. There were no other campers in sight, and it didn't appear that there were any sites set aside specifically for camping. Caleb spotted some signage and a public restroom for visitors.

As the two surveyed the situation, Caleb said "Well, why don't we just leave your SUV here at the entrance, while we take off in my truck to search for horses."

"Good idea!"

She picked up her point and shoot camera along with a six pack of energy drinks and some snacks, and hopped into Caleb's truck. He pulled in past the restrooms and drove over to the big welcome sign. There was a big map of the entire reserve, along with rules for the park.

"It looks like we're already past highway 75 for the big loop around the perimeter. Should we go back, or should we just drive up the middle and see what we can find there?"

"We are already here, so let's just drive in a few miles in and see what we can find close by."

"Okay, sounds like a reasonable approach."

He proceeded cautiously up the road to the north while Angie scanned the countryside with Caleb's binoculars. More and more sheep were gathered in sizable flocks as they proceeded along the mustang viewing loop.

Caleb asked, "What are all these sheep doing here?"

"I don't know. Maybe this is what they've been talking about in the papers, with the government deliberately allowing livestock to crowd the refuge."

"Why are they doing that, why would they do that?"

Angie answered, "I don't know, it doesn't make any sense to make a refuge and then deliberately displace the animals that the refuge was created for in the first place. It's just like Montana, it's all the old ranching money working behind the scenes for their own benefit, at the expense of wildlife and the tax payers."

"Hey Caleb, I think I see a small band of mustangs up ahead and to the right of the road."

"Perfect, according to the map that's exactly where we should be headed!"

Caleb continued along the rough dirt road until they crested a hill with a full view of the horses in the valley below. Now with a better view, it became apparent that there were actually two small bands with a watering hole in the center. Caleb and Angie watched in amazement as both bands moved toward the water. Angie monitored the action with the binoculars, while Caleb set up his tripod and big zoom lens.

Caleb asked, "Do you think both bands will be able to get a drink, or will they fight over it?"

"I don't know, I really don't know much about wild horses other than the little bit I've read in the newspapers."

Trotting out to meet the other herd was a powerful tri-colored brown and white painted stallion. His approach seemed to beckon to the patriarch from the second herd, and the two met in the middle. Both horses reared up in the most threatening posture possible. Caleb was intent upon capturing the entire scene, including a fight if one ensued. On this day though, it seemed neither stallion was in the mood for battle. The aggressor backed down from the big brown and white stallion, who then led his mares down the embankment to the water. In one way Caleb was disappointed that he didn't get the big money shot, while at the same time relieved that he didn't have to witness a vicious fight between two beautiful horses. The second stallion circled his band as they waited their turn.

"I think the painted stallion is the one they call Winter Storm. I've seen pictures and it looks just like him."

Caleb trained his lens on the magnificent animal and snapped as many compositions as he could imagine. He wanted close up views to capture fine detail of individual horses, and wider angles including the mares and stunning western backdrop to tell the entire story

"Wow, he's beautiful isn't he!" Caleb exclaimed.

"Yes, he's every bit as regal as the stories say he is."

It was midday by then and Caleb felt a twinge of hunger.

"Well, it looks like they aren't going to be moving for a while. Should we get out the cooler and have some sandwiches?"

Angie answered, "Sure, sandwiches sound good. Do you have some camp chairs or something for us to sit on?"

"I do, they are in the truck bed off to the left side."

Angie dragged out the chairs and Caleb followed with the cooler.

"The bread is in the grocery sack if you want to get it while I drain the water out of the cooler."

"Okay, what are we going to use for a table?"

"I guess the tailgate will do nicely," answered Caleb.

"That will work just fine. In the meantime I'm going to catch some rays while we have lunch."

Caleb's jaw dropped as Angie reached to throw off her top. He took a deep breath as he realized she was wearing a swimsuit underneath. Angie noticed the startled look on his face and laughed, "I guess you thought you were about to see a different kind of wild life!"

Caleb laughingly answered, "The thought crossed my mind!"

"Not today," she replied with a coy smile.

They prepared their sandwiches on the tailgate and each grabbed a beer from the cooler. Angie threw back her long blond hair and leaned back to let the warm sunshine stream onto her beautiful face. Caleb did the opposite, pulling down his wide brimmed hat to shade his face. He was outside all the time, so sunshine was definitely not lacking in his lifestyle.

Eventually Winter Storm's band ate and drank their fill, and slowly wandered off. Once it was apparent to the other stallion that the coast was clear, he led his band down to the water for their liquid sustenance. Caleb zoomed out wide and filmed the scene with his camera set to video mode. He continued recording until that group also disappeared over the ridge.

"Well now what?" Angie asked.

Caleb cast a sideways glance at the western sky and said, "I don't know, it looks pretty dark out there."

"Yeah, they say you don't want to get stuck here in a rainstorm. I've heard of people sinking up to their axles in the mud."

"Okay, let's just turn around and head back to the entrance."

Thunder was rumbling in the distance, and it was starting to sprinkle when Angie's SUV finally came into view. An icy wind began to blow from the north and the temperature dropped rapidly.

"Why don't you grab your sleeping bag and pillows, and I'll clear us a space in the camper for us to wait out the weather."

"Good idea."

Caleb pulled the cooler out of the truck bed and put it on the front seat. Angie threw her bedding into the camper, and just as they got inside a torrential rain began to pound the fiberglass ceiling.

As Caleb crawled in and slammed shut the tailgate, he exclaimed "Wow, just in time!"

"Woohoo, I'm glad we aren't out there now! I wonder how long it will take to dry out enough for us to drive on the roads again?"

"I don't know, the air is normally pretty dry out here. I imagine by morning it will be firm enough to drive on again."

They inflated their sleeping pads and propped up their pillows into make-shift chairs as they listened to the storm rage against the camper.

Angie commented, "Golly, I should have grabbed my winter parka out of the car. I didn't know it was going to be this chilly this early in the evening!"

"There's a blanket by your feet, let's pull that over us while we wait this thing out."

Angie pulled up the blanket and exclaimed, "Dang, it's even too cold to drink beer!"

"Fortunately I planned ahead and brought along some brandy for the camp-fire tonight. Let's crack it open early!"

"Brandy sounds really good, what flavor did you get?"

"Blackberry I think," answered Caleb.

They chatted and sipped brandy while the wind buffeted their shelter. The thunder roared and occasionally it appeared that lightning was striking the ground not too far away. Caleb counted the seconds from flash to terrifying roar, noting that it was less than a second on some especially loud crashes of thunder. But with the comfort of companionship and the blanket to retain their body heat, the two felt safe and warm.

Angie asked, "So how did you and Lacey meet, if you don't mind me asking?"

"We met in phys-ed at a running class at junior college out in the Bay Area. I was taking photography and she was in the fashion curriculum. We became friends and I helped her create a portfolio to get her modeling career started."

"Were you two serious out there?"

"Well it was leading in that direction, but then she got a big opportunity in New York followed by an even bigger one in London. That's when I got interested in wildlife and moved to Bozeman and met you. I was as surprised as anyone that she wanted to come to Montana and leave that all that glamour behind. What about you, have you found anyone in Denver?"

"No, you would think it would be easy to find someone to date with all the single people there. Some of my friends have tried online dating services, but I just don't care for the idea. Who knows what people are going to put on those profiles. It could all be bullshit and you would never know."

"Yeah, it seems odd to me too."

"Are you and Lacey married?"

"No, we've talked about it but we both have our separate identities, brands I guess you might call it. I suppose we could figure it out, but it just hasn't reached the top of the priority list."

Eventually the rain stopped and the skies cleared. However by then the sun was dipping low on the horizon, and there was little chance for it to warm up and dry out before morning. There was a long night ahead though, so the two decided to make a fire to pass the time.

Caleb was aware that the Sand Wash was fairly barren, and had wisely purchased a couple bundles of firewood while still in Montana. They soon had a beautiful fire crackling in the darkness to entertain them while they enjoyed the brandy. They snuggled together by the fire and made small talk until time to sleep.

With no curtains in the camper, morning light streamed onto their faces as the sun cleared the bluffs to the east. Caleb right arm felt a bit sore, and when he tried to move it he discovered it was stuck underneath Angie. He could hear her breathing in his ear, and he was surprised how closely they had spent the night. He was torn between savoring the moment, and getting the camera out to capture the sunrise. However the golden glow shining above the mountain tops eventually made the decision for him.

He nudged her and said, "Hey Ang, check out this sunrise!" He liked calling her Ang for short, something he had done since he met her when she was working at the Alpine Tap in Bozeman. She moaned a bit and opened her eyes.

"Well good morning sunshine!" Angie exclaimed as the bright light hit her half open eyes. "Oh boy," she groaned. "What are we going to do about coffee?"

"I have some instant and my one burner propane stove. Let's just heat up some water and we can fill the thermos. I'm going to shoot this sunrise if you want to get the water going. The camp stove is in the back seat along with a pot for the water. There are also some gallon jugs of spring water on the floor in the back seat."

Soon Caleb was done capturing the sunrise, and by then the water was already boiling. They sat together on the tailgate in silence for a while as they watched the sun ascend over the high desert to the east.

Angie eventually broke the silence, saying "What are we going to do today?"

"I was thinking maybe we could go all the way to the north end and see what's going on at the big watering hole. Ironically, I think it's name is Coffeepot Springs."

"Okay, that sounds worth a try."

Soon the pair was packed up and cruising north on road 67 through the reserve. Along the way they saw nothing but sheep, certainly a bad omen for the wild horses. The dirt road was still a bit wet from the day before, but plenty firm enough to drive on.

As Caleb concentrated on the road, Angie scanned the terrain ahead with the powerful 10x binoculars.

"I see some bigger animals up ahead, but I can't quite make out what they are yet."

"That's a good sign, keep watching! I think it's probably at least another hour before we get to the turnaround at Coffeepot Springs."

As they slowly cruised up the rough and rocky dirt road, it became clear there was definitely a band of horses ahead. They appeared to be traveling toward the springs, and Caleb didn't want to get ahead of them and interfere with them getting a drink. He brought the truck to a stop at the top of a hill with a good view of the animals ahead.

Angie commented, "I think that's Stormy's band again. And I think I see one of his mares with a new pinto colt, the one they call Swift Thunder. Thunder is the offspring of Stormy and Spring Rain, and I think he got his name because the first time he was seen was during a spring rainstorm. I think I'll just call them Rain and Thunder. Those two word names are too much trouble to say all the time."

"As far as I'm concerned, you can call them anything you want. I suppose I should use their full names in my story though."

As they watched Storm's band making their way to the spring, they found themselves entertained by the antics of the young ones. Thunder and Dusky were practicing their fighting skills, occasionally rearing up and pretending to do battle. Then one would chase the other until the roles reversed, along with the direction of the chase. The colts were just having fun, but it would be revealed soon enough what the games were preparing them for. Their youthful antics were preparing them for the inevitable life and death battles of adulthood.

"Caleb look, there's another band of horses on top of the ridge. The big stallion is pawing at the ground."

"That can't be a good sign, I hope there isn't a big fight."

Just as Caleb finished his sentence, the opposing stallion charged Storm's band, heading straight for the young foals. Winter Storm was already well aware of the other band, and was willing to meet the challenge head on. He galloped out to meet the attacking stallion and blocked his approach about thirty yards from his harem. Angie and Caleb watched in amazement as the two powerful animals locked in combat.

The terrified foals hid behind their mothers who circled their foals in a defensive formation. The fight seemed to last forever, but in reality was probably less than a minute in duration. When the biting and striking was all over, it was apparent that Winter Storm had beaten back the challenger and the invading stallion turned tail to rejoin his own band.

A visibly shaken Angie commented, "Wow, that was intense."

"Look, Storm is bleeding," added Caleb.

"It doesn't look too bad, he isn't limping or anything."

"I hope he's alright, but I imagine this kind of thing is fairly commonplace out here in the wild."

"I've heard the bands often fight with each other. I guess with such limited resources in this desert they are compelled to defend their territory for their very survival," added Angie.

The two foals recovered quickly, and returned to their antics while the band continued northward toward Coffeepot Springs. The pair followed in the truck at a safe distance, so as not to disturb the already traumatized band.

Eventually Storm and his family reached the springs and walked down for a drink. Caleb steered the truck to the east to capitalize on the morning light for his photography. He soon found a suitable pullout, and he and Angie got out and walked to the nearest vantage point. After capturing a few images of the scene, they sat down in the dirt to watch.

Angie said, "I feel so privileged to be in the presence of such majestic animals. I don't understand how the government can mistreat them so."

"I guess it's just greed. More space for wildlife is less space for their precious sheep and cattle. And it's not like the world is going to starve without these pathetic herds of livestock. There are plenty of sheep and cattle out in Iowa and Nebraska to feed the country without taking over land that should be reserved for the mustangs."

The two sat and watched for a long time while the sun rose behind them. But even as they enjoyed the morning, ominous clouds to the west made it apparent that another rainstorm was brewing. Virga and blowing dust was frequently illuminated by wicked lightning bolts behind the bluffs far to the west.

Caleb commented, "Looks like it's going to storm again."

"Sure does, maybe we should get going."

"Yeah, we don't want to get stuck out here. Have you gotten a phone signal since we got to the Sand Wash?"

"No, I have zero bars," answered Angie.

"Maybe we should go into Craig and get something to eat while we check our messages. I also need to fill up with gas."

"Sounds like a good plan. Let's load up, it looks like the horses are going to take a long rest anyway."

They decided upon the same cafe where they had met when they first arrived in town a couple days before, and soon they were seated at a table waiting to place their order.

"Looks like I'm going to be busy when I get back," said Angie.

"Do you have some customers lined up?"

"Yup, I already have three families wanting showings."

"Will you lose the business if you don't get back right away?"

"Oh, I don't think so. The whole home buying process can take a long time. A day or two isn't going to make any difference. Besides they are my listings, nobody else can really take them from me. It's against the firm's bylaws."

"Oh crap!" Caleb exclaimed.

"What's up?"

"Lacey is suddenly having dizzy spells. She said she was walking across the parking lot to the store and started involuntarily veering to one side. She thought maybe she was dehydrated or low on electrolytes or something, but she stopped for lunch and the dizziness continued. She has a doctor appointment on Friday."

"Do you need to go back to be with her?"

"I suppose it probably isn't safe for her to be walking around or driving when she's dizzy. Let me see what she says."

Caleb sent a text message, "Hey Lace, how are you doing?"

She answered right back, "Not so good. I still can't walk right."

"Do you need me to come back?"

"No, I think you should finish your trip."

"But don't you think it's kind of dangerous to be out driving around when you are off balance?"

"Yeah I guess, maybe."

"Okay I've gotten plenty of good pictures, enough to write my story anyway. I didn't make it out to Denver, but it isn't going anywhere. I can always come back to look for a house once you are feeling better."

"Okay, I'm so sorry Caleb I know you were looking forward to this trip."

"No worries, your health is more important. I'll see you tomorrow sometime, probably."

Angie asked, "Do you have to go back to Montana already?"

"Unfortunately, it doesn't seem too safe for her to be out and about and she needs to get to the doctor."

"Okay, well I guess I'll head home as well. I hope you get to come out to Denver pretty soon."

"Yeah, me too, I was really looking forward to it." They went ahead and ordered lunch and discussed their adventures with the mustangs.

"Will you be able to finish your story with what you have so far?"

"I have plenty of pictures to post an article. Any additional research I need can be done on the internet. If I decide to write a book, of course I'll need much more."

"Okay, I'm looking forward to seeing your article! I'll do what I can to make sure it gets in the right hands."

"That would be a big help! I don't know anyone in Colorado other than you that can get it circulated properly."

They finished their lunch and stood to their feet, each reaching for the other. After a long embrace they said their goodbyes and drove off in opposite directions. As he inserted his card for gas, Caleb wondered if there might be a faster route back to Bozeman. Highway 191 through the park was nice but he knew he would be tired at the end of the day's drive, and the curvy road through the mountains north of Jackson would be an unwelcome challenge.

As the pump was filling his tank, he checked his phone for the best route for the long journey. The maps app indicated that he would need to backtrack on I80 a few miles to Rawlins, but from there it was a pretty straight shot through the high plains all the way to I90. Plus, what had taken him the better part of two days to accomplish on the way down could be whittled down to a little over nine hours.

He wasn't enamored with the idea of backtracking thirty miles, but it was only a half hour delay and would eliminate the need to camp out when there was little chance of sleep anyway. Caleb turned his truck to the north and proceeded with haste to get back home to his long time partner.

Chapter Four

The sun was just dipping below the horizon as Caleb rolled into Bozeman. It had been a long day, but eagerness to see Lacey overcame his stiff and tired legs as he ran up the steps to their apartment. He saw her across the room facing the big window, but he immediately felt a deep sense of foreboding when she didn't arise to greet him. Without even turning around she spoke a feeble greeting, "Hi Caleb."

He dropped his camera bag in the corner and quickly walked across the room, saying "Hey Lace, how are you doing?"

"Not too bad, as long as I'm sitting down. My back hurts and I seem to be having trouble catching my breath. I'm glad you're home, I have an appointment tomorrow at the medical center for a checkup."

"Can I get you something to eat or drink?"

"Would you mind boiling me some water in the teapot? There's some chamomile tea in the cabinet that would be really good right now."

"No problem, I'll get it going. So what do you think is wrong?"

"I don't know, I'm wondering if I have a case of pneumonia or something. I'm sure it's no big deal, we'll find out tomorrow. How was your trip by the way?"

"It was great, I saw the mustangs several times and I'm pretty sure I got some great shots for my article. If I'm going to write a whole book I'll need to do some more research and get some more pictures though. I'll have to add a few shots of Denver and the capital building there so I can include some words about the politics of it all."

"I'm sure I'll be feeling better in a couple of weeks, maybe you can make another trip then."

"We'll see," replied Caleb.

Caleb heard the whistle of the teapot and poured her tea into the cup.

"Would you like some honey in your tea?"

"Honey would be wonderful Caleb, thank you!"

"Coming right up!"

Caleb handed her the cup and sat down on the loveseat beside her. He slid over close and put his arm around her and the two sat in silence as she sipped the hot brew.

Lacey finished her tea and asked, "Would you help me to the bedroom? I've been able to walk around the apartment okay, but I'd feel better with your help."

"Of course."

Caleb helped Lacey to her feet and slowly led her across the room to the bedroom, and helped her onto the mattress.

"I'm going to have a beer and unwind a little bit if that's okay with you."

"Oh, no problem, I just want to get a good night's sleep. My appointment is at 8:30, so could you wake me up?"

"Sure, should I set an alarm for 7:30 or so?"

"7:30 is perfect, thank you."

He turned out the light and walked to the fridge to get a beer before taking a seat in front of the window. He felt his muscles relax as the first few sips of the golden brew hit his empty stomach. Lacey hadn't been sick the entire time he had known her, and he wondered what could possibly be wrong. It was not his intention, but he drifted off to sleep still sitting in the chair.

His eyes opened as the first rays of sunshine streamed through the side window, and as usual his first thoughts turned to coffee. It would be another hour before the alarm would sound, and a quick glance across the street confirmed that the coffee shop was already open.

Brooke was busy preparing the equipment for the morning crowd when Caleb walked through the front door.

"Good morning Caleb, how was your trip to Colorado?"

"It was good, I saw the horse herd in the Sand Wash and got a lot of good pictures for my story."

"I thought you were going to be gone a couple of weeks?"

"I was, but Lacey isn't feeling well so I had to come back. I'm taking her over to the medical center this morning for a checkup."

"Sorry to hear that, I hope she's feeling better soon."

"Yeah me too."

"Black coffee this morning?" Brooke asked.

"You know it, and I think I'll go with the dark roast today and how about one of those cappuccino muffins."

"The muffins are still warm, but do you need me to heat one up a little more?"
"No, I'm sure they are fine."

Caleb took a seat near the window as usual, and watched the street as the small businesses of Bozeman came to life. A few travelers on their way through town occupied Brook's time, which was fine with Caleb. He wasn't in the mood for conversation anyway. Eventually the sun rising higher in the blue Montana sky alerted Caleb that the time to awaken Lacey was drawing near. He left enough money on the table to cover the bill and the tip, and stood up to leave. Brooke spotted him and he motioned that the money was on the table.

"Have a great day Caleb, I hope Lacey feels better soon!"

"You have a great day as well! I'll probably see you tomorrow morning."

Caleb walked outside and took a deep breath of fresh mountain air before walking back across the street to the apartment. He quietly entered the bedroom and touched Lacey on the leg.

"Hey Lace, time to get up."

She moaned and stretched and asked what time it was.

"It's almost 7:30, you have about thirty minutes to get ready for your appointment."

"Oh that's right, I forgot. Can you give me a hand getting into the shower?"

Caleb reached around her lower back and boosted her out of bed. She linked arms with him and he led her to the shower.

With a turn of the handle, the water came on and Caleb took a seat in a chair that Lacey had put by the shower while he was in Colorado.

"How are you feeling today?" Caleb asked.

"Pretty good, not feeling dizzy but I have a backache again."

"I wonder what is causing that, have you been moving a lot of clothes around in the shop?"

"Well I was, but I've had some good help lately for a change, since I hired the two new girls."

"That's good, I hope they stay for the rest of the busy season anyway."

Caleb heard the water shut off and asked, "Are you going to be okay if I give you some privacy?"

"I'll be fine, the hot water has helped a lot."

"Okay, give me a yell if you need me."

Eventually Lacey emerged fully dressed and said, "Well I guess I'm ready."

Soon they were standing at the reception desk at the medical center, filling out the necessary forms.

The receptionist gathered the completed forms and said, "Have a seat and we will call you when we have a room."

Lacey and Caleb sat in silence until her name was called.

The doctor finally entered the room and asked, "What seems to be the problem today?"

Lacey explained the backaches and the dizzy spells, also mentioning shortness of breath.

"Did this just start up all of a sudden?"

"Well the dizzy spells are new, but my back has been hurting for a while. I was doing some lifting at my store, so I didn't think anything of it."

The doctor felt around and eventually said, "Well, let's get some pictures to rule out any serious problems. Let's have you lay on your stomach and we'll do some x-rays. Sir, you'll need to sit outside for a few minutes."

About a half hour later, the doctor emerged and asked Caleb to come back in. The pictures were up on the computer, and with a deeply furrowed brow the doctor stared at them intently.

"You have a few spots on your spine and lungs that I'd like a second look at. I don't want you to panic, but I'm going to send you over to the cancer center for a preliminary screening. In the meantime though, let's take some blood so we can check for any bacterial infections."

On the way home Caleb said, "There's no way you have cancer, you have always taken care of yourself. You eat healthy and don't smoke. I think it's probably just an infection."

"I hope you are right," she answered.

The appointment at the cancer center was the next day, and the excruciating wait until then was the longest day of Caleb's life. The two passed the time walking around town and sipping coffee at the cafe.

Brooke asked, "Did you go to the doctor yesterday?"

Lacey answered, "We went this morning. They found some spots on my x-rays and I'm supposed to go over to the cancer center tomorrow."

"Cancer!" Brooke exclaimed. "That can't be right, you are so young and healthy!"

"That's what Caleb said too."

Caleb wasn't allowed to accompany Lacey into the screening room, and passed the time reading cancer literature in the waiting area. Eventually he had read every brochure available, and sat staring out the window wondering, "*What could possibly be taking so long?*"

Finally after what seemed like hours, a tearful Lacey emerged from the back accompanied by a pleasant looking woman in a white coat. The woman put her arm around Lacey and spoke the most terrifying words Caleb had ever heard, "I wish I had better news, but our tests show advanced invasive ductal carcinoma that has spread to the spine and lungs. The original tumor seems to have escaped notice because it formed so deeply inside on the chest wall. But don't panic yet, great strides have been made in treatments for this type of cancer, and Lacey is young and strong."

"What can you do at this point?" Caleb asked.

"With surgery to remove the main tumor plus chemo and radiation, we can kill the cancer cells in the lungs and spine, and hopefully after a few months of treatments she will be cancer free. In the meantime we will set you up with our counselor to help guide you through the process."

Back at the apartment Lacey was quiet, and Caleb had no idea what to say. He led her to the loveseat and asked if she would like some tea or something.

She replied, "No, I think I'm going to take a nap. I didn't sleep that well last night."

Caleb gazed into her beautiful face as she drifted off to sleep. His weekly article for the Gazette was due, but he had no strength to work on it. The pictures of the Colorado mustangs remained on the memory cards where they remained unprocessed since the end of the last photo session in the Sand Wash. As she slept, Caleb mustered the ambition to at least copy the raw files onto his computer. He wondered if Angie had made it home safely and fired off a text message.

"Hey Angie, did you make it home okay?"

Soon came the response, "Yes thank you! I'm back to the old grind today, taking care of some paperwork at the real estate office. How's Lacey?"

"Well I'm afraid we have some very bad news. She has stage 4 metastatic cancer."

"Oh my God Caleb, I'm so sorry to hear that. Can they treat it?"

"At the screening center they said they could do surgery and chemo. I don't know though, they found cancer in her chest wall, lungs, and even her spine."

"How did Lacey take the news?"

"It's hard to tell, she has been very quiet since we got the news. She's sleeping right now."

"So what's next?"

Caleb answered, "Tomorrow we are supposed to meet with a counselor, whatever good that is going to do. I don't know, maybe it will help Lacey. After that I guess we just start the treatment."

Angie asked, "What are you doing today?"

"I'm finally copying the pictures from the Sand Wash onto my desktop computer. I have an article due at the Gazette, but no pictures ready for me to work with yet."

"I can't wait to see them!"

Despite the best efforts of the oncology department, Lacey continued to lose weight and weaken throughout the summer. Eventually she was unable to walk on her own, and the hospital gave her a wheelchair. Caleb took her for walks every day, and she always enjoyed the warm sunshine streaming through the windows at the coffee shop. The atmosphere there was pleasant, and Brooke was always patient and kind during Lacey's extended visits. There was no elevator up to their apartment but by then she had withered to 80 pounds, and it was no strain for Caleb to carry her up and down the stairs as often as necessary.

By August Lacey was in constant pain and required strong medication to endure the relentless advance of the disease. Caleb spent every waking moment assisting her, and was unable to continue contributing his weekly wildlife article at the Gazette. While she was still strong enough to finalize the sale, Lacey had found a buyer for the boutique and the online sports fashion enterprise. Fortunately she made enough money from the sale to support her and Caleb through the ordeal.

The couple found it to be a great relief to be able to concentrate on Lacey's health full time, and Caleb hoped that applying his full attention to the cancer battle would tip the scales in Lacey's favor. He researched natural cures day and night, hoping he would discover the perfect concoction to heal her strain of the disease.

As the summer dragged on and the nights grew colder, Caleb wondered what winter with the wheelchair would be like. *"Would Lacey still want to walk to the park, or would life consist of just a short walk across the street to the coffee shop?"*

Caleb had begun to wonder if the treatments were working at all, and it began to sink in that his best friend in the entire world was not going to be around much longer.

It was Friday, the day before the big end of summer Labor Day holiday weekend. Lacey was awake unusually early, and in a very cheery mood for her condition. The sun was shining brightly and the birds were chirping happily outside. It seemed there was an especially large flock in the trees outside their window, and Caleb wondered if they were already on their way south for the winter.

Caleb asked, "Do you want to go next door for coffee?"

"No, I think I'll just listen to the birds for a while. Would you mind going to get me a caramel macchiato though?"

"Sure, I can do that."

"And my journal is full, could you pick me up a new one at the store?"

"Do you want me to bring your latte first?"

"No, I have some entries I'd like to make right away before I forget. Just get me the journal and pick up the coffee afterwards. Then maybe we could go to the park. It looks like it is going to be a beautiful day."

"Okay, I'll be right back then," Caleb said as he walked out the door.

"Wow, she is really in a good mood today, I wonder if the treatments are finally kicking in?" Caleb thought to himself. He drove to the store and purchased the journal, all the while looking forward to sitting in the warm sunshine at the park. Brooke greeted him as he entered the cafe, and asked "Didn't you bring Lacey today?"

"No she's feeling pretty good this morning, but wanted me to pick up some stuff at the store and order the coffee to bring up to her in the apartment in a few minutes."

"Oh, that's good news! What is she going to have today?"

"Caramel macchiato, she said."

"Okay, coming right up. I assume you are going to have yours black."

"You know me pretty well," smiled Caleb.

"Do you want these in a to go box then?"

"That sounds fine, I'll be back in a few minutes to pick them up."

Lacey was asleep on the loveseat when Caleb returned with the drinks. There was such peace on her face that he hesitated to wake her, but he didn't want the latte to get cold. He called her name, but there was no response. Concern grew as he touched her arm. Still she didn't respond, so he gave her a gentle shake. Finally he gripped her hand and noticed that it was chilly to the touch.

Now in a full panic he called the emergency line, but knew in his heart that Lacey's long fight with cancer was over. Due to the spread of cancer through her lungs and ribs there was no possibility of performing CPR, and Lacey had already signed a Do Not Resuscitate order for that very reason. Seconds later he heard the sirens and became aware that soon his battle against her disease would be over as well, the moment the ambulance crew stepped through the door and took responsibility for her life.

He sat down beside her and held her hand, cold as it may be and said, "Oh Lacey, how am I supposed to go on without you?" He spoke the words aloud to her, but obviously the question was for himself. His thoughts drifted back to the day they met at the long distance running class on the athletic field of the community college in Cupertino. He remembered locking eyes with her after all the other runners had paired up and departed for the course. His thoughts he kept to himself, as he marveled at the amazing adventure that moment would launch. He wondered if they would do anything different if they could have seen into the future that day. Mostly he wondered how it would ever be possible to go on without her. Even though they hadn't spent every moment together, he had felt her presence every second of every day for a decade.

The paramedics put her lifeless form on the stretcher and carried her out. Caleb was no stranger to loneliness during long solo camp outs, but never in his life had he been so filled with such overwhelming emptiness. As seconds passed like hours, his mind could not see past the darkness of the moment and all he could do was sit and stare helplessly into eternity.

As Caleb sat in stunned silence, the walls of the apartment began to feel more like a prison than a sanctuary and suddenly he didn't want to be alone. His hot drink had gone cold and he longed for the cheery sunshine that he knew awaited him at the cafe across the street. He also thought to himself, "*I wonder if Brooke saw the ambulance out front? She is probably wondering what happened.*"

He slowly and stiffly arose to his feet and walked across the street. Brooke would be the first of their friends to learn of Lacey's loss. It was a beautiful late summer morning and she had propped the door open to let in the fresh morning air. Caleb walked through the opening and she looked anxiously into his eyes.

She hesitatingly asked, "Is Lacey okay?"

Caleb sadly looked at her and slightly shook his head no."

Tears welled up in Brooke's eyes and she rushed out to give Caleb a hug.

"Oh Caleb, I'm so sorry. I thought she was doing better this morning."

"I did too. It looked like she passed peacefully in her sleep while I was getting her latte. She has been in such pain, maybe the suffering departed for a while to give her a few moments of peace before she passed. She appeared to be completely at rest in her final moments."

"Oh my God Caleb, what are you going to do?"

"I don't know, right now I'm going to just sit and have a cup of coffee."

It is a lucky man that has someone to tell about his daily triumphs and failures, and Lacey had always been Caleb's soulmate. However there was one more person in Caleb's world that he could confide in, and that was Angie. As he sat and sipped his coffee he carefully crafted a text message to her.

"Hey Angie, I have some bad news. Could you give me a call?"

A few moments later Caleb's phone rang and Angie said, "Good morning Caleb, what's up?"

"Well I'm sorry to say, Lacey passed away in her sleep this morning."

After a long pause, Angie said "I'm so sorry Caleb. I know how much she meant to you."

"Yes, we've been together a long time. But at least she isn't in pain anymore."

Angie answered, "Right, she is in a better place and you will see her again on the other side."

"I know, she was such a sweet spirit but I guess God needs her in heaven for some reason. She sure didn't deserve the pain she endured these last few months, and I've never seen someone face death with more courage and dignity. I'm sure going to miss her."

"What are you going to do now, will you get your job back at the Gazette and stay in Bozeman?"

"I don't know yet, I haven't given it any thought."

"Well you know, the offer to come and stay with me in Franktown still stands. Even if you just want to get away for a while, maybe take a break and see some new countryside?"

"I'll definitely give it some thought. Right now I guess I'm going get through the funeral and see what comes to me."

"Okay, well I've got a showing in a few minutes so I'd better get going. Call me later if you want to. You don't have to just send text messages. I think it's better to actually talk to someone in times like this."

Caleb answered, "Okay, sounds good. I'll talk to you later then."

Brooke noticed his empty cup and asked, "Can I warm that up for you?"

"Sure," said Caleb. "Are you going back to school pretty soon?"

"Yeah, this is my last weekend here at the coffee shop until the Christmas break."
"Man, summer flew by fast didn't it?"

"Sure did, my first day here last spring seems like it was yesterday."

Caleb got up to leave and said, "I'm sure I'll see you again before you leave for school, but good luck if I don't!"

Caleb had two more stops to make that morning. The hospital called about filling out some paperwork, and he would need to stop by her church with the sad news. He thought about going down to Yellowstone, but it was already late morning on a holiday weekend. The traffic in the park would be horrendous, and in the end he decided to just go over to the Alpine Tap for a beer.

He was glad to see Joanie behind the bar, and he felt comfortable just pulling up a seat in front of her work station.

"Good to see you Caleb, how are you today?"

"I've had better days," he said. "Lacey passed in her sleep this morning."

"I'm sorry to hear that Caleb. I know she was having a rough summer. Are you having the usual?"

"Yes thank you, but I don't really feel like eating anything right now."

"I understand, I'll just get your beer."

"With nowhere else to go and nothing else to do, Caleb spent the rest of the afternoon and evening sipping dark beer and chatting with Joanie when business was slow. Finally the day came to an end and Caleb returned to his dark apartment to face the rest of his life without his best friend.

Caleb awoke before dawn and again felt the need to escape the apartment. Lacey didn't usually go with him on his excursions to Yellowstone, so he thought he might find peace there. He quickly loaded up his camera gear and headed south to Gardiner. He wondered if Michelle had gotten her job in the park, or if she would still be waiting tables at the cafe.

That question was soon answered when he was greeted by her mom as he walked through the door.

"Good morning Caleb, it's been awhile!"

"Yeah, Lacey was diagnosed with cancer earlier this summer so I haven't gotten out much since then."

"Is she going to be okay?"

"No, they caught it too late for the treatments to work. She passed yesterday."

"I'm so sorry Caleb. What are you going to do?"

"I don't know, Angie wants me to come out to Colorado and give some press to the wild horse herd in the Sand Wash Basin. I guess maybe I'll go out there for the fall colors in the mountains and see what Colorado has to offer. I've never been to Denver, so that might be a nice change of pace."

"I've never been to Denver either. Come to think of it, I've never been anywhere."

"How is Michelle, did she get a job in the park?"

"She did, in fact she's down there today. I think she's patrolling the Lamar, trying to keep the tourists from getting trampled by the buffalo I guess."

"Yeah," Caleb chuckled. "Saving them from themselves mostly! Well that's where I'm headed, so maybe I'll see her. I suppose I'd better get going, I don't want to get caught up in a big jam at the entrance."

"Okay Caleb, it was good to see you again. Have a nice day in the park!"

"I will!"

Caleb drove in darkness on the curvy road through the mountains to Tower Junction, before turning east along the Lamar River. Sunlight was just spilling over the horizon when the wide river valley came into view. He usually spent his days there driving back and forth along the Grand Loop looking for wildlife, but on this day he thought he might pull out a camp chair and just sit. He found a pullout near Bison Peak and planted his chair on a high point with a good view of the valley. Soon he heard the mournful howl of a wolf in the distance, which seemed strangely comforting at the moment. The bison down by the river heard it too, but didn't seem too concerned.

Caleb attached his camera and big lens to the tripod and explored the forest edge on the opposite side of the river. His 800mm lens was formidable, but no match for the vast Lamar Valley. The wolves in the distance were little more than tiny dots in the viewfinder, and as the sun rose higher in the sky those dots retreated into the dense pine forest.

Suddenly he heard a familiar voice calling his name, "Caleb, is that you?"

"Michelle! Your mom said you might be working the Lamar today. It's so good to see you, how do you like your new job?"

"I love it, you can't beat spending your days in the forest with all these beautiful animals!"

"No, I imagine not."

She asked, "It's been awhile, what have you been up to?"

"Well early in the summer Lacey was diagnosed with cancer and she went downhill pretty fast."

"You sound like you are speaking of her in past tense. That doesn't give me a good feeling."

"No, she passed peacefully in her sleep yesterday morning and I'm out trying to clear my head today. If you have a day off, her church is gong to have a memorial on Tuesday at four in the afternoon."

"I wish I could come, but I'm scheduled to work on Tuesday."

"That's okay, I'm not a big funeral person anyway. I'll be trying to escape as soon as the service is over."

"Well I'd better get on down the line, but it was good to see you again. Maybe you can visit me in the park more often now?"

"Yeah, maybe. As I told your mom, Angie wants me to come out to Colorado to work on the problems with the wild horse herd."

"Well don't leave without saying goodbye then!"

Caleb replied, "I won't."

As he took in the magnificent scenery it became more clear in his mind that he would go out to Colorado, maybe for the entire winter. He had heard the winters in Denver were relatively mild due to the warming Chinook winds spilling over the Continental Divide, and that sounded inviting. By the end of the weekend his mind was made up, he would make a new start in Colorado.

The time had come to leave the park and return to Bozeman to prepare for the memorial service at Lacey's church the next day. He didn't really know anyone from the church, but knew he would be expected to attend.

Caleb was ravenous by the time he got to Gardiner, but didn't want to take the time to stop and eat. He had heard of delicious ready to go meals in the hot deli at the local market and wanted to give one a try. A couple of energy drinks might also not be a bad idea for the long drive back to Bozeman. He chose a check stand that was attended by a couple of friendly looking young women who seemed happy to see a new face. He fumbled around trying to be cool as he placed his items on the counter, nearly dropping one of the drinks. His quick reaction in catching the bottle before it hit the ground saved the moment, and provided some entertainment for the quite obviously very bored clerks.

Laughing, one of them said "Hey, I'm impressed!"

Caleb laughed too, saying "I guess I've still got it!"

As he strode toward the door, one of them said "Come back soon!"

Caleb looked back smiling, and said "I will!"

Once back at his apartment, Caleb sent Angie a text saying "I'm thinking of coming to Colorado after Lacey's funeral."

There was no immediate response and Caleb drifted off to sleep. In the morning he checked his messages and Angie had replied, "Great, let me know when you get to Colorado, and we can arrange to meet somewhere."

"Okay, I think I might stop off at the Sand Wash for a couple of days first."

"Good idea, I won't be able to get away this time though."

"No worries, I know the lay of the land now."

Angie answered, "Okay then, I'll see you next week!"

"I'll keep you updated on my progress."

"Okay, I'll be watching for your messages."

Chapter Five

Caleb watched in silence as the casket was lowered into the ground. The preacher spoke a few last words before Lacey's parents tossed flowers into the grave and the crowd began to disperse. Caleb had never met her parents and they also knew little of him. Lacey and her parents were both Catholic and found common ground with the other members of the church, but Caleb had never warmed up to her friends there. Following the eulogy they proceeded to the church basement for the reception. Caleb sat by himself near the back of the room and slipped out when the preacher began to pray over the food, thinking no one would miss him at that point. Lacey's parents had already gathered up her belongings from the apartment, so his obligation to them was complete. Their plans were to leave for home immediately following the service and he felt no need for final goodbyes.

Caleb found it laborious rather than comforting to mingle with people at a time like this, and longed for the open road. His gear was still packed and his apartment secured from the previous weekend in the park. There was nothing more to hold him, so he started up his truck and headed east out of town toward the Highway 89 turnoff. He hoped to make it to Gardiner before the end of Michelle's shift in the park. He could call from there to see if she might sit with him awhile before he departed for Colorado. Although he found the crowd at the reception stifling, an hour or so with Michelle at the cafe seemed inviting.

As his truck hit running speed on the freeway he felt a sudden rush of freedom, the kind of freedom one can only feel at the beginning of a long journey. He had not experienced this exhilaration since the day he left the San Francisco Bay Area so many years before. He enjoyed the sound of his well tuned engine growling as the miles slipped past. His thoughts drifted back to the day he left Sunnyvale on his way to West Yellowstone. He chuckled to himself as he remembered that mistake, when he arrived in wintertime to find the west entrance of the park closed for the season. He marveled at the events that had led him up to Bozeman where he met Angie working at the Alpine Tap, and found an unexpected new home north of the Yellowstone National Park

Before he knew it, he was rolling into the tiny town of Gardiner. He decided to stop at the cafe and have a cup of coffee while trying to reach Michelle on the cell. Michelle wasn't there, but her mom spotted him as he strode through the front door.

"Good afternoon Caleb, how are you today?"

"Oh I'm doing well, how about you?"

"Another day another dollar. What are you having this afternoon?"

"How about a cup of black coffee?

"Coming right up!"

"Is Michelle working the Lamar Valley today?"

"Yes she is, she has a couple more hours before the end of her day."

"Okay, do you know if she's planning on coming back to Gardiner tonight?"

"I imagine so, she comes home every night after her shift. Why don't you give her a call?"

"I'll do that!"

Caleb dialed the phone and listened to the ring tone. After a couple of rings he heard Michelle's familiar voice.

"Hi Caleb, what's up?"

"Well, I skipped out of the funeral early and I'm on my way out to Colorado. I was hoping to see you a few minutes before I leave.

"Sure, do you have time to spend the night? There's a campground in Gardiner west of town along the river. I'd have you meet me down here in the park, but my shift is almost over and I'd like to get back over the pass before it gets late."

"That sounds like a good idea, I'll go over there and get set up. Do you want to pick us up a couple of hot meals from the market on your way? I'll pay you back when you get here."

"Sure, what kind would you like?"

"How about the ribs if they have them. Otherwise I don't care, they are all good."

"You got it! I'll text when I get close."

"Awesome, I'm looking forward to seeing you!"

Caleb finished his coffee and headed for the campground. As he cruised past the market, it occurred to him that some brandy to warm their insides, and wood for a campfire might be a welcome addition to the evening. After making the purchase he proceeded to the campground to check in. Luckily there was a nice quiet spot still available, down close to the Yellowstone River. There wasn't much involved in setting up camp since he was just using the camper topper, but he passed the time getting kindling and wood prepared for the fire, and checking his stock image statistics on the campground Wi-Fi.

Just as the sun was disappearing behind the mountains to the west, he received a text from Michelle.

"I'm back home in Gardiner, pulling into the market now to pick up the food."
"Okay, great! See you in a few minutes."

Caleb lit the fire and fanned the flames, hoping to have a nice blaze going by the time she arrived. His timing was perfect and the fire was just getting nice and warm as she pulled in. Caleb rose to his feet and walked over to greet her at the door of her little SUV.

"Let me help you carry those over to the picnic table."

"Sure, I grabbed us a couple of soft drinks as well."

Once their hands were free of food and drink, Caleb and Michelle both reached for a hug.

"How are you doing, was it a nice service?" Michelle asked.

"It was really nice. Lacey's parents came in from out of town and the whole church congregation seemed to be there. Nobody really noticed me which was fine, I'm not a big crowd kind of guy. Actually I slipped out as soon as I could. I hope nobody noticed that I left early."

Michelle laughed, "That sounds like you. Hey let's eat, I'm hungry! I had a long day chasing after the tourists!"

"I'll bet you have your hands full with all the people and their selfies."

"You have no idea the stunts they pull, especially with the bison. Most people have the sense to stay away from the grizzlies, but for some reason they think bison are tame. Did you know that buffalo are the most dangerous animal in the park?"

"Yeah, I've seen some dumb things on a few of my visits."

"People actually walk up to them and try to pet them, unbelievable."

Caleb answered, "I know, it's crazy. Hey these meals are pretty darn good."

"Yes, they are very popular with the tourists, and us locals like to grab them after a long day of work too."

Soon they were done eating and Caleb offered to carry the containers to the trash.

"Let me grab the trash, the bear proof containers are tricky here."

Michelle responded, "Okay, well I need to use the restroom anyway."

Caleb and Michelle walked side by side to the restroom area, making small talk along the way.

"Here's the code to the restroom door," Caleb said as he handed her the paper given to him when he checked in.

"I'll meet you back at the table."

"Okay," she responded.

He opened the brandy, and looked for a couple of shot glasses while he waited. Soon he saw her walking back across the open yard and poured a couple drinks.

"I picked us up some brandy to warm our bones."

"That sounds great after the day I had."

They clinked glasses in an unspoken toast to the day, and Michelle said "I'm going to miss you. You've been coming down here since I was just a kid."

"I'll miss you too, but I'll be back."

"How long are you going to be gone?"

"I'm not sure, I want to stop off at the Sand Wash for a while. I need some alone time to sort things out in my head. Then Angie invited me to come and visit in the Denver area for a while. You remember Angie don't you?"

"Yes, we met a couple of times. She's pretty."

"She is pretty isn't she! Well anyway, she's a real estate agent now and Lacey wanted to move out to Denver to try to expand her business. I don't know what I would do there now, I guess I'll just take things one step at a time."

"That sounds like a wise approach."

"How did the wolves do this year? I've been so busy I haven't checked."

"We lost a few that strayed outside the park to hunters last winter. Plus a couple got killed in fights with other packs, but other than that our population is staying pretty stable for now."

"That's good, I still haven't recovered from the loss of Luna and her mate. I know there will be others to take their place, but she was the star of the show."

"Yeah, that was an awful winter. I wish they would put them back on the endangered list in all the states and leave them on it forever."

"Me too, I keep writing letters," replied Caleb.

After a few minutes of silence, Michelle commented "The fire is nice."

"I thought it might be a fitting end to the day."

"Well, I have to work early. I guess I'd better get home and get some sleep."

"Yeah, I imagine I'll be up with the sun as well. I want to make one more pass through the Lamar Valley, so maybe I'll see you herding tourists! From there I'll go out through Cooke City and down to Cody. It's a quick trip to the Sand Wash Basin from there."

Michelle stood up to leave and gave Caleb a long embrace before saying, "Well good luck out in Colorado, and once again I'm really sorry about Lacey."

"Yeah, me too. Well I hope you have a good winter in the park. The snowy months were always my favorite season for taking pictures."

"I'm sure it will be fine," Michelle replied.

"Okay, I know you have my number so give me a call anytime you want someone to talk to!"

"I might take you up on that! Sometimes it gets pretty slow around here in the winter. I could use a call once in a while,.to pass the time in the snow."

Caleb departed before dawn and was well past Tower Junction before the first rays of sunshine cleared the mountains to the east. However today he vowed not to stop for mundane sightings commonly experienced in the valley. He would bypass the bison waking up and walking down to the water for a drink. Wolves watching from the edge of the forest in the distance would also not command his attention. Montana and Yellowstone both still reminded him of Lacey, and he was just not prepared to face so much sadness in such familiar surroundings.

Nothing he saw that morning was worth delaying the road trip to Colorado, and before long he had arrived at the tiny settlement of Cooke City. He would be entering the vast expanse of central Wyoming after this, and thought it a good time to stop for some gas and a bite to eat. Cooke City had been his turnaround point on many an excursion through the Lamar Valley over the years, and his face was well known at the local coffee shop.

Heather saw him come through the door and said, "Good morning Caleb, how are you today?"

"I'm well, how about you?"

"Same old, same old."

"Are you out getting some fall pictures today?"

"No, the leaves aren't quite ready yet. Actually I'm on my way to Colorado. I have some friends out in Denver and thought I might spend the winter there."

"Man, I would love to get out of here for the winter. I've always wanted to see Denver."

Caleb laughed, "Well load up, the tour bus is leaving in a few minutes."

"Aww the kids would probably miss me. Otherwise I swear to God I'd pack today!"

Caleb put his thermos on the counter and asked, "Can I get this filled before I head out?"

"Of course, what kind do you want? We have breakfast blend, dark, light and of course the house blend."

"Oh, how about the breakfast blend. It's still breakfast time isn't it?"

"Close enough, you got it!"

"Well I need to get going, so I'll see you next time. You take care of yourself, okay Heather?"

"I will, and you have a great trip. Drive safe and send me an email now and then. Or even better, send a postcard and I'll tack it up for all of us to see!"

"Okay, I will!"

Caleb suddenly felt empty as he steered his truck southeast toward the Highway 296 junction to Cody. Even though he was looking forward to a new chapter in life, the mountains of Yellowstone in the rear view mirror felt like a dream was dying. However he was still not yet willing to submit to the grieving process. He knew he would have plenty of time for that in the Sand Wash, waiting and watching the magnificent wild horses he had seen prior to the terrible events of summer.

As he meandered through the mountains of northwest Wyoming he was reminded of his first trip to Yellowstone so many years before, after Lacey had left for New Your City to advance her modeling career. He remembered the emptiness that he had felt then too, except that then Lacey was still alive. However the miles between them were so great that for a while anyway, it occurred to him that it felt almost as bad as if she had died.

The hours passed and by late afternoon he was rolling into Rawlins, where it would be a good time to take a break for gas and food. He was in no mood for a sit down meal, so it would just be a quick in and out at the truck stop.

Craig was only a couple more hours down the road, and Caleb was eager to get those miles behind him. He had good memories of his visit to the Sand Wash Basin with Angie, and believed that place would be ideal for healing his spirit. It held memories not rooted in the past, and also not yet completely grounded in the future. Caleb thought it to be a perfect crossroads, a portal between his life with Lacey and an unknown future without her.

A quick stop in Craig for gas and a visit to the grocery store would be sufficient for a few days in the wide open space of the wild horse refuge. Caleb wasted no time gathering his supplies and heading west to the campsite where he and Angie had stayed. The site was his goal for the day and he had not considered any plans beyond that. While he was reminiscing about his Colorado trip with Angie, it occurred to him that she wasn't yet aware that he was in Colorado.

He messaged, "Hi Angie, thought I'd let you know that I made it to Colorado today."

She must have been sitting with phone in hand, the return reply came back so quickly, "Wow Caleb, I didn't expect you this soon!"

"Yeah, I just had this overwhelming urge to get away."

"Where are you?"

"I'm in Craig right now, thought I'd spend some time in the Sand Wash before heading over to Denver."

Angie responded, "I don't have any more time off just yet, or I would come out and join you."

"That's okay, I need some time to myself for a bit anyway. It was a rough summer."

"I'm sure you do. Well I hope you get to see the horses while you are there."

"Me too, well, I'm off to the campsite. If I remember right we didn't have a signal there, so I'll be incommunicado for a couple days."

The sun was low in the sky as Caleb pulled into the site, and he hurried to prepare a fire before darkness completely engulfed the countryside. By the time the sun dipped below the horizon, a warm blaze illuminated his temporary home. With the addition of a camp chair, he was set for the evening.

Caleb sipped brandy from the bottle as he sat in silence. The Sand Wash Basin was all but silent though, the sound of coyotes singing could be plainly heard in all directions. Caleb wondered at the sound of flapping wings in the darkness, "*Owls perhaps, maybe bats,*" he wondered to himself.

The enormity of the summer's tragedy slowly engulfed Caleb's spirit, and tears began to flow freely. He tried, but there was nothing he could do to stop them. There was no sobbing and no audible acknowledgment of their presence, just water involuntarily flowing down his face. Eventually a profound but welcome numbness began to settle in to take the place of the tears. He didn't know if it was the brandy or if it was the sensation of his soul hardening against the loss. In any case, the tears eventually stopped flowing and only the numbness remained.

The last embers of the fire grew dim, and Caleb climbed into the camper shell hoping for a good night's sleep for a change. Soon images of wild horses captured his imagination, and he once again began to feel a small measure of hope and anticipation as he drifted off to sleep.

Wild horses running free may have been on his mind as sleep overtook him, but it was a vision of he and Lacey running free that filled his dreams in the darkness. As dawn approached, in his night vision he and Lacey were once again running along Steven's Canyon Road at the base of the Santa Cruz Mountains, just as they did on the day they met so many years before. The dream was so vivid that it was disorienting, and when he awoke it took a few seconds before it sank in that it wasn't real. He slowly realized that he was in Colorado and not California, and he would never experience the joy of running with Lacey again. Not in this life anyway.

He propped up the back window and lowered the tailgate to greet the new day. The crisp air of a Rocky Mountain autumn morning filled the camper, and the bright Colorado sunshine warmed his shoulders as he sat on the tailgate surveying his surroundings. He leaned back into the truck bed and pulled out his one burner propane stove. Normally he would be eager to grab the camera bag and head out in search of wildlife, but on this morning there was no pressure to write an article, and no words to type into a new book. There was only the sunshine and the mountains, a fitting backdrop for the vast expanse of uncharted time that now lay before him.

Hunger pangs gnawed at his stomach as he filled a pot with water to heat for coffee. He had groceries and fixings for a hearty breakfast, but opted instead for the simplicity and convenience of a granola bar. He sat on the tailgate and stared in wonder at the rugged hills and bluffs surrounding him. The aromatic smell of coffee soon jolted his senses to life, and the welcome infusion of caffeine rejuvenated his foggy mind and weary body.

Caleb finished his java and leaned back in the camp chair. The sun was well above the mountains to the east, and he had finally worked up the ambition to go out and explore. He and Angie had seen the mustangs on the inner wildlife loop on their visit at the beginning of summer, and that seemed like a good place to start on this day.

With his backpack in the front seat and camera resting safely on the back seat, he drove north along the rough dirt road. At each high point he stopped and scanned the horizon for the mustang herd, but it was not until he reached the watering hole on the northern boundary did he see any sign of the majestic beasts. By then the Colorado sun was burning hot, and a couple of the horses were already lying down for a nap. Many others it appeared, were already resting on their feet.

Caleb pulled out a camp chair and attached his camera and long lens firmly to the tripod. He also grabbed his binoculars so he could watch the action in comfort through both eyes. There was no mistaking the big tri-colored stallion watching intently over his herd. Caleb easily recognized him as Winter Storm, the patriarch of the band. Now that he knew for sure he was looking at the same group he and Angie had spotted earlier that summer, he also knew to look for the stallion's offspring

It didn't take Caleb long to find Swift Thunder, the pinto that was becoming so popular with the herd's human friends. His mother Spring Rain was resting nearby watching her son frolic with the other colts, and Caleb made the best of the moment with his camera. He was elated to find all three of his favorite animals alive and healthy, and looked forward to telling Angie of his observations.

Soon the young ones also grew weary of their antics in the hot sun, and they too lay down among the adults. Caleb watched for a while, but soon grew bored with the inactive animals. He was hungry and anxious to check his phone for messages and sales updates on his books and stock images.

Since he had no idea when the mustangs would arise, he decided to drive on into Craig and have lunch. He wondered if there were any other good places in town to eat, but eventually decided on the usual cafe. The food was good and the Wi-Fi signal strong, and he thought to himself, "*Why take a chance?*"

The server asked, "Can I get you something to drink?"

"Sure I'll have a draft beer, and why don't we get a burger ordered while we're at it."

"Coming right up."

Caleb was soon enjoying a glass of cold beer while he sent a message to Angie, "Hey Angie, how are you today?"

He didn't receive an immediate response, but wasn't worried. Angie was a busy woman, he thought "*She might be with a client or on the road to a showing.*"

The server soon arrived with his order and said, "Here's your burger sir, is there anything else I can get for you?"

"How about some steak sauce?"

"Sure, I think we have some, I'll go check."

Eventually Caleb heard the message alert on his phone, "Hi Caleb I'm doing well, how are you?"

"I'm okay, sitting at the usual cafe in Craig at the moment."

"Did you get some good pictures of the wild horses?"

"It's was hot and sunny, and the horses were pretty lazy this morning."

"Well that should be coming to a quick end, have you checked the weather lately?"
"No, is there a change blowing in?"

"Yup, we are supposed to get one of those big Colorado September surprises. A massive winter storm front is coming down from Montana and Wyoming, and it's supposed to hit Colorado tomorrow afternoon. You don't want to get caught up in the Sand Wash when the snow starts piling up. You could be stuck there for days!"

"No, waiting out a snowstorm in the middle of nowhere seems like a bad idea."
"Why don't you just come on in to Denver?"

"I suppose I could, I don't think the horses are going to be doing anything in the hot sun this afternoon. I guess I'll just finish my lunch and head that direction."

"You should go through Rocky Mountain National Park, it's beautiful this time of year. The tundra should be turning all sorts of colors on the high peaks"

"I'll definitely do that!"

"Okay, I'm looking forward to seeing you! I gotta go though, I'm supposed to meet a client in a few minutes."

"No problem, I'll message you from the road!"

"Sounds good, drive safe and watch out for cell phones!"

"Yeah, it would be a shame to get taken out by a phone before I even get a chance to see the mountains up close!"

Caleb brought up a map of the park on his phone and planned out a route. The same highway that took him from the Sand Wash back into Craig also continued through town and all the way to Granby. Just north of there was the junction for Highways 40 and 34, the main route through the national park. According to the maps, Granby was only a two and a half hour drive and suddenly Caleb was eager to hit the road.

As he drove east out of town, a great sense of peace came over his spirit. Any doubts he had been harboring about visiting Angie had vanished with the completion of their last conversation. His thoughts soon turned to the road, and his imagination was filled with visions of the high peaks of the Colorado Rockies, which he had previously only explored on topographical maps and in his imagination.

Caleb had made the transition between past and future. The past had been reckoned with in the desolate solitude of the Sand Wash Basin, and the majestic high peaks of the Colorado Rockies and his future lie just ahead. Steamboat Springs was less than an hour away, and he wondered what attractions the historic ski town would hold for him. One thing was for sure, it would be much busier than the high desert sprawling across the landscape west of the Continental Divide.

Chapter Six

Caleb reached the ski town of Steamboat Springs by mid afternoon and was immediately surprised by the throngs of people milling around, even though it wasn't even ski season. He was intrigued by all the activity and considered resting at a pub or local microbrew for a while. However he was soon dissuaded from that idea by packed parking lots and crowds everywhere he looked. He slowly rolled through town making a mental note of places he might want to visit another time.

By the time he reached the end of the business district he was in no mood to turn around, and the towering peaks in the distance ahead held far more allure. He was now looking forward to reaching the little town of Kremmling, less than an hour away. It was important not as a stop, but as the milestone for the turn toward the rugged Continental Divide. Highway 40 veers east toward Highway 34 at this crossroads, the pass more widely known as Trail Ridge Road. Trail Ridge is of course the famous highway that traverses the high peaks of Rocky Mountain National Park.

Kremmling would also alert him that the Colorado River was just ahead. All his life he had read stories of the great river, which over the eons had carved out world famous Grand Canyon before continuing on to the Gulf of California. He looked forward to finally seeing these renowned waters for himself.

Soon the tiny town of Kremmling was behind him and he was keeping a sharp eye out for the famous waterway. Colorful yellow and red aspen leaves lined the river bed ahead, and it was only a matter of time before the deep blue waters of the river would become visible. Suddenly there it was, a beautiful section of pristine water that opened up toward the southeast. Upon viewing this scenic section of water, he looked for a place to stop and capture it's beauty.

He reached back into his pack in the seat behind him and pulled out his wide angle lens. A short trek took him down to the riverbed where he lay down on the bank to shoot from the lowest angle possible. He was so close to the fabled river that he could almost taste the crystal clear water. A quick look at the LCD screen on the back of the camera revealed the river's shimmering surface in the foreground, with the colorful leaves of autumn illuminating the background. The blazing blue Colorado Rocky Mountain sky peeking through the branches rounded out a stunning capture.

Caleb wanted to stay and take in the scene for a while, but shadows were beginning to lengthen and there were still miles to go before his intended destination, the Stillwater Pass Campground at the base of the park.

Time flew as the truck rolled past stunning gold and red aspen leaves, interspersed with an occasional splash of blue when the river veered close to the road. A beautiful shimmering lake appeared before him, reflecting a view of mountain peaks that rivaled the magnificence of the Grand Teton Range. He was relieved that such stunning views less than a day's drive from Angie's home would be available to photograph for his stock photo business, anytime he desired. For a few moments all his recent struggles seemed small against the magnificence of the towering peaks of Rocky Mountain National Park.

As he neared the town of Grand Lake, he noticed a strong signal lighting up five bars on his phone. It was late in the day, and well past time to find a place to spend the night. He thought perhaps he could pick up some supplies and maybe directions to the Stillwater dispersed camping area.

He followed the signs indicating gas and food and pulled in. He checked his oil as he filled the gas tank, and then went on inside.

He asked the clerk, "Where's the best place to camp around here?"

"There's a nice place just ahead. It has showers and laundry if you need it."

"Cool, how do I get there?"

The friendly clerk answered, "Just stay on the main road and follow the signs. They will take you right to it."

"Okay, thank you!"

Once back at the truck, he checked his camping app to see if he could locate the campground. The Stillwater site was already a few miles behind him now, so he decided to keep on going ahead to the pay site mentioned by the clerk. He thought to himself, "*A hot shower would feel really good right now. Probably well worth the few extra bucks the commercial campground would cost.*"

The next morning Caleb was awakened by the sound of pots clanking and the smell of bacon wafting into his nostrils, as other campers prepared their morning meal. Breakfast on the camp stove was tempting, but he wanted to be inside the park before sunrise. However a couple of miles back to the station didn't seem like too great a price to pay for a full thermos of hot coffee to begin the day's travels.

Soon Caleb was headed north along the Colorado River, toward world re-nowned Rock Mountain National Park. Mist filled the valley between the mountains to the west and the high peaks of the park to the east. He hoped he would be able to capture some amazing images of massive elk or moose, before the road veered east and climbed to the summit of the Continental Divide.

Just ahead at the Beaver Creek picnic area, a crowd seemed to be gathering. Caleb of course was well aware that where there is a crowd, there is likely to be an animal at the center of it. He pulled in and leaped out of his truck with his camera to investigate. Sure enough, there was a big cow moose with her two calves feeding in the water. He was amazed at the amount of green foliage the huge beasts were able to pull up from the bottom of the pond. Each time the big cow plunged her head into the water, she would emerge with a loud whooshing sound and a massive mouthful of green.

He captured each moose in action, water cascading down their faces after each dive. The big herbivores moved slowly across the pond as they ate, until finally they reached the other side where they left the water behind and disappeared into the dense pine forest. Caleb sat for a few minutes at a picnic table, thumbing through his captures to make sure he had gotten the shot. Once satisfied with his results, he got back into the truck and turned toward the rugged peaks.

Soon the road veered east of the river and began the long climb to 12,000 feet at Milner Pass on the Continental Divide. The view from there was magnificent and he longed to linger and take it all in. However it soon became apparent this wasn't going to be a pleasant stop. As he tried to exit the truck, a gale force wind blew the door back onto his legs. Now better prepared for the harsh alpine climate, he made a second attempt to get out the door. This time he was successful, leaning into the wind as he proceeded toward the overlook.

His eyes were watering from the wind and it was almost impossible to keep the camera still, but he still managed a few captures of the incredible view. In the distance toward the east, a rugged peak towered over all the others. He wondered, *"Is that the 14er known as Long's Peak?"* There were fourteen thousand foot peaks in California too, but they weren't prominent in a fashion photographers mind and he paid them little attention at the time. Just as he was gaining interest in hiking the California mountains, he left his climbing friends behind for a new life in Montana.

Colorado however is famous for high peaks, and climbing them is a state-wide passion. Caleb knew Angie was an avid hiker and hoped maybe they could climb to that fabled elevation before winter set in.

A couple miles later the visitor center came into view, and he thought it might be a nice idea to pick up a souvenir for Angie from his drive over the highest continuous paved road in the country. As he approached the gift shop, he noticed people pointing over the edge of the safety rail. Far below was a herd of elk grazing on the alpine tundra. He wondered why the herd had climbed so high to forage, when there was plenty of grass in the meadows at the base of the great mountain range.

He and Angie had enjoyed sipping pints when she was the bartender at the Alpine Tap, so Caleb picked out a couple of nice 32 ounce mugs sporting carvings of bull elk. Perhaps they could use them at her house while he visited. Caleb was interested in the hiking trail leading up to the summit just north of the gift shop, but getting down to the campground seemed more urgent. Perhaps one day he would return to this place and explore the trails.

He packed up the mugs and began the thirteen mile descent into Estes Park. He considered taking the drive down Old Fall River Road, until he saw the one way sign. Apparently the narrow dirt road could not accommodate traffic in both directions, and was only available for those ascending the pass from the east. The stunning scenery on the way back down from the nation's summit demanded several more stops for pictures before signs of Estes Park began to appear.

A bunch of parked cars suddenly came into view and he wondered what the attraction might be. It seemed too steep for a herd of elk, but perhaps there was another attraction that might be of interest. He found a parking spot and walked on the sidewalk down to the overlook where most of the people had gathered. From that vantage point the entire expanse of the eastern plains of Colorado were visible. Beautiful aspen trees were turning to gold, and little ground squirrels were scurrying about looking for crumbs offered to them by the tourists.

He found a place to sit and craft a plan for the next few hours of his journey. His first priority was finding a place to sleep, and it appeared there were still a few available spots. A place called Moraine Park kept appearing in his searches, along with videos of elk herds roaming the banks of the Big Thompson River Valley. There was a campground by the same name that would be very close to the action, and he set his heart on a site there. After stretching his legs with a good walk, he returned to the truck and headed for the national park campground at Moraine Park.

A few small gangs of elk dotted the highway along the way, but the afternoon light was fading and clouds were rolling in. It was apparent that the storm Angie warned him about was at hand, and he was eager to get settled into a campsite.

Shortly after turning onto Bear Lake Road, Moraine Park came into view. There was only a primitive campground with limited facilities, but it was plenty sufficient for Caleb's needs. He drove past all the big RVs and trailers, hoping to find tent sites suitable for his pickup and topper. He was nearing the end of the road when he heard the unmistakable sound of elk bugling in the distance for the rut season. He soon found an open tent site and pulled in. The spot was right on the edge of a ridge with a valley full of elk below. *"Perfect,"* he thought. *"Maybe I can just hike down in the morning and get some pictures as sunshine fills the valley."*

A few snowflakes began lazily drifting down from the sky, and he wondered if he would be snowed in by morning. *"No matter,"* he thought. *"If worse comes to worst, I'll just hike on foot to the valley from here."* As the cold settled in, he suddenly felt tired and alone. Colorado was beautiful, but it seemed so very far from home. Montana too had seemed far from anything he had ever known, but the miles between them had never broken the bond between he and Lacey. She was always just a text message or a phone call away. A world without Lacey in it seemed empty, almost too much to bear. As the snow fell outside, Caleb reached for the bottle of brandy. The liquid warmth did little to fill the gaping void, but each sip brought sleep that much closer.

Caleb was awakened by the unmistakable sound of a bull elk bugling. There was no hint of sunlight yet, and his mouth was parched from the brandy the night before. He pressed the illumination button on his watch to find out the time, hoping that it wasn't still the middle of the night. He was gratified to discover that it was 5:30, only an hour before the first vestiges of sunlight would be peeking over the hills to the east. He reached for the water bottle to sooth his dry throat, and wondered where he had put the one burner propane stove for heating his morning coffee.

He flipped on the LED lantern and lowered the tailgate. It was already cold in the camper topper, and he shivered as even colder predawn mountain air rushed in. He quickly found the new parka that he had purchased at RSI for the journey, and threw it over his shoulders. The one burner was still in his duffel bag from his stay at the Sand Wash, and he hoped the propane tank wasn't empty. He shivered again as he grabbed the water jug and moved it out to the snow covered picnic table. He cleared he snow with his arm and placed the stove on the table. The gratifying hiss of propane reached his ears as he opened the valve and with a pop, orange and blue flames illuminated the wooden picnic table.

He quickly cleared a spot on the cold bench to sit on, and glanced at his phone hoping to check his messages. Unfortunately however, there was not even a hint of a signal in the primitive campground. Bright stars overhead indicated that the big storm had not significantly developed on the eastern slopes. Perhaps the towering peaks of the Continental Divide had held the cold front at bay.

Soon the water was boiling and he poured it into the awaiting thermos. He let the hot water sit for a few seconds and then poured it back into the pot for reheating. He knew from experience that the metal thermos would be ice cold, and the water would lose much of it's heat before he ever got a chance to add the coffee crystals. When the water began to boil once again, he turned off the burner and poured it back into the thermos as he stirred in the instant coffee crystals.

By then a faint glow began to appear to the southeast, well before any light was able to penetrate the darkness under the pine canopy. He took his thermos to the truck and laid it on the tailgate while he reached for the binoculars to investigate the welcome glow. Long before the rest of the peaks received any light, one peak punched through the predawn darkness. He surmised it must be the famous climbing destination of many 14er enthusiasts named Longs Peak, after it's discoverer Stephen H. Long. Soon a notch in the mountain became visible, confirming his assumption. He thought, *"The notch must be the famous Keyhole,"* a dangerous stretch of trail etched into the side of the great mountain, and passage to the famous Narrows.

All the while, the bugling of bull elk pierced the crisp early morning air. He wondered if the males ever got any rest during rut season. Between defending their harems against marauders and the endless task of rounding up cows, it seemed there was no time for the bulls to sleep. As the first rays of light began to shine through the pine branches, he was reminded that it was nearly time to make his way down to the meadow for pictures. As the rest of the campground began to come to life, he fired up his truck and drove down to the Moraine Park meadow near the headwaters of the Big Thompson River.

Several gangs of elk dotted the wide valley, with the largest male standing close to the road. Cars and trucks already lined the paved road, and photographers dispersed across the hillside with their tripods and massive lenses. A park ranger was already on scene directing traffic and commanding onlookers to keep their distance from the huge animals. The elk were apparently accustomed to photographers, however he surmised their patience wasn't infinite especially during the highly stressful rut season. An angry fifteen hundred pound bull elk could turn a pleasant vacation into a life and death fight in a fraction of a second.

He drove on past the line of cars and turned around to find a spot of his own. It would be a quarter mile walk back with his equipment, even at this early hour. He was glad he hadn't waited until it was light to start the day. He heard talk as he made his way back to the herd and apparently the big bull closest to the road was known as the Big Kahuna, the reigning king of the valley. A few bachelors were willing to mount a bluff charge, but on this morning none of the challengers had an appetite for a fight with the mighty boss with the huge rack.

Caleb trained his long lens on the big bull and waited for him to stop and bugle. He had seen pictures of the majestic animals with vapor escaping from their mouths during full bugle, and wanted to capture one of those images for himself. It didn't take long to get the shot. The herd's patriarch was running to and fro, keeping the cows from straying too close to any other bulls, bugling loudly all the while.

Soon he heard the ranger lady yelling, "Let them through!" Caleb looked up from his camera to see a line of cows right in front of him. It quickly became apparent that they were wanting to cross the road to gain access to the wooded area on the edge of the hills behind him. Photographers scrambled to pack up their tripods and make a pathway for the cows. With the Big Kahuna urging them on, the females soon worked up the courage to gallop past all the people and cars, eventually thundering loudly across the pavement. The big bull gazed suspiciously at the crowd for a few moments, then he too charged across the clearing and into the western meadow.

Soon all the other photographers were moving their gear to the other side of the road, and Caleb followed suit. The beautiful orange glow of morning light now fell directly upon the animals, which were beginning to settle down a bit. Another bull called out from the other side of a knoll to the south. The Big Kahuna heard the challenge and trotted up to the top of the hill where he could watch over the herd while making sure the interloper knew who he would be messing with.

Caleb kept his lens focused on the big bull, wondering if at any second a fight might break out. He heard the bulls would fight to the death to protect their harems. Caleb didn't want to see such a vicious fight, but knew he would be compelled shoot it if one developed. On this day none of the bachelors were up to taking on the King of the Valley, and there were no major skirmishes.

A quick glance at his watch revealed that a couple of hours had already passed. It was mid morning and whatever snow had fallen was quickly succumbing to the intense Colorado sunshine. The cows slowly made their way into the trees where they picked out a soft spot in the shade for a nap. He wondered if the big bull would finally get some rest, but it was apparent that he wasn't about to let his guard down just yet. Eventually though, the heat of the day calmed the herds and even the bachelors lay down for a mid morning nap.

Caleb thought this might be a good time to take a break and head into town. He had never seen Estes Park and was eager to see what the small mountain town had to offer. A quick pass down the main drag revealed a number of nice restaurants and coffee shops, and he picked an inviting cafe on the east side of town.

A pretty brunette met him at the door and asked, "One for breakfast?"

"Yup, just me this morning."

"Okay, table or booth?"

"How about that little table over by the window?" Caleb asked.

"Sure, would you like something to drink?"

"How about a cup of black coffee this morning?"

"Coming right up. We have breakfast blend and dark roast."

"I'll try the breakfast blend."

He sat down at his table and looked out at the crowds gathering on the sidewalks. He noticed an art gallery and gift shop across the way, and made a mental note to check it out when he finished eating.

The waitress soon returned with his coffee and said, "I'm Megan and I'll be your server this morning. What's your name cowboy?"

He laughed and answered, "My name is Caleb."

"Are you in town for the elk rut?"

"Me and everyone else in the state it seems!"

"Yes, the elk rut draws quite a crowd."

"It certainly does!"

"Are you from around here?" Megan asked.

"No, I'm on my way through from Montana to check out the Denver area."

"Oh, How long are you going to be in town?"

"I don't know, I guess until I'm confident I have the pictures I want!"

"So you are really thinking about moving to Denver?"

"I don't know, is it really that bad?"

"Lots of traffic, the brown cloud, and too damn many people if you ask me!" Megan answered.

"Estes Park seems like a cool town, maybe I should settle down here!"

"If you are a wildlife photographer, Rocky Mountain National Park is the place to be."

"I'll keep that in mind!"

"Look me up if you decide to stay," Megan said.

Caleb smiled and said, "I'll be sure to do just that!"

"Well what will you be eating this morning?"

"How about a short stack of pancakes."

"Plain or blueberry?"

"I'll try the blueberry."

"Coming right up!"

He pulled out his phone and saw a message from Angie, "Did you get stuck in the storm?"

"No, I made it across Trail Ridge and got camped in Moraine Park before the snow hit. There really wasn't much snow here."

"It's a good thing you got out of the Sand Wash. It was a western slope storm and they got dumped on over there."

"Yeah, that would have been a mess."

"Where are you now?"

"Right at the moment I'm having breakfast in Estes Park."

"Oh nice, I love Estes Park! Are you coming down today then?"

"I don't know, how long of a drive is it?"

"Oh, I think you could make it down in a couple hours."

"That's not bad. I guess I'll finish eating breakfast and head that way."

"I can't wait to see you!"

"Me too!" Caleb responded.

He wanted to explore the park a bit more, but was also tired of being on the road and eager to get on with his life. He finished his coffee, paid the bill and walked across the street to explore the art gallery and gift shop. He was amazed at the beautiful framed photographs of wildlife and scenery from the park. He wondered if someday he might be able to display some of his work there, or *"Was it an exclusive club only available to local artists?"* In any case, it was a question for another day. Right now he was content to enjoy the beauty of the artwork and examine the materials used to display the works for future reference.

The town was filled with eclectic shops and all manner of clothing and trinkets that might entice tourists to make a purchase. There were t-shirts, beautiful sweatshirts with artwork depicting magnificent wildlife and landscapes from the park, handmade jewelry, specialty coffees and local delicacies to eat. He wondered if he should pick up something else for Angie. He couldn't remember her wearing any kind of jewelry, and thought a Rocky Mountain National Park hoodie might be appropriate.

After he had finished with the art galleries and gift shops, he decided to stop in at an interesting local winery. Perhaps a bottle of mountain wine would be a good gift that both he and Angie could enjoy later in the day. *"What to pick though, white or red?"* He eventually decided upon a nice bottle of chardonnay with a catchy local label. By this time the urge to get back on the road was becoming overwhelming. Any thoughts of another night in the campground were quickly dismissed, and Caleb was soon on his way out of town.

The phone maps recommended a route south on Highway 36 down to Lyons but Caleb settled on the most simple route, follow the Big Thompson River east to Loveland and then go straight south on I25 all the way through Denver to Franktown. He was a bit low on gas, but was confident he could make Loveland with no trouble.

Any interest in exploring Loveland was quickly overcome by his desire for the open road. Angie said it was only a two hour drive, so it would be no trouble to return to Rocky Mountain National Park any time he wanted. Soon he was on I25, flying southward at 75 mph. Little towns came and went between long stretches of wide open prairie. Caleb was surprised at how far away the mountains seemed from the main north and south artery through Colorado. On the map it appeared that the highway ran right along the foothills.

Small towns he had never heard of flew by, and soon he could see the Denver skyline through the brown haze. By this time it was mid afternoon and Caleb just wanted to get to the other side of the city before rush hour traffic developed. He quickly learned to pay close attention to the overhead signs, as there were many ways to get boxed in and accidentally herded off the freeway by oblivious drivers.

He had not seen a labyrinth of highways like this since leaving the Bay Area many years ago. It seemed to him that California drivers were a bit more cognizant of their surroundings though. People there would make way for cars getting on and off the freeway, while Denver drivers appeared to be actively trying to prevent other travelers from doing so. Instead of allowing cars from the on ramps to enter, they seemed to be speeding up and slowing down to intentionally block them. One guy in a small truck had to slam on his brakes and stop on the shoulder to avoid being run off the road. He began to wonder if he was in an episode of Mad Max.

He eventually learned to stay in the second lane from the left behind a big truck. Not many people wanted to cut in front of him only to be stuck behind a semi. Even then a couple of maniacs were still willing to risk life and limb to cross multiple lanes of traffic, while narrowly missing his front bumper. He began to wonder if he had made a poor choice, leaving the relative quiet of rural Montana, resolving to avoid downtown Denver whenever possible. Perhaps it would be more to his liking in Douglas County where Angie lived.

Soon the skyscrapers were behind him and the traffic began to thin out. Earlier, he had examined the route and had set the GPS to direct him over to Parker and Highway 83, which would then take him south to Franktown.

By then Caleb had developed a splitting headache from the exhaust fumes and perhaps maybe a little dehydration from the arid Front Range climate. Not long after turning south on Highway 83, he spotted a discount drug store on the west side of the road, and pulled in thinking *"Good time to stop and pick up some aspirin."*

He also grabbed a cold drink and some chips before going back out to sit in his truck for a short rest. While he sat recovering he sent a message to Angie, "Hey Angie, I'm in Parker. Is this a good time to meet, or should I find something else to do for a while?"

He was surprised by an immediate response, "This is perfect Caleb, where exactly are you?"

"I'm stopped at the drug store near Lincoln Avenue."

"Okay, there's a restaurant called the Stage Line, right at the corner of Highways 83 and 86. Why don't you meet me there and I'll have you follow me to my house. It's kind of a pain in the butt to find the first time."

"Okay, how do I get to the restaurant?"

"Just get back on 83 and head south. You will go through Parker and then past the Pinery to your left. Then you have about four miles of open space before coming to a little gas station and shopping complex on the west side just north of the intersection. Pull in there and you'll see the restaurant.

"Okay, I'll see you in a few minutes!"

As Caleb drove south through the hilly open countryside, he found himself thinking *"Now this is more like it!"* Caleb knew he was getting close when a stoplight on a major intersection came into view in the distance. He slowed as he passed a gas station and looked to his right for the restaurant. A split rail fence marked the boundary of the parking lot and he pulled in. There were a few cars and a long row of motorcycles near the entrance. *"A biker bar?"* Caleb wondered. He spotted Angie's SUV without her in it, and assumed she must have already gone inside.

He couldn't see a thing as he walked out of the bright sunlight into the darkened bar. He was standing at the entrance for a few seconds while his eyes adjusted, when suddenly a woman appeared out of the darkness and wrapped her arms around him.

Angie said, "So good to see you again! I've reserved a table over here in the corner. How about a beer before we head on over to my house?"

"That sounds like an excellent idea! It's been a long day already."

"How was the drive down?"

"It was okay, the traffic through Denver got a little dicey a couple of times but I pretty much just cruised right on through."

"That's good, how long has it been since you've done any city driving?"

"Not since I left California."

"You'll get used to it again."

Caleb asked, "Is the food any good here?"

"Yes, actually it's not bad. They have good pizza and the burgers are pretty decent too."

"Do you want to eat before we go up to your house?"

"Sure, I haven't really put any thought into dinner tonight so yeah, good idea!"

He looked over toward the other corner and saw a dance floor and musical instruments, apparently awaiting a band.

"Looks like they have a band tonight."

"Yeah, I think they do have music tonight. What day is this?"

He glanced at his watch and answered, "It's Friday." With a chuckle he added, "I've kind of lost track of the days."

"They always have live music on Fridays, so should we stay and watch a while?"

Caleb answered, "That would be great!"

Caleb and Angie ate their meal and sipped draft beer while catching up on old times. They talked about the long hours they had spent chatting at the Alpine Tap, when she tended bar there after Caleb had arrived in town. Angie put Caleb in contact with the newspaper there, and also helped get him set up in his apartment. They also reminisced about wildlife meetings, and working hard to protect the Yellowstone wolves from hunters and trappers.

Soon band members and a few more patrons began trickling in. Angie and Caleb relaxed and watched as the band tuned their instruments and practiced a few riffs. Eventually they were ready to play, and started their first song.

By then the pair had downed a few glasses of brew and Angie was ready to dance.

"Come on Caleb, let's dance!"

"Well, it's been a long time since my feet have been on a dance floor, but I'll give it my best!"

After a few minutes Caleb was back in the groove and after another beer or two he realized he was actually having fun, something he never dreamed possible just a few days ago. Angie seemed to be having a lot of fun as well, and he couldn't take his eyes off the slender blonde beauty.

As he watched her dance he thought to himself, "*No wonder I spent so much time hanging around the Tap when I first got to Bozeman!*" The song ended and he heard the lead singer say, "Okay, we are going to slow it down." With no words exchanged, Caleb and Angie drew near and pulled each other in tight.

After a couple more sets, Angie said "It's getting late, should we head up to my house?"

"Good idea, I'm actually pretty worn out."

"Okay, just follow me then. The turns are hard to identify in the dark."

Soon they were in front of Angie's house, and Caleb marveled at how big and nice it was. Angie noticed his surprise and said, "One of the perks of being a real estate agent. We are on the fast track for availability and financing."

Caleb answered, "Maybe I'm in the wrong business!"

"Come on in, I'll show you around!"

It was a beautiful home with sliding glass doors to a deck with what was obviously going to be an amazing view in the light.

Angie added, "The deck overlooks Castlewood Canyon. It's about as close to living in the mountains as you can get in Douglas County."

Caleb smelled the fresh air and said, "I can smell the pine trees."

Lastly Angie showed him the spacious living room, complete with big screen television.

"Wow, this is nice, I believe I could get used to this!"

Angie asked, "Should we watch a movie or something?"

"Sure," answered Caleb. "Should we both sit on the couch?"

Caleb sat down and Angie snuggled in close. It reminded him of that first Thanksgiving in Bozeman when she had invited him over to celebrate with her family. He remembered her squeezing in next to him on the couch between him and her sisters while they watched holiday movies with her family. The similarity made him wonder if he and Angie were destined to be together from the beginning.

Perhaps they were tired, perhaps it was the alcohol and dancing at the bar or maybe they were just comfortable together. Whatever the reason, the two were soon fast asleep in each other's arms.

Caleb awakened to the clank of a pan in the kitchen. Angie had awakened early and was fixing breakfast.

"We're having pancakes for breakfast, is that okay?"

"Pancakes will be awesome."

Angie added, "We can eat out on the back deck. It's beautiful outside this time of morning."

Caleb walked over to the sliding glass doors and slid them open. He stepped outside and took a deep breath of crisp autumn air.

"I never would have expected such a beautiful place so close to the city!"

"It's Castlewood Canyon State Park. Cherry Creek cuts a valley through the Palmer Ridge, and pine trees have lined the riverbanks. It's one of Colorado's best kept secrets, which suits me fine."

"Is there any wildlife in there?"

"Not much I guess. I've seen a few deer wandering past, but that's about it. Okay, the food is almost ready. Are you ready for a cup of coffee?"

"Definitely!"

"Have a seat at the table and I'll bring it out."

Angie brought in the coffee first and the plates a few seconds later. She sat down and said, "Boy, life does take some twists and turns. I can't quite believe you are sitting in my living room, a thousand miles from Bozeman. It seems like yesterday that we were shooting the breeze at the Alpine Tap."

"It does!"

She followed up saying, "Well, I've got a couple showings so I need to get going. Here's an extra key if you want to get out and look around the area."

"I think I'll go over and check out that park!"

"Great, I'm sure you'll like it! There are some neat features and beautiful scenery there, so don't forget your camera. Make sure you check out the old dam ruins from the big flood years ago."

"I will!"

Angie gave Caleb a big hug and rushed out the door. Caleb sat back down on the deck to sip coffee and gaze out upon the beautiful canyon. His mind could hardly absorb the changes that were taking place, and he needed a few minutes to wrap his mind around his rapid change in fortune.

Chapter Seven

It was a warm sunny autumn morning in the Sand Wash Basin. Winter Storm's band began their day as they did every other day, by grazing on desert grasses growing in the arid hill country given to them by their human benefactors. Snow was beginning to accumulate on the distant peaks of the Continental Divide, but the ground was still warm in the desert at the relatively low 6,000 feet of elevation in the basin. However during this fateful season, grass for horses was growing ever more scarce as hundreds if not thousands of domestic sheep allowed into the horse management area had chewed much of it to the ground.

Winter Storm was watching over his family when he heard the dreaded sound of helicopters in the distance. It was a sound he had heard before, and he knew that the terrible beasts in the sky meant danger for him and his band. The mares and their offspring also heard the fearsome noise and looked up from their feeding. Out in front of the helicopters, other bands of Sand Wash mustangs ran in terror, searching desperately for a way to escape.

Winter Storm knew from experience not to run with the mass of horse flesh charging toward him. Instead of joining the animals running west, he ran back and forth to herd his band north. The chopper pilots saw what he was trying to do and swerved to give chase. However as they did so, the rest of the fleeing horses began to scatter. Eventually Storm and his family were allowed to escape, while the roundup of the main herd continued.

Morning Mist, Winter Storm's mother was not so fortunate. She was caught in the middle of the stampede, unable to keep pace with the younger animals because of her advanced age. As she was jostled from all sides by bigger and stronger animals, she began to stumble. Eventually she lost the battle to keep up and fell to the ground. The rest of the herd was too terrified to pick an alternate path, and Morning Mist was trampled beneath their thundering hooves.

Winter Storm's father was also caught up in the stampede along with his mate. He was advanced in age too, but still big and strong enough to hold his own. He charged ahead with the young horses, but even they weren't immune to prairie dog holes in the ground. Several had gone down with legs horribly mangled when their feet plunged into the open death traps. To the right and left, magnificent animals writhed on the ground in agony.

Others ran dripping with sweat from the sweltering heat, eventually collapsing from heat exhaustion. When it was all over eleven horses lay dead, many others dying and still more on the ground screaming in pain from their injuries. Riders on ATVs scattered out to survey the carnage, shooting injured horses and dragging dead ones to the holding pen where they could be disposed of. Little attention was paid to whether any of the downed horses were still alive, and several unfortunate animals were dragged to their death with the carcasses.

Storm's father Lightning Bolt made it to the holding pen, where he kicked at the fence with anger at being confined. The rest of the horses with him were left in the holding pen without food or water until they could be herded onto trucks for removal. Winter Storm watched and learned. He would not be easily fooled by the brutal techniques of uncaring humans charged with the safety and protection of the Sand Wash herd.

It was still dark in Angie's living room when Caleb's eyes first opened on a beautiful late October morning. He arose from the couch where Angie had arranged for him to sleep, and went into the kitchen to turn on the coffee pot. As he waited for the morning java to brew, he checked his messages and social media accounts for the latest news. "Eleven dead, dozens injured," was the headline on the Sand Wash Mustang forum. He read the terrifying account word for word, while also checking corroborating accounts of the tragedy. He wondered if any of the dead and injured were horses he'd grown familiar with on his recent visits to the basin.

Angie was still asleep in her room when Caleb finished his morning brew, so he decided to head out into the early morning light on a trek through Castlewood Canyon. He grabbed his camera bag and stepped out onto the deck to take a deep breath of the chilly morning air. It was only three steps down to the rocky table top on the east side of the park, and another half mile or so before the steep descent into the deep canyon. The warm glow of morning sunlight was reflecting on Cherry Creek when he finally reached the old dam ruins. Instead of continuing on when he arrived there, he decided instead to sit on a rock by the water and contemplate the news he had just digested. He thought to himself, "*Something really needs to be done to help those beautiful animals.*" He also remembered how Angie had organized the meetings for the wildlife advocacy group at the Alpine Tap in Bozeman. He was sure she would have an idea about what could be done.

Angie was awake and getting ready for work by the time he returned from his walk along the creek.

"Good morning Caleb, did you have a nice hike?"

"Yeah, not too bad. The mornings are definitely getting chilly! I'm going to have to rethink my outdoor wardrobe pretty soon." After a long pause he added, "I saw some bad news on social media this morning,"

"Oh really, what's that?"

"Seems they did a roundup at the Sand Wash and a bunch of horses died. A bunch more were trucked off to the holding pen at the prison in Canon City."

"Oh my God, did they say if Winter Storm was killed?"

"They didn't mention him by name, but I don't know for sure. I was thinking, maybe we should put together some kind of group like we had for the wolves out in Bozeman."

"Yeah, maybe we should. I have an early meeting this morning, but let me think about it a little bit. We should be able to come up with something. What do you have going today?"

"I don't know, I guess I'll do a little research and put together an article about the horse slaughter for my column in *The Current*."

"That's a good idea, did they say why they decided to kill the horses?"

"Well I don't think they set out to kill the horses outright, but it doesn't seem like they cared too much about the outcome. Remember all those sheep we saw last summer?"

"Yes, I remember we wondering what they were doing there."

"Well apparently as a result of the sheep sharing the grass, the government felt there wasn't enough food to sustain the herd."

"Why didn't they just move the sheep off the land, isn't it supposed to be for horses?"

"Yeah, I don't know. I guess that's one of the things we can look into."

"Okay, well I need to get to work."

"Have a great day Angie!"

"You too Caleb!"

Angie stepped out the front door and Caleb went back to his computer to see if he could learn more about what had happened. By lunch time he had compiled enough information to publish an article on his column at his online news agency, *The Current*. He was getting a bit restless after sitting at the desk so long, and was eager to explore his new city a little bit. Angie had been busy and hadn't really had time to show him around very much.

He had seen advertisements for a couple of camera shops up in the south Metro Area, and decided today would be a good day for a field trip. One of the stores was a nice locally owned shop with very friendly staff. The store reminded him of the camera shop in the East Bay where he had purchased his wildlife lens years before. There were pictures hanging on the wall behind the counter that he assumed were captured by staff members, and a couple of nice photo albums on the counter. He was particularly fascinated by beautiful images of bighorn sheep along a river, and asked one of the staff where they had been photographed.

Jonathon the clerk answered, "Those were taken out at Waterton Canyon."

"Cool, is that nearby?"

"It's about 10 miles west of here. You can get there by taking C470 out to Wadsworth and then turning south down to the town of Waterton. Watch for the turn when you get to Waterton Road, or you might end up at the gates of a big aerospace facility. They won't let you in there."

"Okay, maybe I'll run out there and have a look! Can you drive into the canyon, or do you have to walk?"

"No, cars aren't allowed. You will have to walk, or you can ride a mountain bike like I do. The sheep are usually a couple miles in, so it's pretty far on foot."

"Oh okay, I've been wanting to get one of those anyway."

"There's a couple of pawn shops up on Broadway that always have a few sitting outside. You should be able to get a pretty good deal on a good bike at one of those shops."

Caleb spotted the rack of film behind the counter and asked, "Do you sell pro color film individually, or do I need to buy the whole brick?"

"Yes we sell individual rolls, what would you like?"

"How about one roll of the 160 speed?"

"You got it. Do you have an account here?"

"No, I just moved to the area."

He set up an account and purchased film for his old film camera, before heading north on Broadway to look for a mountain bike. A bike rack in front of a pawn store caught his attention, and he pulled into the parking lot for a look. He was amazed to find one in new condition with disk brakes and front shock absorbers. He was kind of hoping for both front and rear shocks, but the price was right so he made the purchase and loaded it into the back of his truck.

Then it was off to Waterton Canyon for a little exploring. A big lake appeared on the left and he thought to himself, "*That must be Chatfield Reservoir that they were talking about at the camera store.*" He began watching for the Waterton Road exit, which became obvious as he neared the end of the four lane. He quickly found the big parking lot and pulled in.

The seat on the unfamiliar bike took a bit of adjusting, as did the derailleurs and brakes. Despite the short delay, he was soon pedaling and shifting smoothly and ready to ride up the rough dirt road along the South Platte River. He stuck a water bottle in the holder and slung his backpack over his shoulders. After a quick stop at the road crossing, the path opened up into a wider dirt road and he was off to search for bighorn sheep. To his left was a beautiful blue river cascading out of the mountains, and he was enjoying the ride immensely. He wondered, "*Where are the sheep?*" It was an extremely hot day for the time of year, and he surmised that the bighorns might come down to the water for a drink, if he could be patient enough.

As he pedaled along, a small rock fell from the cliffs above. Caleb looked up to see if there were more rocks to worry about, and spotted a small herd of ewe bighorn peering down upon him from an outcropping. He wondered if they had kicked rocks down at him on purpose. He laid his bike down beside the road and got out his camera. He then proceeded to work the scene, trying to get both blue sky and cliff in the background for the most colorful composition possible.

Eventually he crossed to the other side of the road for a different angle, and that's when he spotted a big brown colored bear sitting in the water. His heart skipped a beat as he crouched down so as not to alarm the bear. He could not believe his eyes when he saw a pair of cubs on the opposite bank, playing and watching their mother cool off in the water.

As fast as he could operate his camera's controls, he shot every composition he could think of just hoping for at least one capture that would do the sighting justice. He knew this special moment was not going to last and he wanted to make the most of it. The mother bear soon spotted him, eyeing him suspiciously before slowly making her way back to shore. Her cubs followed her upstream as she stopped to eat chokecherries whenever she found them. Soon the big mother bear and the two little ones began the climb up a steep rocky cliff, where they finally disappeared into the forest on the other side of the ridge.

Caleb was astonished at his good fortune and he felt so blessed to be living close to such an amazing place. By then the afternoon was wearing on, and it wouldn't be long before Angie was home from work. He couldn't wait to tell her about the canyon and show her the pictures he had captured.

Her SUV was already in the driveway when he arrived, so he assumed the sliding doors in back were open to the living room. He grabbed his camera bag and walked around back to climb the wooden steps up to the deck. She was already in the kitchen fixing dinner when she saw him approaching the glass.

"Hey Caleb, how was your day?"

"It was great! Picked up a mountain bike at a pawn shop and rode up Waterton Canyon. Have you ever been there?"

"I've been there a couple times. Once for a 10K run up to the dam and back."
"Did you get to see the bighorns?"

"No, they weren't out when I was there. I got to see a couple of beavers though."

"Well today there was also a mother bear and two cubs by the river."

"Cool, did you get some nice pictures of them?"

"I did, come and look!"

"Let me get dinner in the oven and we can sit down and look at them."

"Okay, I'll get the camera out."

Soon Angie came and sat on the couch, squeezing close to Caleb so they could both view the LCD screen on the back of the camera.

"These are amazing Caleb! I especially like this one of the little bear standing on the rock next to his mama."

"Yeah, I couldn't believe it when they both popped up over the rock together. I was sure my hands were shaking too much to get a clear shot, but it looks like I got it after all!"

Angie said, "We should go out there together sometime."

"Do you have a mountain bike?"

"No, I never found the time and money to get buy one."

"They had girls bikes at the pawn shop too. Maybe we can get a good deal on one for you as well. It's a lot easier to ride up the canyon than it is to walk. The wildlife is pretty far upstream."

Angie added, "That sounds great, maybe this weekend."

The timer on the oven sounded and she said, "We're having chicken, maybe we should get out that bottle of chardonnay that you brought home from Estes Park on your way through?"

"That sounds nice, I'll open it up."

Angie lit a candle and Caleb was captivated by the golden light of the flame illuminating her beautiful face. She soon noticed him staring and said, "What are you looking at?"

"You look amazing tonight," he replied.

"How do you think of me Caleb?"

"What do you mean?"

"Well, over the years we've sat together closely on the couch, slept in the same tent and spent countless hours talking about our hopes and dreams, and you've never really touched me."

Caleb sat quietly for a moment trying to think of the right answer and finally replied, "Well, it's not for lack of wanting to. Remember that first Thanksgiving in Bozeman when we were sitting together on your parent's couch? I was really thinking we might have something together. But then you moved away and Lacey came back into my life. Her quitting modeling totally caught me by surprise, by the way."

"I have to admit, I was thinking the same thing that night. Then life happened and suddenly there was 700 miles between us."

"Yeah," replied Caleb. "Lacey was in London and you were in Colorado, and I felt like I was starting all over again. I honestly had no idea Lacey would leave her dream job behind and move to Montana."

"Do you miss her?"

"Of course I do, we were practically just kids when we met. But that doesn't change how I feel about you. I've loved you since the day we met."

"How do you like Colorado so far?"

"What's not to like, the weather is great, you have the mountains, you have the cities if you need things, and best of all you are here!"

"Do you think you might want to stay permanently?"

Caleb answered smiling, "I let you slip away once and that's not going to happen again."

"You won't miss Montana?"

"Oh I'll miss the park, but it's only a long day's drive away if I really want to go there."

"What about your apartment?"

"I was thinking about that. Maybe we should go out and visit your parents for Thanksgiving. I could turn in my notice and clear out what little I have left there."

"That's a great idea Caleb, I haven't seen my family in a while!"

"Okay, let's plan on it then. Maybe we could swing by and see the horses at the Sand Wash on the way. Perhaps we can find Stormy and his family, of course if it hasn't snowed too much by then."

"That would be great."

"Okay, it's a plan then. Should we look for a movie for tonight?"

"Sure!"

Caleb and Angie snuggled on the couch while they checked the movie listings.

Angie said, "Wow, this is the most peace I've felt in years."

Caleb gazed into her beckoning blue eyes and leaned over to kiss her. Angie wrapped her arms around his neck and met him halfway. Four years had passed since they first learned of each other in Bozeman, and this was the first time they had ever kissed. After a long heart throbbing embrace, they finally came up for air and stared at each other's faces.

Angie said, "I think maybe you don't need to sleep on the couch anymore."

"I was hoping you might say that." Caleb replied. "Suddenly I'm feeling like going to bed early to tonight!"

Angie smiled and took Caleb by the hand as they walked through the bedroom door. Four years of longing and waiting came to an end on that late October evening.

For the first time in months Caleb slept through the night, until the sun rising in the east illuminated the long white curtains in Angie's room. Angie moaned softly and smiled as he slid out from under her naked body.

"I'm going to start the coffee," he said.

"Okay, then come back to bed. I'm not done with you yet!"

Caleb laughed and said, "Okay, just don't hurt me."

It was mid morning by the time the two left the bedroom to come out onto the back deck for their morning java.

"Well nobody can say our relationship is moving too fast," said Caleb.

"No, four years should be enough to satisfy even my parents. I guess I'll call Mom and let her know we are coming."

"How long are we thinking about staying?" Caleb asked.

"I don't know, let me see what Mom says. What are you doing today?"

"I haven't really thought about it yet, I might go back out to Waterton. Seeing the bear and the sheep was pretty cool!"

"That sounds like a good idea. I've got an appointment pretty soon, so I've got to run."

"Okay, I'll see you later then."

Chapter Eight

Frigid air had descended upon the Sand Wash Basin when Caleb and Angie were passing through on their way to Montana for Thanksgiving. Winter was fast approaching and they had brought along supplies for any kind of weather, including cold weather camping gear. They were both eager to spend a couple of days with the wild horse herd.

As they passed through Craig Angie commented, "I wonder if Storm and Lightning survived the roundup, Morning Mist too?"

"I don't know, they didn't give any names after the roundup."

"Well I guess we will find out shortly."

The miles swiftly disappeared behind them, and soon Caleb turned onto the main road into the horse management area.

Caleb said, "There's a little snow, but I don't think it's cause for worry. We are only going to be here a day or two, and there is no additional snow predicted for Craig in the forecast."

"That's good, let's just drive back a ways and see what it's like."

The desert wind had swept the road free of snow, and the ground below was frozen hard. Caleb's four wheel drive had no trouble negotiating the rough frozen dirt and as they slowly cruised along the wildlife loop, Angie scanned the horizon with the binoculars searching for wild horses in the distance.

"Hey, I think I recognize Stormy's band just ahead."

"That's awesome, I'll try to get closer so you can see better."

As they approached the band Angie exclaimed, "Is that him? I think it is, I think I see Winter Storm!"

Winter Storm had survived the roundup when he wisely led his family in the opposite direction of the stampeding herd. He and all his mares and young ones remained free and all together, peacefully grazing on winter grass in the afternoon sunshine. Caleb drove toward the mustangs and looked for a vantage point with a good view, far enough away to avoid disturbing Stormy's band.

"Here's a nice spot on top of this hill. What do you think?"

Angie answered, "I think it looks perfect!"

Caleb parked and retrieved his tripod and long lens. Angie pulled out a camp chair and watched through the binoculars.

"It looks like the whole band is still intact. I wonder how Stormy managed that?"

Caleb answered, "I don't know, he must have outsmarted them somehow. I'm glad I wasn't here to see it. I think it would have been awful."

Angie watched intently and commented, "I see Spring Rain, Thunder's mom. Oh and look there he is, the colt Swift Thunder. It looks like Stormy did a great job protecting his family."

"I wonder if Storm's parents survived? They would be getting pretty old by now. Come to think of it, Stormy is looking a little long in the tooth himself."

Angie replied, "I don't know, maybe we should take a little drive around and see what other horses we can find."

"That's a good idea. It looks like Stormy is going to take his mares over the hills to the east. We won't be able to see them on the other side anyway."

Caleb and Angie wound their way around the hills and up past the Coffeepot Springs watering hole where they caught the perimeter road.

"I guess we can just take this back to the highway and come back in through the main entrance to claim a campsite."

As they cruised back around the south end of the refuge, a man made object in the distance came into view.

Angie saw it first and exclaimed, "Hey, what's that structure up ahead?"

"I don't know, let's go take a look."

Angie could see better with the binoculars and said, "It's a corral and there are horses in it. I wonder if it's a holding pen for captured mustangs?"

They had not seen another person all day, and there was no one attending the corral either. In fact it didn't look like anyone had been there in some time. There appeared to be no food or water, and the horses looked gaunt and weak.

Angie said, "Hey look, I think that's Stormy's dad Lightning Bolt."

"Do you see Morning Mist?"

"No, I don't see her anywhere. I wonder if she was one of those killed?"

"I don't know, could be."

"I don't think anyone is taking care of these horses Caleb."

"Damn, that's just not right. Let's go check it out."

They parked near the gate and got out to investigate.

Angie said, "I wonder if we should call someone?"

"I don't know, they don't seem to care very much. Looks like the gate is locked, or I might be inclined to just let them go."

Angie looked more closely and said, "It's just a little padlock and a chain."

"I could easily cut that with my bolt cutters."

"Let's go back out to the highway and back to our campsite to see if anyone is around."

"Okay," responded Caleb.

They didn't see another car all the way back to the highway, and there were none on the pavement either.

"You know what," mused Caleb. "We should hang out at the camp site until dark and then sneak back in. I'm going to cut the lock and let them all go."

"Oh my God Caleb! Aren't you worried we'll get in trouble?"

"How will they know? Let's cut the lock, herd them out and split!"

"We can get on Highway 40 over to Dinosaur with all the other holiday travelers. Nobody will be the wiser. We'll just be another car heading west."

"Okay, let's do it. These animals don't deserve to be treated this way."

The two found a suitable place to camp and pulled in. Even though they had no plans to spend the night, they still wanted to heat up some food on the camp stove and maybe catch a short nap. Caleb set up the stove on the tailgate while Angie pulled a couple of dried meals out of the supplies. All they had to do was boil water and add it to the packages of dried food for a nutritious hot meal.

They ate their dinner and climbed into the camper topper to escape the wind. They also took the opportunity to snuggle a bit while they made small talk and watched the Milky Way grow brighter in the beautiful southwestern sky. Eventually darkness descended upon the Sand Wash Basin, and it was getting uncomfortably cold in the camper.

"I didn't think it was going to be this cold," commented Caleb.

"I didn't either. We'd better get out our parkas and gloves."

"There still hasn't been anyone around here," noted Caleb.

"Nope, let's pack up and get this done."

The horses were restless when they returned to the corral. It was as if they could sense that something different was afoot. Caleb clipped the padlock and pulled away the chain. The horses seemed frightened and wouldn't come near the opening to freedom. Caleb countered by walking around to the back of the enclosure. The mustangs warily moved closer to the gate, but their attention remained on Caleb.

"Caleb, jump the fence and walk toward them. Maybe they'll go out."

"Okay, here goes."

He didn't want to start a stampede and cause them injury, so he climbed the fence and stood still for a few moments. The animals didn't panic, so he slowly moved toward them. Suddenly Lightning Bolt discovered the open gate and nickered. He peered through the opening for a moment before going out and whinnying loudly at the remainder of the herd. A few animals ventured out, followed by a couple more adventurous mustangs, and soon the entire herd was out of the pen and galloping northward to freedom.

"Holy crap Caleb, we did it!"

"Yeah, grab the lock and chain and let's get the heck out of here!"

They raced back to the truck and headed back toward Sunbeam. Caleb commented, "I hope we don't see anyone before we can get to Highway 40."

"Me too, let's just keep going!"

Luck was on the side of the daring duo, and they saw no headlights until they were well down the road toward Dinosaur.

Angie commented, "I wish we would have had time to tear down that stupid corral. Just get rid of it."

"Yeah, me too."

"Should we get a motel room in Dinosaur?" Angie asked.

"No, I don't think we want our license number on any receipts until after we get to Utah. In fact, we probably shouldn't stop for anything except gas until we get close to Salt Lake City. We can get a room there if we need to."

"Okay, I hope it doesn't snow along on the way."

"We might have to find a rest stop if it does start snowing, but if everything goes right we should be near Salt Lake by about two in the morning," said Caleb.

"Okay, that's not so bad"

Caleb drove on through the hills of eastern Utah as Angie drifted off to sleep. He finally spotted a motel east of Provo and turned into the parking lot. Angie stirred a bit from the activity and asked, "What time is it?"

"It's a little after two."

"Wow, I can't believe I slept all the way. Are you doing okay?"

"Yeah, getting close to Salt Lake gave me a jolt of adrenaline. Does this place look okay to you?"

"Yeah, I'm ready for some electricity and a comfortable bed."

Morning came, and the sun was shining brightly by the time Caleb awoke. He looked around and noticed that Angie had left the room. As he surveyed his surroundings, he noticed that she had made coffee in the little complementary pot. He assumed she would be back soon, so he just sat by the table and sipped some morning brew. Soon he heard the door swing open and she was back with a couple of plates of pastries.

"They had complimentary breakfast," she said, smiling brightly.

"Awesome! This will get us by until lunch. Another hour or so and we should be on I15 and we can roll all the way almost to Bozeman on that. Did you happen to notice a newspaper?"

"No, why?"

Caleb laughed and said, "I just wanted to see if we are fugitives yet!"

"Oh my God, right? Hey, can I ask you a question?"

"Sure, what is it Angie?"

"Why did we take the lock and chain?

"Well, if we had left it they would know it was cut. Maybe this way they will think somebody just forgot to lock it."

"Good thinking!"

"Well if are you ready we should hit the road! I guess we should stop for gas and fill the thermos. It's still about four hundred miles to Bozeman."

"Yup, let's hit it."

They made the long drive with only one stop, and by nightfall Angie was knocking on her parents door. Angie's mom Kate opened the door with a big smile and said, "Oh, it's so good to see you! Hi Caleb, it's been a long time!"

"Yes it has! I don't think I've been here since that first Thanksgiving after I moved here."

"Well come on in!"

Angie went in and Caleb said, "I'll go get our bags."

"I'll help you," offered Angie's dad, Robert.

When they returned with the bags Caleb asked, "Where should I put these?"

Angie's mom replied, "Angie is going to sleep in her old room, and Caleb you can have Emily's room for now. She won't be back from college until the day before the holiday. We'll figure something else out then."

Caleb wasn't sure what the sleeping arrangements were going to be, and he cast a glance at Angie who responded with a shrug. He decided it wasn't worth an argument, and just put his luggage in Emily's room.

Angie asked, "Is Jessica coming home too?"

"Yes, she will be here on Monday. Somebody needs to pick her up at the airport."

"I can do that," offered Caleb.

"Are you sure?" Kate asked?

"Sure, it's no trouble."

Kate asked, "Would you like a glass of wine or some snacks?"

Angie answered, "Sure I'll have some wine, how about you Caleb?"

"Yes thank you, a glass of wine sounds pretty good right now."

Angie and her parents got caught up on the latest in each other's lives, while Caleb checked his phone for the latest news from Yellowstone Park. He discovered that a recent carcass was attracting the Lamar Valley Pack, and he was eager to get down to see them.

"Does anyone want to run down to the park with me tomorrow to see the Lamar Pack on an elk carcass?"

Angie and her mom said no, but Robert was game for a road trip.

"Sure I'll go, it's been a long time since I've been down to the park."

"Okay, I'll be leaving before sunrise if that's okay."

"No problem, I haven't slept past sunrise in years!"

Caleb replied, "Okay then, I'm pretty tired from the trip. I think I'll turn in early if nobody minds."

"Good night Caleb, I'm going to stay up a little while and talk to Mom."

"Okay, 'night everyone!"

Robert and Caleb were on the road before sunrise in hopes of seeing the wolves at Druid Peak, before the crowds had time to gather and scare the pack back into the forest.

"Do you need to stop in Gardiner for breakfast?" Caleb asked.

"No, let's just fill the thermos at the gas station and get on down there."

"Yeah, I was going to stop in Gardiner and ask Michelle's mom if she was on duty today, but I imagine she will be at the carcass directing traffic if she is in the park this morning."

Robert commented, "Hopefully we can be at Tower Junction just as the sun clears the mountains in the east."

It was still dark when they made the turn at Tower Junction. Soon after, the Lamar Valley opened up before them just as light began to spill into the broad valley. Bison were gathering along the river bank on their way across to a clearing on the north side, while pronghorn frolicked in the distance.

"As much as I'd like to stop and shoot the bison, I'd rather keep on going to find the carcass and the wolves," Caleb commented.

"Yeah, I've probably fulfilled my lifetime quota of seeing buffalo in the park. Let's keep going and find the wolves, like you said."

The two continued on through the valley until they spotted a forest service vehicle pulled over near a knoll just off to the right.

"I'll bet that's Michelle," commented Caleb.

"I don't know, let's pull in and find out. This is probably where the carcass is anyway."

"Okay, looks like we got here in plenty of time to find a good parking place. Did you bring your binoculars?"

"Got 'em!"

"Hey look," said Caleb, pointing across the clearing. "That's Michelle standing over there."

As Caleb and Robert walked toward her, Michelle exclaimed "Caleb, I wasn't expecting to see you so soon!"

"Well I made it out to Colorado to see Angie, and we decided to come back and celebrate Thanksgiving with her parents. Speaking of parents, Michelle this is Angie's dad Robert. Robert meet Michelle, our favorite park ranger!"

Robert smiled and said, "It's nice to meet you Michelle."

Michelle replied simply "Likewise."

Caleb asked, "So what's the story here today?"

"Well the Lamar Pack took down a big old bull elk with a bad leg. They've been feeding off of him for a couple of days, and gathering quite a crowd for the off season."

"How are the wolf packs doing this season?"

"Not too bad so far. We've been fortunate to fight off the Turner Administration efforts to completely delist them. We're still worried though. Whether he wins next year or not, his administration will push delisting through since they won't have to worry about reelection. Did you get to see the wild horses? Have you been able to get anything done to help them?"

Caleb briefly chuckled. He was dying to tell Michelle about cutting the lock at the corral, but as a ranger Michelle was an official government representative and Caleb thought it better for everyone if she didn't have that information.

"I saw the horses on my way through to Denver, and they were okay then. However there was a big roundup not too long after I got settled in at Angie's. I guess a bunch of the wild horses got killed and even more injured, and they had to put a number of them down. It was pretty tragic and was in all the papers. I hear Winter Storm and his band somehow managed to survive.

"Too bad about the deaths. Why do they have to treat them so badly?"

"Just like the wolves I guess, the horses have big money enemies. Angie is helping me set up an email campaign, and we are going to get people to write the governor about making changes. We feel like he will be sympathetic to our cause."

"That's good, I hope you can do something for them."

"So where are the wolves?"

Michelle answered, "The carcass is just on the other side of Trout Lake. I'm going to hike in on the trail to stop people from walking around the lake while the wolves are feeding. You should be able to get some good pictures with your long lens from this side of the lake."

"Great, well I guess we'll walk in with you then."

"Okay, It looks like a few cars have already pulled in after you did so we'd better get moving."

Caleb asked, "Are you up for a hike Bob?"

"Got my boots and my binoculars. I'm ready to go!"

The trio began the short trek up the snow packed trail to the south shore of the frozen lake.

"Is the ice thick enough to walk on?" Caleb asked.

"Probably, but we aren't allowing people to walk out there at least until after the wolves are done with the carcass."

"There they are, can you see them?" Michelle asked.

Caleb positioned his tripod on solid footing and attached the camera, while Robert scanned the other shore with the binoculars.

"I see them," Robert said.

"Oh yes, I see them now," responded Caleb.

Caleb snapped away as the wolves each went to the carcass, in order of their standing in the pack. The alphas of course ate first, followed by the others and then finally the omega was allowed to partake.

The entire pack had eaten it's fill by mid morning and were preparing for a midday nap. In the meantime, Caleb had captured plenty of images and Michelle was busy herding visitors away from the north side of the lake.

"Well Robert, what do you say we head for home."

"Sounds good to me. I got to see wolves so I'm good."

"Okay, I'm going to say goodbye to Michelle and then we can hike out."

Caleb walked over to where Michelle was working and said, "We're heading out, it was great to see you again!"

"It was good to see you too Caleb! Send me a text if you are coming back to the park before you leave. Maybe we can have lunch or something."

"I'm not sure of our plans, but I'll definitely try to get back down here!"

Michelle gave him a hug and was promptly interrupted by an inevitable tourist disturbance.

Back in Denver, complaints about the lack of compassion for the wild horses in the Sand Wash holding pen had been inundating the governor's mail box. Eventually the issue became too big to ignore and the governor sent out a small contingent of state wildlife personnel to look into it. When the group arrived however, they were astonished to find the pen completely abandoned.

Meanwhile the feds had apparently gotten wind that their operation was being investigated by the state, and decided to show up and protect their interests.

Upon arriving and finding the pen empty, one of them said to the Colorado rangers, "Did you guys release the horses?"

"What horses, the corral was empty when we got here."

"No it wasn't, you cut the lock."

"What lock?"

"We had a lock and chain on the gate, where is it?"

"There was no chain on the gate, I guess your men must have forgotten to lock it."

"Oh we locked it, somebody must have cut it off."

"Well it wasn't us. I guess if you are that worried about it you should have had somebody monitoring the pen. We've been getting reports that you all weren't even feeding or watering the animals. I guess that fact that someone was able to free them without you even knowing proves that."

"There's going to be an investigation," threatened one of the feds.

"Maybe you should investigate why the animals weren't being cared for."

"Well this isn't over."

"Go ahead, make a big deal out of it and embarrass yourselves. Maybe we will look into neglect charges. We also want the names of those responsible for this egregious lapse in oversight."

Lightning Bolt and the other bands had simply spread out with their own families, and returned to their own favorite grazing spots. Lightning bolt mourned the loss of Morning Mist though, and continued to move his band around to all their former pastures looking for her. Broken hearted and advanced in age, he eventually lost the will to go on and found a place to lay down and cross the Great Divide. His mares scattered and found other bands to join, and there was no one to mark the end of Lightning Bolt's reign in the Sand Wash Basin.

Back in Franktown, Caleb had discovered a new book store where he could spend his free mornings enjoying the holiday atmosphere and sipping hot caramel macchiato drinks, while catching up on photography periodicals. At the table next to him, he overheard some office people in suits and ties discussing the Sand Wash Basin. He thought it sounded like they were talking about the holding pen incident so he asked, "Are you talking about the mustangs that escaped?"

"One of them answered, "Yes, pretty cool huh?"

"For sure, have they found out how they escaped yet?"

"No, the state and the feds are blaming each other but neither one can prove who's fault it was."

"Awesome," Caleb replied.

Caleb eventually finished his drink and went about his assigned task. Angie wanted to fix turkey on Christmas Day, and he was supposed to purchase a boneless breast and some white wine at the health food store. The remainder of his day was uneventful, but he continued to revel in the successful breakout at the Sand Wash Basin earlier in the season.

On Christmas morning, Caleb continued his long tradition of going hiking on big holiday mornings. Angie was still asleep when he slipped out the front door into Castlewood Canyon. However he made just a single quick lap through the trail system, knowing that she would be excited to open presents first thing.

He had already returned by the time she came out of the bedroom, and they sat in front of the tree and opened presents on the first Christmas they had spent together since that lonely Christmas Eve at the Alpine Tap so long ago. Eventually they snuggled together on the couch, and watched Christmas movies and made small talk for the remainder of the day.

"The office is throwing a New Year's Eve Party, do you want to go?"

"I don't know, is it important to you?"

"Yeah, I kind of want to be there. It will be the first time since I started working there that I will have a date!"

Caleb laughed and said, "Yeah, I can probably survive it. Are you going to be working every day this week?"

"No, there isn't going to be much going on at the office. I might have to go out on a showing if someone calls, but I plan to take some time off and rest up for the new year."

"That's good, maybe we can try out some new places for lunch."

"That would be nice Caleb, I haven't really had a chance to show you around. We should go up to the little refuge north of here and see the deer. Then we could go into Parker for some lunch. There's an old historic restaurant downtown that I like."

"Isn't that refuge in a gated community?"

"I think they would like it to be, but it isn't. In fact delivery people use those roads as a shortcut over to Democrat Road."

"Okay, we can give it a try. I could use a good source for deer pictures for my stock image portfolio."

The week passed quickly and the two enjoyed their time together. Caleb fell in love with the little five acre refuge, finding it full of deer, fox and coyote early in the mornings. He took the opportunity to capture hundreds of wildlife images to upload to his stock library.

New Year's Day was in the middle of the week that year, which resulted in a somewhat muted celebration. Caleb and Angie were last to arrive at the party, and were greeted by a loud cheer from her friends who rushed over to meet Caleb. He was a bit embarrassed at all the attention, but felt oddly comfortable around her co-workers. They were eager to find out about his books and wildlife adventures in Yellowstone, however neither he nor Angie made mention at all of the Sand Wash rescue.

The evening passed quickly, and suddenly the time was at hand. Champaign glasses were handed out and filled with the bubbly. The DJ was keeping the official time and counted down the seconds to the big event. When the spraying of champaign finally subsided, the DJ spun the traditional Scottish ballad, Auld Lang Syne. Caleb and Angie danced closely, locked in a long kiss as they swayed to the music.

When they finally came up for air, Angie stared into his eyes and said "I love you Caleb."

He also gazed deeply into her blue eyes and returned the declaration, "I love you too Angie."

Chapter Nine

On a cold January evening, Caleb was looking over a new website while he and Angie ate dinner. He was fascinated by the site that described every 14er in Colorado, along with directions to get there and descriptions of the most common routes to each summit. Members could also submit climb reports and log all their successful summit achievements.

"Have you ever climbed a 14er?" Caleb asked.

"I climbed Mount Bierstadt with some friends not too long after I moved here. Why do you ask?"

"Well apparently a winter climb is a special category on this 14er site. We should do a winter climb."

"You're nuts, that would be awful!"

"Well a lot of climbers are summiting Mount Elbert in winter. It's the highest peak in Colorado, but it's Class 1 all the way to the summit. It's a nine mile round trip trek, but the trail is supposed to be hard packed snow requiring only microspikes all the way to the summit."

"Sure, I guess that could be fun if it wasn't too cold."

"Next week is supposed to be in the upper 20's all week in Leadville."

"Okay, but we are going to have to find a place to stay. We'll need an early start on the mountain and I don't want to get up at two in the morning to do it."

"Maybe we could find a nice bed and breakfast in Bueny or Leadville."

Angie answered, "All right, if you can get it arranged I'll do it."

"Cool, I'm going to join this 14er site then. Do you want me to sign you up also?"

"Sure, go ahead. I guess if I'm going to climb it, I might as well have a record of it. Maybe it will give us incentive to climb others in the summer."

"Awesome, I'll get started tomorrow. By the way, do you have microspikes?"

"No, I have never been anywhere they were necessary."

"Okay, I'll check RSI in the morning."

Caleb was successful in planning the climb and on a beautiful winter morning in late January, the couple stood at the trailhead to the summit of Mount Elbert. Both were eager to begin their snowy adventure on Colorado's highest mountain.

Caleb looked into her eyes and asked, "Are you ready for this?"

"I'm ready, let's go!"

"Okay, you lead the way. Don't start out to fast though, it's a long way to the summit!"

The trek started out easy enough. There were a couple of miles of forest service road to cover before beginning the steep ascent up the side of the mountain. They covered that ground with ease and made the turn onto the single track path just as the sun began to illuminate the trail.

"Wow, this is steep," commented Angie.

"Yeah, let's just take it easy."

"What if we are going too slow?"

"Well, this is our first winter climb, so no pressure. If we run out of time we'll just turn around and go back down. We should probably set a hard turnaround time."

"That's a good idea, I don't want to end up camping up here."

"No," answered Caleb. "We are going to be sleeping in a nice warm bed tonight. This is supposed to be fun, not something to risk our lives over."

"Okay, what time do you think?"

"Let's call it at noon. If we aren't on the summit or really close to it, we'll turn around and call it a day."

"Sounds like a plan."

The pair easily covered the first few miles on packed snow. The views were stunning and the snowy mountain was beautiful. A Canada jay followed them along the trail for a while, hopping from branch to branch to keep pace.

"I wonder if people feed him? He seems to be quite interested in our progress," Caleb commented.

"I imagine some do. Should we stop and rest for a minute and eat a granola bar? We could give him a couple of crumbs. They are organic, so I don't think they would be bad for a bird."

"Let's go sit on that fallen tree and see if he comes over."

As they sat down and opened their packs, it became obvious what the beautiful gray bird was up to. Their little avian trail companion flew right down beside them and landed on the fallen log, only a few feet away.

Angie asked, "I wonder if these are the birds they call camp robbers?"

Angie tossed the little fellow a small crumb from her granola bar, which was quickly devoured. Caleb also tossed him a crumb which too was immediately consumed. Then just as Caleb was about to take his last bite, the little bird took flight and stole it right from his hand. The jay seemed happy with his prize and flew away with it in his mouth.

"Well if these aren't called camp robbers, I guess they should be from now on," commented a startled Caleb.

"He sure fooled you!"

"Yes he did! Okay, we'd better get moving, it's already 9:00 and we aren't even at the tree line."

Caleb and Angie made steady progress all the way to the tree line. As they prepared to tackle the high elevation above tree line, a huge clearing appeared before them with no discernible trail to guide them across the sea of snow. Apparently during the night the wind had blown a thick layer of snow over the path.

"Too bad we didn't bring snowshoes," commented Caleb.

"Right, I don't know how we are ever going to traverse this. We'll sink up to our necks in powder."

"Well I don't know, I assume the packed trail is still just under the surface of the snow. Maybe we can pick our way across by poking our poles into the powder to locate the path."

Angie replied, " Okay then, let's give it a try. If we can't find the trail I guess this trek might be over with."

Caleb took the lead and stabbed the snow with one of his ski poles. It sank effortlessly into the deep powder. A second stab yielded better results, and he took a tentative step forward. A couple more stabs at the snow resulted in a few tentative steps forward.

"I think this is going to work," commented a hopeful Caleb.

Just then he stepped off the packed trail and sank to his waist in the deep powder. He struggled, but could not pull himself out on his own.

"Hand me the end of your pole and pull me out!"

Angie extended the end of her ski pole and pulled with all her strength. The effort was successful and Caleb was soon back on the trail.

"I hope I don't fall off again, that wasted a ton of energy!"

In this manner the two picked their way across the open meadow, only occasionally sinking into the deep snow. This short segment required the better part of an hour and a lot of their reserve strength to cross. However they eventually managed to make it to the other side where the packed trail became visible once again.

"We made it!" Caleb exclaimed jubilantly.

"Wow, that was tough!"

"I hope we don't encounter any more of these obstacles."

Soon they cleared the tree line and hiked as quickly as they could toward the summit. It was almost noon by the time they reached the top, only to discover that it was a false summit. The trail continued on before them, with what appeared to be perhaps another mile before the real summit.

Another hour passed before they reached the next high point, and heartbreaking discovery of a second false summit. It was well past noon by then, but with the summit so close they decided to continue. They pushed on, but at this elevation they could only take a few steps at a time before stopping to replenish their oxygen level.

Well beyond their mandatory turnaround time of 2:00, the trail stretched endlessly before them. When the couple encountered yet a third false summit, Caleb finally said "It's getting late, maybe we should give it up."

"Maybe so, let's just climb to the top of that little hill and see what's up there"

It was an easy five minute walk to the top of the hill and suddenly there was no more mountain in front of them, just a vast expanse of snow covered peaks in all directions beneath them.

Caleb exclaimed, " I think this is it, I think we are at the summit!"

"Holy crap, we did it!"

It was an eerie scene at 14,433 feet above sea level. Sound itself struggled to survive in such thin air and deep snow. The sky was so blue it was almost black, and there was nothing in sight but a magical winter wonderland in all directions. On top of Colorado's highest peak in January there was no sign of life, not even the birds dare venture there.

"This is amazing," commented Angie.

"Yes it is, I've never experienced anything like this."

Caleb reached into his pocket and knelt down beside her. However she was too busy looking at the scenery to notice until Caleb spoke her name.

"Angie, will you marry me?"

Angie turned around as Caleb held out a simple gold band that he had purchased in Montana, in case he ever found the opportunity to propose to Lacey.

"Angie answered without hesitation, Yes, oh my God Caleb of course!"

Caleb slipped the ring on her finger and the two embraced in a long hug. No words were necessary for the next few moments., their beaming faces said it all.

Joy however was soon tempered by the bitter cold and thin air, from which even the best high tech insulation was no match. They were well past their hard turn-around time, and at risk of not reaching the trailhead before dark.

Caleb finally broke the silence, saying "We'd better start down. We don't want to spend the first day of our engagement frozen to death."

"Yes, it's getting cold fast."

"Hopefully it will start warming up after we get a mile or so down the slope."

Going back down the mountain was easy compared to the ascent, and the two quickly covered the miles back to the tree line. A pair of campers were setting up a tent at the clearing that almost prematurely ended Caleb and Angie's day.

One of them asked, "Did you make summit?"

"We did!" Angie exclaimed!. She showed him her ring and said, "Look what he gave me at the summit!"

"He proposed to you on the mountain?"

"Yes!"

"Whoa, how cool is that!"

"Yeah!" Angie answered simply as she stared at her hand.

The other camper asked, "How is the trail to the summit?"

Caleb answered, "It's snow packed and marked by a steady stream of micro-spikes. Plus the snow isn't deep up there, it appears the wind has blown most of it away."

"Cool, we are going up in the morning then."

"Good luck!"

Caleb and Angie reached the end of the single track just as the sunlight was extinguished by the pine canopy. They were exhausted but with only two miles to go and the jeep road to guide them, they found the strength to push on. Another half hour after what they had already accomplished seemed inconsequential compared to a brutal bivouac in the snow and cold at 11,000 feet.

It was Angie who first spotted the truck, exclaiming "There it is, I see the truck!"

"Wow, that's a relief, I was starting to worry that we were going to be camping out tonight."

"Speaking of tonight, why don't we just go back into Leadville and stay at the bed and breakfast again. We can get a hot meal and a good night's sleep instead of driving the mountain roads in the dark."

"That's a great idea," commented Caleb.

They were both too tired to even discuss their engagement. With a hot meal in their stomachs they fell asleep immediately, and didn't awaken until morning hunger pangs provided the incentive to throw back the bed covers.

On the way back over Freemont Pass Angie finally asked, "When do you think we should have the wedding?"

"I don't know, I guess we should wait until May so that everyone can get here without having to worry about a snowstorm."

"I don't want a big wedding, just a small ceremony with family will be fine. I especially don't want a big reception, I don't want my parents to think they need to spend a lot of money."

Caleb answered, "Maybe we could have the wedding in Montana. Your sisters will already be at home, or at least close by. We could just have your minister say the vows, and then have a little get together at the Tap."

"That's a great idea Caleb, I think that would be perfect! I'm going to call Mom right now and let her know. Wait, what about your family?"

"I guess I could invite Michelle and her mom."

"Okay, at least you will have someone there on your side of the aisle."

Caleb could hear the phone ringing from the other side of the truck.

"Hi Mom, guess what! Caleb and I are getting married!"

"Oh Angie, that's wonderful! When is the wedding?"

"We want to come up to Bozeman in May and have a simple ceremony at our church. It's just going to be just our close family, and Caleb is going to invite Michelle and her mom from Gardiner. We can a small reception at the Alpine Tap and that should be enough."

"Are you sure you don't want to have it in Colorado?"

"No, there's nothing special about Franktown. I don't even go to church there."

"Okay, I'll tell Robert and your sisters. I can set it up with the minister and get a reservation at the Tap."

"That sounds perfect Mom! I'm going to let you go, we are probably going to lose our signal in the valley pretty soon."

After Angie hung up the phone Caleb said, "This doesn't have to be your actual wedding ring. I actually got it for Lacey in case the moment arose. But when she got cancer I put it away. Marriage would have messed up her health insurance, and considering the cost of the treatments it was simply out of the question."

"It doesn't matter Caleb. That you would give to me something meant for someone you loved that much is actually an honor."

"Well just the same, it is kind of plain."

"We'll worry about that later okay? But I don't see any reason why it wouldn't be the perfect ring."

There was silence in the truck the rest of the way over the pass. However on the north side with phone signal restored, Angie began calling her friends and co-workers to tell them the news. Caleb was suddenly glad the wedding was going to be in Montana, a Colorado wedding sounded like it could get out of hand in a hurry.

Chapter Ten

By the end of March, warmer weather had conquered the Front Range winter. Angie was busy preparing for the wedding, but not too engrossed in the preparations to miss the annual rite of spring for Colorado athletes. For the sports minded adventurer, the Cherry Creek Sneak was the official kick off for the summer season.

As they sat in the afternoon sunshine on the deck, Angie said "Caleb, we should run the Sneak this year!"

"What's that?"

"It's a five mile run through the city of Cherry Creek. Thousands and thousands of runners participate every year, and it's a lot of fun."

"Well, I'm not in shape for a run. How about you run and I take pictures?"

"Well okay, but you will be missing out on a beautiful run through the cherry blossoms."

"That's okay, I'll get pictures of them too. When is it?"

"It's usually in late April. I'll have to check the running schedule to get the exact time and date."

"Okay, just let me know when it is exactly and I'll add it to my calendar so I don't schedule something else."

Angie commented, "Let's run up to the mall and get a late lunch at the food court. I want to hit the running store and look at shoes. Mine are getting pretty ragged and I'd like to have some new ones for the race. Plus I can sign up for the race there and pick up a packet to make sure I don't chicken out."

"Sure, no problem. I wouldn't mind stopping in at the camera store as long as we're there. I need to pick up some ink and paper for the printer. Plus my vest is wearing out, the pockets are all full of holes and I'm afraid of losing things."

"Sure, I guess that would be fun too."

Caleb pulled the truck into the parking lot close to the food court and they walked through the mall entrance hand in hand.

They each found the cuisine they wanted and met at a table in the center of the dining area.

Angie asked, "So how did Lacey actually get started in modeling?"

"She was in the fashion curriculum at the school, and I was taking photography classes. When I found out she needed pictures done, I got jealous thinking about another photographer getting to do them. So I bought a used camera and opened a studio not too long after graduation. Then I showed her my setup and proposed shooting the portfolio pictures for her. We arranged them into a nice book and took them to one of the big modeling agencies, and they liked them."

"Do you think I'm pretty enough to be a model?"

"Of course, you would be a perfect model. You're tall, slender, and have a great face. You are just what they are looking for, why do you ask?"

"Oh, I saw a story online about a local fitness model and thought it looked like fun."

"Well, I still have all my lighting equipment from back in my fashion photography days. We could set up a studio in the den if you want to give it a whirl. I could also use the studio to pick up some extra cash doing high school senior pictures and family portraits. I could also talk to the agency while we're there about shooting for them."

"Do you know an agency in Denver?"

"I know there's a pretty well known one near downtown Denver. We could shoot some pictures when we get a nice day for it, and I could take them in for you. Or we could both go, they would probably want to meet you anyway."

"That would be a blast!"

"Boy, this brings back some memories," commented Caleb.

"Oh, I'm sorry. I didn't mean to cause you any pain."

"Oh no, they're good memories. I've actually been kind of missing the excitement of those times, when I was first starting up my photography studio."

"Okay, let's do it then. I'll arrange the den so you have some space to set up your equipment."

"You know a modeling career comes with a lot of rejections, especially at first. You need to be emotionally prepared for that."

"I know, I just want to try for the fun of it."

"The first time I went in to the agency with pictures, they wanted Lacey but not me."
"Were you okay with that?"

"I was already making good money on my own, so I wasn't too upset about it. They had some specific requirements for the pictures for her book, and we just kept working at it. They were eventually satisfied with our work and signed both of us."
They finished their meals and wandered into the running store. Angie walked up to the counter and asked the salesman about the race, asking, "Do you have race applications for the Sneak?"

The salesman reached under the counter and handed Angie a plastic bag with some running swag and asked, "What size t-shirt would you like?"

Angie picked out some shoes and they ventured back out into the main corridor. As they strolled along Caleb asked, "Should we walk through the mall?"

"No, I'm kind of tired today. Let's just go home."

"Sounds good to me."

Caleb was awakened the next morning by the sound of water boiling, and the pleasant aroma of coffee brewing. Angie was already rummaging around in the spare room making space for Caleb to set up his lighting equipment.

"Wow you are really on top of this aren't you!" Caleb exclaimed.

"Yeah, I guess I'm kind of eager to get this modeling thing going!"

"Okay, I'll bring in my boxes from the garage and see what I can find. I know I moved it all out from California, because I used it to shoot Michelle's high school pictures. I hope I kept my backdrop stand and some of my big muslin backdrops, especially the gray one."

Angie went about clearing out the room, and Caleb went out to the garage to bring in his boxes from the apartment in Bozeman.

"Where do you want me to put these?" Caleb asked.

"Let's go ahead and unpack them. It won't do any good to just stuff boxes in the closet when we don't even know what's inside."

"Good point."

One by one the boxes were opened and unpacked. Caleb spotted a gray cloth in a big tote and commented, "Here's the big gray muslin I was talking about. I haven't seen this since I packed up to leave California."

Angie asked, "What's it for?"

"It's a backdrop. If we can find the stand we can set it up near one of the walls. You pose in front of it."

"Oh, okay."

Another box was full of smaller cases and Angie asked, "What's in all these boxes?"

Caleb looked over and said, "Oh good, you found the strobes. Now we just have to find the light stands, which I believe are in these black bags over here. Yup, now we have the backdrop, the stands and the lighting units. All I have to do is set them up and test them out. The stuff in the rest of these totes is either my own clothes or props from the studio in California."

"Well, let's go ahead and unpack it all. You can put your clothes in the closet in spare bedroom. It's still piled up with my stuff from when I moved in, but I need to get organized anyway. I just never had any ambition or incentive to get it done. I suppose we should run into Shopmart and get some hangers. For now let's just stick your clothing boxes in the spare bedroom, and we'll put all your studio stuff in the den."
"Sounds good."

Angie opened another tote and asked, "What are you doing with all these fancy women's clothes?"

"Oh wow, those are the prop clothes that we used for Lacey's portfolio. I didn't realize I still had all that!"

"This stuff is cute! I love the bustiers, do you think they will fit me?"

"They should, you are a little taller than she was but otherwise probably about the same."

"Oh look at this!" Angie exclaimed about one little garment. She held it up and said smiling, "Sorry, I have to go try this on right now."

"Go ahead! Hey I found my light meter, so I'm going to set up the flash units and start working on light ratios."

Soon Angie returned wearing a sexy garter and a slinky black bustier.

"So how do you like this?"

"Wow, that is one hot outfit! I don't know whether to take your picture or jump your bones!"

Angie laughed and said, "How about both?"

"Let's set up the backdrop and pull the love seat over in front of it. We can take some test shots and make sure everything is working right."

Angie wasn't shy at all in front of the camera, and worked the loveseat like she had been modeling all her life. Caleb was glad she was comfortable in front of the lens, which made his work much easier.

"Where did you learn to pose like this?"

Angie laughed and said, "My sister and I used to dress up and pretend we were supermodels when we were kids."

"Well it seems to have paid off, you are a natural! You know, not everyone can do this, and most people totally freeze up when they are in front of the camera. Myself, I look like I've never even seen a camera in my life when I'm trying to shoot my videos for the channel."

Caleb thumbed through the images on the camera's LCD and said, "Let's put these on the computer and have a look!"

Angie sat down beside him and they went through each image together.

Caleb commented, "These are pretty darn good! I wasn't planning on it, but I think we can actually use some of these to start building your book!"

"That's awesome Caleb!

"I still have a few more things to set up before we really get going. I still have to set up the hair light, and maybe you can pick out a few props."

"Yeah, I'm worn out right now though. Maybe we should just go find a movie and snuggle or something. We can go into town tomorrow to get some hangers, and maybe have lunch somewhere."

Caleb replied, "That sounds like a good plan. One of the first things I learned with Lacey's pictures is that agencies want to see a lot of natural looking outdoor settings. Maybe we could shoot a few on the old dam, and on the foundation of that old concrete building at the entrance to the park."

"Funny you should mention that. I've always wanted to play around on that old foundation. This modeling thing is going to be fun!"

"There might not be a lot of money in it at first," Caleb cautioned. Even in New York, Lacey used to complain that the money wasn't that good. Which I think is probably why she ended up quitting and launching the clothing line."

"Oh I know, I just want to have some fun. I'm not going to quit selling houses."

"Okay that's a relief, I was starting to feel some pressure there for a minute. It took a lot of time and effort to get Lacey going. You know she was working as a dancer in a club to supplement her income until the money started flowing."

"She was a stripper?"

"No, it was a bikini dance club in Sunnyvale. It was a fun place, but she was really glad when she could finally quit and model full time."

"Yeah no worries, we are just going to do this for fun. If I can make a few extra bucks along the way, it will just be a bonus."

Caleb answered, "We are definitely going to have some fun!"

The weeks passed quickly and it was soon time for the big race. The traffic on race day in Cherry Creek was horrific, and parking seemed impossible.

"Why don't I just drop you off at the starting line and I'll go find a parking spot at the mall. Which wave are you in just in case I can't find you before the start?"

"I'm in wave B, right behind the elite runners."

"Okay, I'll see you in a few minutes."

Fortunately they had arrived early, and Caleb was able to pull right in to a spot in the shopping center parking lot. He got out of the truck, slung one strap of his backpack over his shoulder and wandered over to the starting line. Groups of runners were congregating near their wave in preparation for their starting time. Luckily he quickly spotted Angie stretching on the grass beside the road.

"Hey Angie, are you ready to go?"

"I think so, I wish they would get this thing going. The elite runners are starting first, so you might want to get into position to catch their wave."

"Yeah, this looks like a pretty big deal. I suppose I should get a little serious about the pictures so I can get some stock images, and maybe write an article. Well, good luck, I'll be watching for you!"

Caleb went down the street about fifty yards where he knew from experience there would be enough separation between runners to get a dramatic image of the mass start. Unfortunately there were a lot of other photographers with the same idea, and he was worried they would ruin his captures. The utility posts beside the road were supported by a concrete base, with just enough room for a foothold to stand on. Caleb thought to himself, "*I'll jump up there just as the group gets close, and hang on until the wave has passed.*"

He heard the starting horn and looked up to see the elite runners approaching fast. There were no other photographers in his line of sight so he just started shooting. He scanned the group with his wide angle zoom lens, looking for artistic patterns of runners until the wave had completely passed. A quick check of his viewing screen revealed that his choice of exposure settings resulted in pleasing captures with no blown highlights.

Now it was time for Angie's wave. He zoomed all the way in to the maximum 105mm of focal length, and scanned the crowd for his blonde fiance. Luckily she was on the outside edge of the pack where he could easily get a full body shot as she ran by. The horn sounded and the group left the starting line at nearly as fast a pace as the elite runners. Just as Angie was nearing the best angle, another photographer jumped right in the way. Caleb quickly went to Plan B and jumped up on the concrete light stand. He trained his lens in on Angie and started shooting.

Angie noticed him on the pole and waved and smiled as she passed. Soon her wave was past, and Caleb turned around to look for an artistic compilation as the group faded into the distance. It was a beautiful day along the Cherry Creek Trail, which was lined with pink blossoms in full bloom. Caleb thought to himself, "*It would actually be difficult to shoot a bad picture in this kind of scenery!*"

Caleb knew it would be at least fifteen or twenty more minutes before the elite runners would approach the finish line, so he snapped a few environmental captures before wandering back to the banner. There was a big crowd of photographers amassed at the finish line, so Caleb walked up the street a few yards until all the other cameras were behind him. His plan was to get a tight shot of the lead packs of both men and women, before widening out his field of view for some environmental captures of the professional runners.

He knew Angie would be running about six minute miles and he calculated the approximate time of her arrival, exactly 30 minutes from her starting time. "*She might run a little faster, so I'd better be ready five minutes ahead of time,*" thought Caleb. He looked up the street for the perfect background to accentuate her flowing blonde hair, and spotted a wide patch of blue sky between the buildings.

Then all of a sudden, he saw her come flying around the corner. For her pictures he would concentrate mostly on tight shots, hoping for the perfect capture. He was glad to have the morning sun at his back, beautifully illuminating the runners in a soft golden glow. "*Her hair is going to look amazing in this light,*" thought Caleb. As she neared, he zoomed in to the maximum focal length of his lens and began to shoot short bursts of images at 15 frames per second. He didn't want to accidentally fill the camera's buffer and miss the best capture, so he kept his bursts to a second or less. He checked his watch and saw that she was running very close to her planned pace. "*Maybe she will set a PR this time*" he mused.

On this pass she wasn't looking around for Caleb. Her determined eyes were fixed upon the finish line, and he made sure to capture the intensity of the moment.

The crowd began to cheer even more loudly when they became aware of her effort, which spurred her on even more. By the time she crossed the finish line she was running full speed. She crossed the line and quickly slowed to a walk as she passed through the chute. He ran past the crowd, eager to meet her on the other side.

She was all smiles by that time and said to Caleb, "I did it, I broke my previous PR time! First time I ever beat a six minute pace on this course!"

"That's awesome Angie! I knew you could do it!"

"I wasn't sure at first, but after about a mile or so I hit my stride. Then with about a mile to go I was still running strong and started to think I could do it."

"I'm so proud of you! Hey, there's a band playing in the park. Should we get some snacks and listen to the music for a while?"

"Yes, it's a beautiful day and I want to watch the awards ceremony. I think there's a chance I could win an age group medal. I don't really remember seeing any women passing me."

Caleb replied, "That would be pretty cool!"

Angie and Caleb enjoyed their morning in the sun as they listened to the music, and she did indeed win first place in her age group. Caleb looked on with pride as she strode up to the podium to receive her award. He followed close behind so he would be sure to get a picture of the announcer putting the medal around her neck. She turned to him and held it high so he could freeze that moment in time.

After the pictures Angie commented, "Well, I guess that's about it. Should we head back to Franktown?"

"Sounds good to me."

"Maybe we could go up to the old house in the canyon this evening and get a few pictures. I'm kind of eager to see what we can do with that place."

Caleb replied, "Sure, as long as the sunshine holds out there should be some pretty nice lighting in the late afternoon. We should probably pick up some fresh AA batteries for my flash trigger on the way home, ."

When they got home Angie went to the shower and Caleb rummaged around looking for the flash trigger. Without that he wouldn't be able to remotely fire the flash to provide the key light. He liked to use natural sunshine from behind as a hair light, while using a strobe to provide the key light. Fortunately the trigger was still in the bag along with his 200 watt second strobes, and he installed the fresh batteries and set it up for the low light of a waning spring afternoon.

Angie came out of the shower and asked, "Do you want to sit out on the back deck for a while?"

"That sounds like a great idea. I'll get us a couple beers, and maybe we can catch a little nap."

In just a few minutes, Caleb could tell from the sound of her breathing beside him that Angie was already snoozing. They had gotten up very early for the race and he knew she had to be tired. Soon the warm sunshine on his shoulders soothed his mind and muscles and he was asleep as well.

Caleb awoke to the sound of a blue jay calling to it's friends. He looked over, and Angie had already gone back into the house. He could see that the sun was getting low in the sky to the west and called out to her, "Angie, do you still want to do the pictures this afternoon?"

"Yes, I'm putting on my makeup now."

"Okay, I'll gather up the equipment."

The sun was rapidly sinking in the sky and there was no time to lose. They rushed out the door and hopped in the truck. Even though it was only a mile or so to the old ruins as the crow flies, it was a ten mile trip on the road. By the time they arrived at their destination, Caleb estimated they had about 45 minutes to shoot before the background would be completely black in the images.

"Let's have you pose in the doorway first."

Angie went over and worked the doorway like a pro. Caleb's 200 watt light system had no trouble firing every half second and before long he and Angie were completely in sync, shooting one lovely pose after another. Caleb was astonished at how quickly he and Angie learned to synchronize pose with capture. It was a skill that had taken he and Lacey a hours to develop.

"That's great Angie, you're a real pro!"

"Oh stop it, I've only been modeling for like five minutes now."

Caleb laughed and said, "It doesn't matter how long you have been doing it, only how well you do it!"

Angie laughed too and said, "Well you're the boss, so if you say so!"

"Is there any way you can climb up into the upper window frame?"

Angie looked up at the window and said, "No problem!"

Once again she worked the window frame like a pro, finding a dozen different ways to bend her body into professional looking poses for Caleb to capture. In the meantime the sun had dipped below the ridge to the west, and the light on the ruins was rapidly dissipating. Caleb thought about an alternative location, and remembered a split rail fence on the east side of the road on the approach to the park.

"We've lost the light here, so let's go back to that old fence we saw about a mile back."

"Sure, that sounds like fun!"

Caleb climbed the fence so he could use the beautiful sunset as a backdrop. Lacey followed, and leaned against the fence in another amazingly alluring pose. With the strobe's power turned down to provide only fill light, the pink and golden sky provided the most beautiful backdrop Caleb had ever seen.

"Man, this Colorado sky is something else!"

"Yes, I don't think there are even words to describe the beauty of a Rocky Mountain sunset."

"Okay, work the fence and I'll just stand here and shoot! We are only a half hour into your new career and I hardly even need to say a word! You are doing great!"

Eventually the sun dipped below the horizon and the color faded from the sky. In that short time Caleb had managed to collect over two hundred beautiful captures of his new fashion partner, and said "Well that was a great session. What do you say we take them back to the house and have a look?"

"Sounds good to me. Wow, that was fun!"

"I had fun too. I think we may really be onto something here!"

The pair got back in the vehicle and drove the ten miles back to the house in the dark. Caleb imported the pictures into the computer and brought them up on the screen.

"Angie, come and look!"

"Wow Caleb these are beautiful! You are an amazing photographer!"

"Well, being a photographer is easy when you have such an amazing subject to work with! You really caught on fast, quicker than some of the agency models that I used to work with out in California."

"Seriously?"

"I am serious, you are really good! Did you and your sisters play runway model too? The catwalk takes a lot of practice to get just right."

"Oh yes, there's not a whole lot to do in the winter in Bozeman. We did it up big when we put on our make believe shows!"

"Cool, it's going to take me a couple hours to get these all processed. Are you wanting to take them up to Denver tomorrow?" Caleb asked

"Sure, I'd like to have my book done before the summer house buying season gets in full swing. I have appointments on Wednesday so we can do it either tomorrow or Tuesday, if you need the extra time to process them."

"Let's do it Tuesday, that way we can call tomorrow and set an appointment. We might go all the way downtown for nothing if we aren't actually on their calendar."

Angie answered, "Okay, well why don't we just get a glass of wine and watch a movie for a while."

"Sure, why don't you pick one out while I back these files up. These are way too good to take a chance of losing to a hard drive crash."

The next day Caleb called to set an appointment, and the receptionist checked the calendar while he waited.

"I can get you in at 4:30 today, will that work for you?"

"Angie, they want to see the pictures today. Is that okay with you?"

"Sure, what time?"

He set the appointment with the agency and went about processing and printing the best of the images. It was already one in the afternoon by the time he was ready and he said, "How about we head on up and get some lunch."

"Sure, I already have my hair and makeup done so let's go! I'm so excited I can't stand it!"

"Okay just remember, they are most likely going to be non committal and will ask for some more pictures. I'll bet you ten dollars they want to see swimsuit pictures on the beach."

"All right, I'll try to contain myself."

Caleb laughed and replied, "Well I don't know about that, just remember this is only the first step in a process."

Angie asked, "Where should we eat?"

"Do you like Mexican food?"

"I love Mexican food."

"I heard there's a good place up on 3rd not too far from the agency."

"Are you talking about the Old Town Brewery?"

"That's the one!"

"I love that place. The girls and I have lunch there once in a while. I hope you like hot food though, like really hot!"

"Sounds perfect!"

Angie and Caleb walked into the agency and were met at the door by Ashley the receptionist.

"You must be Angie, and is this Caleb? I'm Ashley."

"Yes I'm Angie, and this is my photographer Caleb."

"Come on in and have a seat. I'll let Amanda know you are here."

After a few minutes a pretty middle aged blond woman walked out of one of the offices and said, "Hi, I'm Amanda the lead rep here. Come on back."

Angie and Caleb followed her into her office and took a seat in front of the huge wooden desk.

"Is that your book?" Amanda asked.

"I'm still working on it, but that's what I have for now."

"Well, let's have a look!"

Angie handed the loose leaf binder with pictures inside clear plastic sleeves to Amanda, and said "I can get more if you need them."

Amanda put on her glasses and slowly turned the pages. After looking at a few she looked over the top of her glasses and asked, "These are really good, where did you get your training?"

Angie responded, "I haven't had any formal training, but I've done a lot of practicing on my own."

"How about you Caleb, where did you go to school?"

Caleb responded, "I took photography at a California Community College in Cupertino. I shot for the Kristi K agency for a while before I moved out of the area."

"Well Angie, I think we can find a place for you in our lineup. What I would like you to do is go out and get some more pictures. We would like to see at least four different looks including one set in swimwear, perhaps on a beach in natural light. Will that be any problem?"

"No, I can get that done. I'm traveling out of town early next month to get married, so it might have to wait until after that."

"That's fine. Let me get your packet of paperwork. You can take it home and get it all signed. Will you be able to get it back to me this week?"

"Oh absolutely, I'll get it done right away!"

"And can you also bring me copies of these pictures when you return?"

Angie asked, "Caleb, can you make copies with your computer?"

"Sure, no problem. We might even have time to shoot another look before we have to leave for the wedding."

Amanda responded, "Great, I'm looking forward to working with you Angie! Now Caleb, how would you like to do some shooting with us?"

"I would love to!"

"Good, let me get some paperwork for you as well."

Amanda handed Caleb a contract packet and walked them both to the door.

On the way to the truck, Caleb said "I can't believe this, you got a contract on your first visit. That's amazing! Do you have any idea how amazing that is?"

"I know right? My head is in the clouds right now! I know we have a wedding to plan, but I really want to get this going. Do you think we could get those beach pictures before we leave for Montana?"

"I don't think that will be a problem. Tomorrow is supposed to be sunny and warm, maybe we could run out to Chatfield or up to Cherry Creek Reservoir. Cherry Creek has that cool looking lifeguard stand that I think would make a great prop."

"I don't even have a swimsuit. Let's stop off at Shopmart on our way home and see if they have the summer stuff out yet."

Caleb replied, "Of course, I need to pick up some more batteries as well."

They spent the next few hours planning a photo session and the wedding, both of them nearly in disbelief at how fast their plans were coming together.

Chapter Eleven

The time had come for Caleb and Angie to depart for their wedding in Montana. Her mom and dad had completed all the planning necessary for the ceremony at the church, followed by the reception at the Alpine Tap.

"Angie, do you think we should stop at the Sand Wash on the way out to Bozeman?"

"No, I just want to get out there. In fact let's just take the interstate all the way. We can stop and camp at the Sand Wash on the way back. That way we can just enjoy ourselves with no pressure to be somewhere else."

"Sounds good, are you ready to go?"

"Yup, I just need to put some drinks in the cooler. Should I throw in a few beers or should we just wait and get some in Bozeman?"

"Go ahead and put a few in. If we take the interstate I'm pretty sure we can make it in one day, but we'll be rolling in late and the liquor stores might not be open."

"Will you help carry this out to the truck? With the ice and the drinks it's pretty heavy."

"Of course, is that the last thing?" Caleb asked.

"This is it!"

"Okay then, let's lock the door on our way out and hit the road! Do we have any need to go through Parker, or should we just take 86 straight over to the freeway?"

Angie answered, "Let's just go straight over to Castle Rock and get on I25."

It was still dark on that Monday in early May as they pulled out of the driveway.

Caleb commented, "Hopefully we'll be all the way through Denver before it even gets light.."

"Yeah, it would be great to beat the traffic."

They sped past the outlet stores and through the Tech Center before sunlight began to glow in the sky to the east. Traffic near downtown Denver was just starting to intensify, and soon the skyscrapers were but twinkling lights in the distance behind them. By the time the sun had cleared the horizon, Angie and Caleb were well on their way to Loveland.

"What do you think about pulling off at Loveland for a little breakfast? The thermos could use a warm up too."

"That sounds fine Caleb, whatever you think. You are doing the driving."

"Can you do a search for breakfast places?"

"Sure," Angie replied. She looked at her phone and added, "I don't really see much in the way of breakfast. If it were lunch time we'd be in business."

"Well there's always The Mountain View truck stop right along the highway. That's probably better anyway, we can get gas, food and fill the thermos all in one stop. That way we won't burn up too much time."

With full stomachs and a hot thermos full of coffee, they were back on the freeway heading north to Cheyenne.

Caleb asked, "Did you remember to bring the thumb drive with the music?"

"I did, do you want to hear some tunes?"

"Sure, we have nothing but wide open space in front of us. What do you think, some country?"

Angie answered, "Out here on the high prairie, it kind of reminds me of life back home. Country seems right."

They passed Cheyenne with three quarters of a tank of gas remaining. There was no need to stop, and Casper was the next big town on the route.

"Maybe we'll be ready for a rest in Casper. Do you want to get a nap in? I'm probably going to need a break for a couple hours between there, and maybe Sheridan."

"Yeah, I am feeling a little sleepy. I'll see if I can get some shut eye."

Angie grabbed a pillow and a jacket for a blanket from the back seat, and leaned her seat back. Caleb turned down the music, and it wasn't long before he could tell from her steady breathing that she was asleep. He set the cruise control for 75 mph and settled in for a two hour stretch across the Wyoming high prairie.

Caleb was still feeling strong with plenty of gas in the tank when they cruised right past Casper. Angie finally began to stir as the vehicle slowed when he eventually made the turn into a truck stop near Sheridan.

"Where are we?" Angie asked as she opened her eyes and looked around.

"Truck stop in Sheridan."

"Wow, I slept hard!"

"Yeah, I was doing fine when we got to Casper so I just kept going. Are you hungry, or should we just make a quick gas stop?"

"I don't know, how far is it to Bozeman?"

"Let's see, it's one in the afternoon now, I imagine we'll be in Bozeman around five this afternoon."

"Yeah, let's sit down and get something to eat. With a little jolt of caffeine I think I can drive the whole stretch through Montana."

They were soon on the road again, and the monotonous drone of the motor knocked Caleb right out. Angie switched the station to classic rock, and her thoughts drifted off to her family awaiting her in Bozeman. By the time Caleb began to stir, the Gallatin Range dominated the view to the west.

"Looks like we must be close," commented Caleb.

"Yup, we just passed Livingston. The last sign I saw said Bozeman 20 miles, so we are definitely on the home stretch."

A few minutes later Angie was pulling the pickup into the driveway of her childhood home. Her mother was watching for them, and rushed out to greet them before they even had a chance to open the doors..

Her mom greeted her asking, "How was your trip?"

Angie answered, "The miles actually went by pretty fast!"

"Well, come on in! We can bring in your stuff later. Robert is here of course, and your sisters will be coming in later this week."

Angie asked, "Are Michelle and Julie coming up from Gardiner?"

Caleb replied, "I talked to Michelle earlier this week, and she said they were definitely coming up for the ceremony."

"Okay good," responded Angie.

Kate commented, "Joanie is going to be our bartender for the reception at the Tap."

Angie added, "Good, she is my favorite."

"Sounds like we are all set then!" Caleb said.

"I think so," replied Kate.

Robert greeted Angie and Caleb inside and asked, "Can I get you a beer?"

Caleb replied, "A beer sounds pretty good right now!"

Angie's mom was scurrying around getting the sleeping arrangements ready when she said, "I suppose you two are sleeping together now, or should I get a second room ready for Caleb?"

"Oh Mom, we've been living together for months. Do you honestly think Caleb is still sleeping on the couch?"

"Oh I know, but I just wanted to be sure."

Caleb finished his beer and said, "I'm going out to bring in the suitcases."

"Do you need any help?" Robert asked.

"No, I'm just going to bring in the two overnight bags and my camera."

As Caleb stowed the bags in the bedroom he commented, "I think I'll run down to the park in the morning, if that's okay with everyone else."

Angie's mom replied, "That's fine Caleb. We assumed you would want to get down there and see the wolves."

"Hey Mom, guess what."

"What?"

"I got a new job!"

"You did, what are you going to be doing?"

"I got signed as a model with an agency in Denver!"

"Can you make any money doing that?"

"Oh I don't know. It doesn't matter, I'm not going to quit selling houses."

"I remember you girls putting on those pretend shows. I always thought one of you would try to be a model."

"I couldn't have done it without Caleb and his camera. They signed him as a photographer to shoot for them as well."

Caleb said, "I'm going to keep up with my writing too. Out in California I had plenty of time for both."

"That's great, I'm glad you two can find things you can do together."

Angie replied, "It should be fun."

Eventually Caleb's eyelids grew heavy and he said, "I'm going to turn in."

"You go ahead Caleb. I'm going to sit up and talk wedding plans with Mom for a while. I'm sure we would bore you to death anyway, and you probably want to get up early to go down to the park."

"Yeah, weddings aren't my strong suit," commented Caleb.

Caleb was on the road before sunrise in the morning. He always liked to be in the Lamar Valley when the first rays of sunlight began reflecting on the crystal clear water of the river. But this time he wanted to check in at the cafe first to see if either Michelle or Julie were working.

Julie was behind the cash register when Caleb walked in.

"Hi Caleb, I was hoping you would be stopping in this week!"

"Yeah, I wanted to see Michelle and of course you as well."

"Black coffee this morning?" Julie asked as she seated Caleb at a table.

"You remember! I think I'll have some scrambled eggs and toast too."

Julie typed in the order and brought Caleb his coffee.

"So are you and Michelle coming up for the wedding Saturday?"

"We sure are! Michelle has the day off and I found someone to fill in for me here at the cafe. We are looking forward to it!"

"I'm glad, you and Michelle are like family to me."

"Your family isn't coming?"

"No, I didn't even bother to tell them, they wouldn't come anyway."

"That's sad."

"Naaa, I'm used to it. I haven't seen them since I got back from the war."

"Well it's still sad."

"I'll have you and Michelle there. I'm closer to you than I ever was my own family."

"I'm glad we can be there for you."

"Is Michelle working down in the park today?"

"She said she would be patrolling the Lamar Valley again today."

"I'll probably run into her somewhere along the river then."

The early morning glow was reflecting on a placid Lamar River as Caleb descended into the valley. Bison were already on the move along the river bank, and pronghorn were grazing on the slopes to the north of Highway 212. Caleb pulled over immediately when he spotted a grizzly with two cubs approaching the river from the south.

Caleb leaped out of the truck and fired off a few shots to be assured of a record of the sighting before the animals had a chance to leave. While he was shooting he heard footsteps behind him, and a sweet young voice saying "Hey Caleb, are you getting some good pictures?"

He knew immediately who it was and responded, "Hi Michelle, how are you this morning?"

"I'm good, how are the wedding plans coming along?"

"Angie's mom seems to have everything under control. The ceremony is set at the church for Saturday, and she has the Alpine Tap reserved for the reception I talked to your mom this morning at the cafe, and she said you are planning to come up."
"Yes, we both managed to get the day off and will be riding up together Saturday morning."

"I'm so glad you are both going to be there."

"We wouldn't miss it for the world!"

"So how are things in the park, did the wolves survive the winter okay?"

"We had a pretty good winter. They are still protected by the Endangered Species Act, but as I said before, the Turner Administration is lobbying hard to have them removed from the list. We've been able to prevent that action so far, and there are only a few more months to the election. If he wins again though, all bets are off. If we lose the ESA I don't know what will happen to the wolves."

"Boy, that's a double edged sword. Either the Republicans win and destroy the environment, or the democrats win and destroy the economy and shred the constitution. Ansel Adams had it right when he said, "It is horrifying when you have to fight your own government to protect the environment."

"Yeah, sometimes it's like trying to stop the wind with a broom."

The bears eventually became nervous when a crowd began to form along the highway, and wandered back to the south toward the dense forest. A few wolves from the Lamar Pack had come out to the edge of the clearing to survey the valley, hoping for an opportunity for a meal. Bison were feeding between the forest and the river, but didn't appear to be disturbed by the presence of the wolf pack.

Caleb asked, "Have you been up toward Cooke City yet this morning?"

"No, I'm headed that direction now. Are you going to continue east?"

"Probably not. I don't think I'll be much help with the wedding plans, but I suppose Angie might need me at some point. Mostly I was just hoping to see you for a few minutes today."

Michelle Answered, "Okay, well I guess I'd better move on down the line."

"All right then, I'll see you in a couple days!"

As he neared Tower Junction on the return trip, he heard the plink of a text message arriving on his phone. It was Angie letting him know that her sisters had arrived, and she said "Hey Caleb, Jessie and Emily just got here. Will you be back in time to go to lunch with us? We are going to go over to the Alpine Tap so we can talk to Joanie for a few minutes."

"That's great! Yes I'm on my way back now, so I should be there by 11:30 or so. Will that be good?"

"That should be perfect. I'll see you in a little while then."

Caleb was satisfied with his captures of the bears and a few bison, and turned his truck back toward Tower Junction. In the meantime in Bozeman, the three girls were busy fitting dresses and preparing for the rehearsal. Caleb wasn't particularly interested in all that, but he didn't want to appear indifferent either. He thought there might be some kind of lunch arranged, and wanted to get back to Bozeman before the girls all left the house so they could all go together.

The drive took a bit longer than Caleb was expecting and the driveway was empty when he arrived. Caleb walked up to the door and saw a note that said, "Meet us at the Tap."

Joanie saw him walk through the front door and rushed over to give him a hug, saying "Look who finally made it!"

Caleb replied, "Hi Joanie, it's good to see you! How have you been?"

"Oh you know me, living the dream!"

Emily and Jessie also gave him a warm greeting, and finally Angie invited him to sit with her and order lunch.

"Caleb, come and sit. We've already ordered, but I'm sure you can still get yours in with ours."

Joanie came over and asked, "Do you need a menu Caleb?"

"No, just bring me a burger cooked medium and fries if that's okay."

"No problem, can I get you a beer?"

"That sounds pretty good Joanie, do you still have the dark that I like?"

"We sure do, one dark brew coming right up!"

Caleb sipped his beer while the girls excitedly exchanged ideas, while Caleb was content to just rest and listen. Joanie soon brought out all the food and sat down beside him asking, "So are you guys going on a big honeymoon?"

Caleb laughed, "You bet we are. We are going to stop on the way home and camp out with the mustangs at the Sand Wash Basin."

"That doesn't sound very romantic."

"I don't know, I don't think there's anything more romantic than wild horses running free in the high desert of beautiful Colorado!"

Joanie laughed and said, "Well maybe so, but I think that's a different kind of romantic adventure than you would want for a honeymoon."

"Perhaps, but it suits us just fine."

The rest of the week was a whirlwind of planning and soon Caleb was dressed in a tux and standing at the alter with his friend Michelle, who agreed to be his best woman. Caleb by nature had avoided most people during his time in Bozeman, and Michelle was his only close friend. It was Julie who had noticed and commented, "Caleb, you can't be standing up front all by yourself!"

"Why not?"

"Well because, it just wouldn't look right. You must know someone who can stand up there with you."

"Well other than Angie, my only real friend in Montana is Michelle."

Angie then chimed in, "Well it might be a bit different, but why couldn't Caleb have a best woman?"

Angie's mom followed up with, "I don't see why not."

Angie replied, "Well then, let's give her a call and see if she wants to."

"Works for me," confirmed Caleb.

Suddenly it was time for Caleb to approach the alter. He didn't want to attract attention to himself, so it was agreed he would approach from the side rather than walking all the way down the aisle. Michelle followed close behind and stood beside him. The organist then began to play the processional, and Jessie walked down the main aisle, followed by Emily and then Kate.

A couple of Angie's little cousins were recruited to be the flower girl and ring bearer, and after their entrance there was moment of silence. The bridal march began to play, and soon Angie appeared in the doorway. Michelle squeezed Caleb's hand and whispered, "She looks amazing!" His heart skipped a beat, and for a second he felt a bit weak in the knees.

Michelle giggled a little and whispered, "Do you want to make a run for it?"

"I don't think so, I can't feel my legs!"

"Time to cowboy up my friend!"

"Oh boy."

Angie looked like an angel as she glided elegantly down the aisle. For Caleb the entire ceremony was a blur, right up to the point when the minister said, "You may kiss the bride." The two partners who had experienced so many escapades together through the years now began an entirely new adventure, one of a completely different nature than they were accustomed to. Previous feats were experienced in hiking boots and blue jeans. This new chapter in their lives began with styled hair and makeup, high heels, a formal dress and a tuxedo.

They remained in a tight embrace for a few seconds. The recessional had been playing for a while when Caleb heard Michelle in the background saying, "Hey guys, time to go!"

Caleb looked around in somewhat of a daze before putting his hand on Angie's shoulder to guide her down the steps. Compared to the grace of the processional, Angie practically ran out of the church with Caleb in tow. A small group of visitors were waiting outside, including a few of Angie's childhood friends and of course Michelle's mom. Bird seed was flying everywhere as the couple exited the building, followed by the rest of the wedding party.

A car was waiting for the newlyweds, and soon everyone was gathered inside the Alpine Tap for the small reception. Joanie congratulated the new couple at the door as others began streaming in. Julie and Michelle quickly found Caleb and joined him at a table, while Angie was mobbed by friends and family.

Michelle asked, "Are you going on a honeymoon?"

"We are going camping at the Sand Wash Basin on our way back through Colorado."

Michelle laughed and said, "That sounds about right for you guys. Are you going to be coming back through the park on your way down there?"

"I think we will camp out in Gardner tonight and then tomorrow we'll go through the park to Jackson, and then on down to Rock Springs. We might actually find a nice place to stay in Jackson for our real honeymoon."

"I think you guys owe it to yourselves to have at least one night to celebrate in a nice place! There are a few fun things to do in Jackson, you should definitely do that. I guess I won't get to see you along the Lamar tomorrow morning then."

Caleb replied, "You should stop by the campground tonight."

"Oh, I don't want to bother you guys on your first night."

"We've been together every night for months. Go ahead and stop by, it would be nice for us to have the company!"

"Okay, I might just do that then. Do you want me to bring anything?"

"No, we'll probably get some snacks and a couple meals from the market, and maybe pick up some wine. We'll have everything we need, so just stop in! Bring your mom if she doesn't have anything else to do."

"Okay I will. Looks like Mom is waiting outside, so you have a nice drive down!"

The party eventually wound down and the newlyweds bid farewell to Angie's family. They wanted to make it to Gardiner before the office at the campground along the Yellowstone River was closed for the night. By late afternoon Angie and Caleb were checked in and enjoying a hot meal from the market, while being serenaded by the soothing sound of the Yellowstone River flowing past on it's way to the Mighty Missouri.

Just before sunset a car approached, and Caleb said "That's probably Michelle. She was going to stop by and visit for a bit."

Michelle got out of her car and walked over as Angie greeted her, "Hi sweetie, how was your drive home?"

"It was okay, how is your first evening of wedded bliss?"

Caleb answered, "Good, we each ate one of those hot meals from the market."

Angie offered, "Would you like a beer or a glass of wine?"

"A glass of wine sounds good."

"So how do you like your ranger job?" Angie asked.

"I love it, I just love being in the park every day."

Angie replied, "I'll bet you have a ton of good animal stories."

"Oh my God. You wouldn't believe the stunts people pull."

"We see some crazy stuff on the internet sometimes."

"Yeah, the people seem to think since the bison are just big cows. But bison can get really angry so quickly, and they are so powerful and fast."

Angie asked, "How are the wolf packs faring?"

"So far the numbers are holding steady. We haven't had any like Luna to take her place, but people have all found new favorites in the Lamar and Mollie packs. Hunting has remained fairly subdued with quotas in place, but we lose a few of our park wolves every year. Grizzlies are doing well too, although 399 lost her cubs to a boar attack this season."

"Oh, that's too bad," commented Caleb.

Michelle asked, "Did you hear about the Sand Wash horses?"

"What's that?" Angie asked.

"They had a big roundup a while ago and somehow they all got out of the holding pen."

Angie smiled and answered, "We heard."

Michelle looked at her and got a sudden sparkle in her eyes. She started to ask, "Was that," and then her voice trailed off. "Never mind," she said smiling. "I don't want to know."

Angie asked, "Are you dating anyone, or does your job take up all your time?"

"I get out once in a while but nothing steady. I'm not really interested in a serious boyfriend at this point. A couple guys I was going out with got all whiny about my hours at the park, and I just don't want to deal with it. I'd rather be out here with the tourists," Michelle answered laughingly.

"I don't blame you," Angie responded. "I had that same problem in Denver. I would go out on a date or two and all of a sudden they seemed to think they owned me. That is until Caleb came along of course!"

Caleb said, "I'm too busy with my own projects to worry about what hours someone else is working."

Michelle answered, "Yeah, I need a guy like Caleb."

Angie said, "Hold out for a photographer, they are always off on some new adventure."

"That's a good idea, we do have some cute ones hanging around here sometimes. I've always thought them to be a bit nerdy, but you make a good point!"

Angie changed the subject back to wildlife and said, "I'm surprised the Republicans haven't removed the wolves from the endangered list by now."

Michelle answered, "Not for the lack of trying. They've only been stopped by public outcry. We're worried they are going to wait until just after the election to act. Whether they win or lose, they will be able to act without concern for getting reelected."

Caleb replied, "Well hopefully the public will have enough leverage to stop any drastic action they have in mind."

"I hope so," Michelle sadly replied.

The lively conversation eventually trailed off and the three sipped their wine in silence. After a while Angie said, "Don't you just love the sound of the river?"

Michelle answered, "Yes it's very peaceful, sometimes too peaceful. I wish you guys could visit more often."

Caleb replied, "I know, I've missed you too. I miss stopping in at the cafe and chatting with you early in the morning."

"I know, I always enjoyed your stop overs."

Angie asked Michelle, "Do you get vacation time?"

"I get 26 paid days a year."

"You are welcome to come out to Denver and visit us anytime you like!"

"Seriously, you guys wouldn't mind?"

"We would love to have you. We could pick you up at the airport if you get a flight, and we have plenty of room. You should do it!"

"Maybe I could come out between Thanksgiving and Christmas this year. I'd want to be back home for Christmas though, or my mom would be all alone."

Angie replied, "Make plans, it would be fun!"

"Okay, I will definitely check out some flights, I can't wait!"

Michelle slowly finished her glass of wine and said, "Well, I'd better get going, I have an early day tomorrow."

Caleb said, "Thanks for stopping by, I'm glad we got to spend some quality time with you."

"Yeah, it was kind of hectic at the wedding wasn't it."

Angie added, "Be careful around all those animals in the park, especially the two legged ones!"

Michelle laughed and said, "Isn't that the truth! I will, and you guys have a lovely honeymoon. Try not to get into trouble at the Sand Wash."

Caleb laughed and said, "Staying out of trouble is always our goal."

Michelle waved one last time and rolled away.

Angie said, "She is such a sweetheart. I hope she comes to see us."

"She seemed sincere about wanting to visit. Do you think she knew we were the ones that let the horses loose?"

Angie chuckled and said, "Oh definitely, she knew."

They finished their wine and Angie said, "What do you say we get some sleep. I haven't seen the park since we went camping all those years ago, and I want to get down there early."

"Okay, sounds like a plan."

They had a nice drive through the park and arrived in Jackson just as the sun was slipping behind the Grand Teton range to the southwest. They quickly found a hotel and checked in.

Caleb asked, "Should we go out now, or do you want to grab a nap?"

"Heck no, let's go down to the bar and party!"

Caleb laughed and said, "That's the spirit!"

"I wonder what we should wear," mused Angie.

"I don't know, why don't you call down and see what kind of music they are playing."

Angie called the bar with her questions and said to Caleb, "They have a country band playing tonight."

"Sounds like blue jeans and boots then!"

Angie chuckled and commented, "This is Wyoming after all!"

They got dressed and moseyed down to the bar, stopping to look at some brochures along the way. A pretty brunette met them at the doorway to the restaurant and asked how many would be in their party.

Angie answered, "Just the two of us."

"Right over here."

The hostess led them over to a table for two, right next to the dance floor.

"Will this be okay?"

"This will be fine."

"Can I get you something to drink?"

Caleb answered, "I'll have a draft beer."

Angie asked for a glass of house wine just as the band came back from their break. The band began to play and the two sipped their drinks, which were especially refreshing after a long hot day on the road.

After a couple of lively songs the lead singer said, "We're going to slow it down."

Angie lit up when she heard the song, one of her favorites.

"Come and dance with me!"

Caleb followed his bride onto the dance floor and they locked in a loving embrace as they began to sway to the music. The slow ballad was followed by a two step, and the joy on Angie's face was not lost on Caleb. He too was filled with the joy of a moment that he never dreamed would come following the devastating loss of Lacey. Their food was being served just as the second song was wrapping up, and they sat down to enjoy their meal.

After a few more songs, Angie said "Wow, I'm feeling a bit woozy, take me to bed cowboy!"

"I thought you'd never ask," Caleb replied.

"But doesn't it feel like we've been married forever already?"

"Yeah," answered Caleb. "It seems like we should have been married before you ever left for Colorado. I think it was meant to be all along, from the moment we met at the Alpine Tap when I first moved to Bozeman."

"Strange isn't it, all of life's twists and turns."

Caleb replied, "Sometimes it blows my mind!"

With that, a beautiful day in one of the most picturesque locations in all the world came to an end. As the couple drifted off to sleep in their room, they hoped this was the first day of a long and happy life together.

Both were a bit groggy in the morning, and eager to get out of their room for some coffee and breakfast.

"Do you think we can make the Sand Wash Basin today?" Angie asked.

"Oh, I'm sure we can. Let's look it up."

Caleb got on his phone and checked the distance to Craig.

"Looks like it's only going to be about a six hour drive."

"Oh good, so we can take our time then."

"Right, there's no big hurry to get there. Maybe we can stop and have some lunch somewhere in Rock Springs."

"I wonder what happened to the horses we set free?"

"I don't know, they have to be better off than they were. At least they will be able to get to the watering hole when they get thirsty."

"Yeah, that was awful wasn't it?"

"I don't understand why they have to treat such wonderful animals so badly."

Caleb answered, "Yeah, it's like they don't even care. Maybe they should put a different agency in charge of them. I think Colorado Parks and Wildlife might do a better job, but it's federal land so I guess that's out."

"Well, should we hit the road?"

"Yes, let's get going. The sooner we get started the sooner we'll be there."

Chapter Twelve

The hot Colorado sun was already baking the sand in the basin when Angie and Caleb rolled into Craig. The heat was oppressive inside the cab of the truck, even with the air conditioning blowing full blast. The couple looked forward to a cool drink and some lunch at their favorite restaurant in town.

As they rolled through town Angie said, "Man it's hot today."

"Yeah we usually get a few afternoon clouds, but not today."

"Should we stop for some lunch?"

Caleb answered, "Definitely, I've been dreaming of a malted for fifty miles."

"I was thinking that same thing!"

As they walked through the door of the restaurant they heard the server say, "Seat yourself, I'll be right out!"

As she took their orders, their server asked "Are you here to see the horses?"

Angie answered, "We are, we just got married and are going to spend a few days of our honeymoon out in the desert with the mustangs."

"Well this is a good time to visit. They were going to get rid of a bunch of them, but they somehow got out of the holding pen and scattered."

Caleb commented, "Seriously, do they know how they got out?"

"They don't know. They think maybe somehow the gate didn't get locked."

"Well that worked out well for the wild horses didn't it?"

"I don't know, they will probably just round them up again. They put a bunch of sheep in the refuge and now there isn't enough food for the mustangs."

"Why would they do that, isn't it supposed to be a horse management area?"

"Supposed to be. I don't know, greedy ranchers I guess. They don't want to share the land or the grass, what little there is."

Caleb and Angie were soon on their way west to the Sand Wash when Angie said, "It sounds like we got away with it. No one seems to have any idea what happened. Stealing the lock really threw them off the track."

"I guess it might have been a mistake though. More will be injured or even killed in another roundup."

Angie replied, "When we get back home we need to start an email campaign with a petition attached for people to sign. There must be thousands of people in the metro area that care about wildlife and the mustangs."

"I'm pretty sure there's a chapter of our old wildlife defense organization in Colorado. Have you looked for it?"

"Oh, there's definitely some kind of online presence we can tap into."

As they neared the main entrance, Angie spotted a band of horses on the north side of the roadway. The herd appeared to be split, but as they drew near it became apparent there was only one horse on the east side waiting to cross.

Angie said, "Why doesn't that one cross over?"

"I don't know, is he injured?"

Angie got out the binoculars and peered through them at the lone stallion.

"I think that's Winter Storm. Why doesn't he cross?"

"Is he sick or something?"

"He's moving around okay, and it doesn't look like he's limping or anything."

"Let's get closer and check it out."

Caleb pulled closer to the band and said to Angie, "Should we park?"

"Yes, let's get out and see what's going on."

Caleb pulled off the highway and walked toward the main group with Angie right behind him.

Caleb crossed the road and tried to approach Storm, but his presence clearly agitated the old stallion.

Angie said, "Let me try. Maybe he's afraid of men after all the roundups and mistreatment of his family."

Angie slowly walked toward him, talking softly to him all the while. Winter Storm seemed much more tolerant of her and stood still as she approached. Caleb was astonished when the proud old mustang allowed her to walk up to him and stroke his mane. He watched as she reached into her pocket and took out a few sunflower seeds she had purchased for a snack at a truck stop. Storm sniffed her hand a few seconds and then took the seeds into his mouth. She reached around behind his jaw and slowly led him forward. Soon human and horse were safely across the dangerous roadway and back inside the refuge, and Angie game him a pat on the backside.

Winter Storm sensed that he was close to his band, and sounded out a happy nicker as he dropped his head and danced a little for joy at his reunion with his band. Angie watched for a few seconds and then turned back toward Caleb. Storm quickly joined his band which resumed meandering northward.

Angie commented, "I think he might be getting a little blind in his old age. He didn't seem to focus on me when I got close. However, he responded well to me talking softly to him. Maybe he has been treated kindly by women in the past. I think he was spooked by the embankment, another sign that maybe he can't see very well."

"He looks happy now," commented Caleb.

"He does seem happy to be back with his band. Wouldn't it be something if Storm's last contact with humans turned out to be an act of kindness?"

"That would be amazing after all these years of abuse at the hand of man."

"Well, should we pull in and find a campsite?"

Caleb replied, "I don't know, I don't see many people around. Maybe we should just drive on in and get some pictures while we still have the light. We can always find a campsite later."

"Good point. Let's go see some horses!"

Caleb steered the pickup toward the north side of the Wash, hoping to find an active herd to observe for a couple hours before sunset. Angie scanned the horizon with the binoculars while Caleb watched the road.

"There's a pretty good sized band ahead. It looks like they might be going down to the springs for a drink."

"Okay, let me try to get a little closer and find a pullout."

The couple found a good spot to park, and set up their camp chairs for a nice afternoon of horse viewing. They had a good view of the mustangs as the sun descending in the west illuminated them beautifully.

Caleb asked playfully, "How would you like to practice your modeling?"

"What? I'm not dressed for modeling, I don't even have makeup on."

"Well, you are dressed for horse watching aren't you?"

"I guess so, why?"

"I've decided to write a book about Winter Storm and the Sand Wash mustangs, and I have an idea for a cover with the horses and sand hills in the background. I need you in the foreground to add perspective and illustrate the story. Maybe we can even try a few with you looking at them with the binoculars or a camera with the long lens."

"Okay, I guess I can do that. Just give me a minute to put on some shorts and a nice top."

"I'll grab a flash unit out of the back while you get dressed."

After Angie found a nice outfit for the shoot, she came out and asked "Do you want me to just stand, or should I use a chair as a prop?"

"We could try some with props, but I have a minimalist vision for this cover. I basically want a clear shot of the mustangs and hills with you in the foreground to add context. Although I did get some great shots of you leading Winter Storm across the road earlier, so it's possible I might be able to use one of those."

"Okay, so what if I sit on that big rock over there looking out at the herd? Or I can sit, or stand with one foot on the rock for a few poses."

"That sounds perfect. I can set a flash unit off to the side to light your face. It will just take a minute to get the light ratio dialed in so that it blends well with the background."

Caleb and Angie shot until the animals were but dark shadows in the distance. Caleb took note of the encroaching sunset and said, "Maybe we should get to a high spot and find a site."

"That sounds good and I think we should light a campfire tonight. I bought some marshmallows a ways back for us to toast, when we stopped for gas."

"That sounds perfect. I'd like to get out early and do some more of these pictures at sunrise, if that's okay with you."

"That's fine. I have a couple more outfits I'd like to try. What do you think of the outfit I wore out dancing up in Jackson?"

"That's a great outfit. I think it just might be a prefect fit for the western theme I have planned for the book."

They drove back to the main road and looked for a high spot with a phone signal. There were no other campers so finding a secluded site was no problem. Caleb positioned the truck on a level area and turned off the engine.

Angie said, "Let's get a fire going right away. It will be nice to have some light to help set up camp with."

"Sure, I'll get out the package of firewood while you find the lighter and the marshmallows."

Soon there was a beautiful fire glowing in the pit they had dug, and Angie said "I'll go get the marshmallows. Can you find us a couple sticks?"

"I'll see what I can do."

Soon the newlyweds were sitting side by side toasting sugary treats over the fire, and Caleb commented "Funny how something so simple can be so much better toasted over a campfire."

Angie replied, "Yeah, and look at all those stars. There must be billions showing tonight."

"It is amazing. The sky is so clear it looks like we are right out in space with the stars."

Eventually the fire grew dim and Angie said, "Maybe we should get some sleep. It was a long day."

"I suppose we should dump a jug of water on the fire."

"Sure, we have plenty for a couple days and we can always drive back into town if we need to."

Caleb crawled into the camper shell and rolled out the sleeping bags, saying "Should we zip our bags together?"

"That would be nice, we can keep each other warm!!"

Angie was the first to fall asleep, leaving Caleb to his own thoughts. He lay quietly on his back, staring out the back window at the stars while contemplating the whirlwind experience behind them. He enjoyed the feeling of being married as he pondered what it would be like for them to grow old together. Would their marriage last as long and be as joyous as Angie's parents had been? He drifted off to sleep imagining a lifetime of memories they had already begun to accumulate.

The sound of a big engine jolted Caleb out of a deep sleep. A heavy duty pickup truck had just pulled up in the road next to their campsite. It was soon followed by another, which awakened Angie as well.

She asked sleepily, "What's going on?"

"I don't know, trucks pulling in for some reason. Well we're awake now, we might as well head back into the wildlife area where we saw the wild horses yesterday."

"Yeah, let's get going. It's already getting light and those trucks are making me nervous. I don't know what they are doing here."

The sun had completely cleared the ridge to the east by the time they arrived at the spot they had photographed the day before. Angie got out the binoculars to locate the herd and said, "The horses look nervous today. Usually it's just the little ones dancing around."

"They do, I wonder if there's a predator in the area. I've never heard of mountain lions around here, and I don't think there are any wolves."

Angie replied, "I don't know. Maybe there is a pack of coyotes, although I don't hear any. Coyotes usually make a lot of noise."

The horses grew more restless by the minute, so the pair scanned the horizon searching for some kind of threat that might be disturbing band of horses below.

Caleb asked, "What's that sound, do you hear something?"

"Yeah, kind of a thumping noise in the distance."

"Wow, it sounds like those big military helicopters that fly over our house on their way up to the Air Force base."

Angie cocked her head and said, "I think I hear another one. It sounds like it's approaching from the east."

"There's a dust cloud over there too. What the hell?"

With panic in her voice, Angie exclaimed "Oh my God Caleb, we are right in the middle of a helicopter roundup!"

"Crap, they are trying to herd Winter Storm's band. Hop in the truck, maybe we can head them off."

As the band started to panic and run in the direction of the pickup truck, Caleb and Angie drove toward them hoping to herd them in a different direction. The animals scattered when confronted by the vehicle, only to regroup on the other side. Once they were back together, they continued running in the direction the helicopters were driving them.

Caleb shouted, "Dang it, that didn't work. I don't think there's anything we can do to stop this at this point."

He suddenly stopped the truck and said, "You drive, if I can't stop it, at least I can film it! I'm going to get this whole thing on video."

Caleb ran around the back of the truck and Angie slid over into the drivers seat. As the truck rolled forward, he turned around to grab his camera.

He looked around and spotted a good vantage point with a view of the entire area and said, "Up there on top of the hill, we can film the entire roundup from there."

Angie drove as fast as she could to the top of the hill and spun around so they could see the action. By then they could hear the roaring of ATV motors, which were the source of the dust cloud approaching from the east. As Caleb began to film he saw one of the horses go down, writhing in agony. One of the men riding an ATV rode right past the stricken animal without bothering to even check on it. He could not bear to watch the animal suffer, and turned away to find a new subject to focus on.

The mustangs disappeared over the next hill, and the ATV riders stopped at the top for what appeared to be some kind of discussion. He was still filming their discussion when he saw them turn around and point at he and Angie. Soon one of them was staring at them through binoculars while the others climbed back on their vehicles.

"Oh crap Angie, I think they are coming after us. Get back in the truck, I'll drive."

Caleb threw his camera in the back seat and took off toward the north. He looked for an advantage and sped past a deep ravine that he knew would slow the riders down. So far the helicopters seemed intent on chasing horses, although he half wished they leave the horses alone and chase his vehicle instead.

"We need to get off the main road, maybe make our way up to Highway 4. From there we can get on 7 and head back into Craig."

Angie replied, "The map shows a jeep road going north past Coffeepot Springs. Maybe we can make that before they get those ATVs through the ravine."

Caleb stepped on the gas and said, "Good plan. Keep an eye on those riders and also the helicopters for me."

"I can't believe they are running those animals in this heat!"

"I know right? I guess they really don't care whether they live or die. They probably would be happier if they do die."

"The springs is just ahead and I don't see any sign of the ATVs yet."

Caleb turned north at Coffeepot Springs and stepped on the gas, leaving a cloud of dust behind.

"Caleb slow down, they'll be able to follow the dust cloud! The ATVs are back on the road behind us, so they'll be able to see us pretty soon. Quick, pull in behind this hill. They won't be able to see us back here."

Angie jumped out with the binoculars and scrambled to the top of the hill that was concealing their position. Caleb picked up the camera and followed. At the top of the hill they remained hidden, as they looked down upon the action.

Angie commented, "Look, they don't know where we went. Get down, they are looking up here with binoculars."

"They are probably looking for a dust cloud. That was good thinking, driving slow to hold down the dust!"

"They are pointing west. It looks like they think we got on the perimeter loop. They probably think we are trying to get back to 318."

They watched as the group of workers milled around in confusion for a while before getting back on their vehicles, and Angie said "They are leaving toward the west."

"Okay then, we'll keep going north up to road 4."

Caleb lingered on the hill for a few moments to film the helicopters in the distance, when he suddenly said "Oh crap, they're coming back this way."

"Well they won't be able to see us from the loop, and we are hidden from Coffeepot Springs too. Maybe we should just stay put."

"That might just work. If we take off and kick up a dust cloud they'll find us for sure. Let's get back in the truck and get ready to run, just in case."

They watched anxiously as the dust cloud closed in on their position.

Caleb said, "I have some good footage that I don't want to lose. Maybe I should hide my duplicate memory card. If they catch us they might try to confiscate the memory, or even my whole camera. If they do, we'll still have the backup."

He pulled the backup card out of his camera and handed it to Angie.

"Put this in your sock or someplace they won't look. Not your pocket though. They might make you empty your pockets."

Caleb and Angie watched in amazement as the ATV riders roared past without even glancing in their direction. They continued to watch nervously as the government goons continued north.

"Okay I think they are gone," commented Caleb.

"Looks like they are going to go all the way up to 4."

Caleb responded, "Sure does. Let's go back south and then head for Vermillion Bluff. From there we can try to get back on 318 further west of the Sand Wash. Once we're back on the highway we can make our way up to Wyoming or over to Utah. I don't think we should try to go back through Craig though, they will be looking for us there. I've never been on these dirt roads, so I hope we don't run into any impassable obstacles. Good thing we filled up with gas in Craig!"

Caleb pulled out from behind the bluff and drove south before turning west. They rolled along slowly, being careful not to kick up any dust. The hours passed by as they dodged rocks and sinkholes. Angie noticed a stream on the map and commented, "Caleb, there's a stream crossing in the road up ahead."

"I see it. We should probably stop and see how deep it is before we try to cross."

"I hope it's not too deep, it's a long ways back if we have to turn around."

Caleb parked the truck at the edge of the stream and peered into the water. Angie got out and stood beside him, looking behind for signs of approaching trouble.

"It isn't very wide," he said.

"No, it really doesn't look too bad. Should we risk it?"

"Let me wade out a few steps."

"Okay, be careful."

Caleb stepped into the stream and walked carefully, picking his way out to the middle of the channel.

"Looks like it's only about eight inches deep," commented Caleb.

Angie replied, "Let's just do it, let's go for it!"

Caleb nosed the truck into the stream and was satisfied with the traction he felt on the stream bed. The four wheel drive powered it's way across the channel and soon they were safely on the other side.

Caleb stopped to look back, but Angie said "Keep going! Let's get out of here!"

"Good plan," responded Caleb. "I think we can go a little faster now."

"Yeah, step on it!"

Just as they crested a steep hill, they were confronted by three ATVs blocking the road.

Angie exclaimed, "What are we going to do?"

"I don't know yet. Let's see what they want from us."

Caleb pulled his big knife out from under the seat and removed it from it's sheath. He put it on the dash as he slowed down to greet the men sitting on the ATVs.

"What can we do for you gentlemen?" Caleb asked.

The biggest of the three men had a long scraggly beard and was wearing a baseball style cap with what appeared to be a farm emblem on it. He was the first to speak and said, "Get out of the truck."

"Not going to happen," responded Caleb.

"We've been ordered to confiscate your camera."

Caleb answered, "Where are your badges?"

"We don't need badges, we're in charge of this roundup. Now get out of the truck."

"I don't take orders from sheepherders."

Caleb grabbed his knife as the big man approached.

The sheepherder stopped in his tracks when he saw Caleb's serrated military weapon and said, "Put down the knife and get out of the truck."

Caleb replied, "You aren't getting the camera and if you don't get your asses out of the way, your ATVs are going to be rolling down the hill."

Angie noticed one of the men walking quickly back to his vehicle, where she spotted a rifle barrel sticking up. With panic in her voice, she yelled to Caleb "He's going for his gun!"

Right then Caleb stepped on the gas and opened his door, striking the big guy and sending him tumbling. He sped straight toward the man scrambling to get his gun, who then made a break for the side of the road. Caleb hit the ATV with his bull bar sending the ATV spiraling. As the other two men mounted their vehicles, Caleb spun the truck around and drove right at them, making sure to run over the rifle now lying in the middle of the road. As he sped toward the lead ATV, the driver leaped off just as Caleb pushed it over the edge. The third rider lost his nerve and spun around, heading east as fast as he could with Caleb hot on his trail. Soon they were back at the stream, and the fleeing sheepherder hit the water going full speed. The nose of the ATV dove into the river and flipped, sending the rider flying into the rushing water.

Caleb slammed on the brakes and leaped out of the truck. When he saw that the man was able to stand up in the river he got back into the driver's seat, spun back around and sped back toward the west. They stopped at the location of the original altercation to see where the men had gone, and spotted them making their way down the hill to retrieve their vehicles.

"Looks like those boys are going to have a long walk home!" Caleb said.

"Damn, that was scary! Do you think we'll get in trouble?"

"I don't see how. We were basically being held hostage by a gang of strangers with no credentials, so I think it was a clear case of self defense. Besides, I don't think they were smart enough to get our license plate number."

"No, they didn't appear to be the brightest lights on the porch."

Caleb commented, "I think we should just haul ass over to Utah. In just a couple hours we will already be back on 191. Seems like we'll be starting the trip home all over at square one, but it should be worth it!"

"Yeah, that's a bummer. Are we going to go all the way back up to I80 in Wyoming from there?"

"We could do that, or we could turn back south and find a way down to I70."

Angie answered, "At least we'd be back in Colorado that way. It would feel like we've made some progress toward home. If it gets too late maybe we can stop in Glenwood Springs. The hot springs might be nice."

"That's a great idea. I could use a nice soak after this ordeal."

"Sounds like a plan!"

Angie looked over the map and said, "Looks like if we can get over to Dinosaur, we could take 64 east to Meeker. From there it isn't too far down to Glenwood."

"Okay, let's do that then. It might be pretty late when we get to Glenwood."

"I can drive if you get too tired."

"Okay, why don't you try to get some rest then. I'll be good for a couple more hours for sure."

"Maybe when we get off this rough road."

Caleb stayed behind the wheel until they finally found their way back to Highway 40 near Elk Springs. Once on the highway, Caleb commented "There might be a shortcut on the dirt down to Meeker."

Angie said, "It's only another 20 minutes from here to Dinosaur. I'm tired of the dirt and the bumps."

"Yeah, me too. Maybe we should take a break in Dinosaur and get something to eat. I could use a good cup of coffee too."

"Okay, I'm going to rest my eyes for a few minutes then."

"Good idea," replied Caleb.

Angie's eyes fluttered open as Caleb slowed to enter the town of Dinosaur.

"Wow, that went fast, we made it before sunset," commented Angie.

"Yeah, it wasn't too bad of a drive."

"Are we still going to stop?"

"Sure, let's look for some kind of cafe or something."

Angie pointed ahead and said, "I see some lights, maybe it's a restaurant."

"I see it too, let's check it out."

Fortunately for the tired couple, a cafe was open in the tiny town of Dinosaur, Colorado. Caleb pulled into the parking lot and they got out to stretch their legs. It was already late afternoon, but the rapidly diminishing sunlight did nothing to cool the hot dusty western landscape. As they entered the establishment, they were greeted by a solitary middle aged woman who appeared to be the only staff on duty on that late Colorado afternoon.

"Greetings, how are you all this afternoon? My name is Rhiannon and I'll be your server today."

Angie replied, "We're doing well!"

"Two for dinner then?"

"Yes it will be just the two of us," Angie responded.

"Okay, right over here. I have a table all ready for you all. Can I get you something to drink?"

"I think we'll just have a cup of coffee for now," answered Caleb.

Ange also chimed in, "Same for me, cream and sugar please."

"Here's a couple of menus, I'll bring your drinks right out."

Soon the couple was sipping fresh coffee and examining the menu.

"Man, I can't believe we got out of that mess," commented Angie.

"I know, right? I thought we were going to jail for sure!"

Soon Rhiannon returned and asked, "Are you ready to order?"

"Maybe just a couple more minutes," replied Angie.

So did you get a chance to visit the park at all today?"

"No, we are on our honeymoon," said Angie. "We are just on our way back home from the wedding in Montana."

The waitress cast them a sideways glance and said, "Congratulations! I hope you are having a nice trip!"

"It's been a bit tiring, but we are having a nice vacation as we make our way back to Denver."

"You should have been here earlier! We had quite a bit of excitement for our little town. Turns out the feds are looking for a young couple who disrupted a wild horse roundup."

Angie responded with a coy smile, "You don't say, did they catch them?"

"Not that I know of. I'll tell you one thing though, I wish I'd been there to help them! Nobody is happy about they are doing with those horses. Except for the damn sheepherders of course."

Caleb and Angie finished their meals and soon they were ready to get back on the road.

Rhiannon asked, "So which way are you heading out?"

"I think we are going to head over to Meeker and then on down to I70."

Rhiannon answered, "Good idea. If I were you two, I might want to avoid going anywhere near Craig tonight. Word is that's where they are centering the search for the famous horse roundup couple."

Caleb smiled and replied, "Good tip! We'll keep that in mind!"

"Good luck, and you two have a nice drive back to Denver!"

Soon the newlyweds were back on the road with Angie behind the wheel.

Caleb checked the maps on his phone and commented, "I'm guessing we should be to Glenwood by about nine."

"That will be great, we will have time to soak a few minutes in the hot springs!"

"That'll be a really nice way to end the day. In the meantime, I'm going to rest my eyes for a few minutes in case you get too tired later on."

"Sounds good, I'm going to put on some music. How about some country?"

"Country sounds great."

Caleb closed his eyes and was soon fast asleep. He intended to awake after a few minutes, but by the time his eyes opened he was already looking at the bright lights of Glenwood Springs."

"Wow, we're here already! How long have I been out?"

Angie laughed and said, "You were snoring the minute you closed your eyes."

Caleb responded, "I didn't mean to sleep that long. Do you think we should just switch seats and keep going through the night?"

"No, this is the last night of our honeymoon and I think we should take some time to enjoy ourselves. I'm really looking forward to the hot springs."

"Okay then, maybe we should just get a little closer to the resort and see if we can find a place with vacancy."

"Let's make sure we get someplace nice. I want tonight to be special."

Caleb looked over the listings and said, "Why don't we just go right down to the historic lodge and see if they have an opening."

"Works for me!"

Caleb set his GPS and guided Angie on into downtown Glenwood."

Soon they were settled into their room, and Caleb quickly found his swimsuit and was soon ready for the pool.

Angie smiled when she saw him and said, "Why don't you head on down and find us a nice spot near the springs. I'll be down shortly."

"Okay, I'll see you there!"

Caleb found good spot and spread out the towel as he waited for Angie. He was completely unprepared for the beauty of his statuesque bride as she approached in a sexy one piece suit, with her flowing blonde hair cascading down over her shoulders. As she strode toward him, he thought to himself that she looked every bit as amazing as the hottest runway model he'd ever photographed on the catwalk.

"Wow, you look stunning Angie!"

"Why thank you Caleb, you don't look too bad yourself. Now let's get our aching bones into that hot water!"

As the couple soaked in the hot water, they thought back upon the wild adventure they had experienced earlier that day.

Angie commented, "You know we disrupted them quite a bit today, but it won't be long before they are right back at it. They aren't going to stop until they destroy the entire herd for those dirty stinking sheepherders."

"I know, we need to find a more lasting solution. We aren't accomplishing much with our current approach."

"Right, maybe we should try out our fundraising ideas and maybe we can even get some support from the state. Colorado has an interest in preserving that beautiful mustang herd. They are a big tourist attraction and they have to be bringing some local dollars, at the very least for the town of Craig."

Caleb answered, "Exactly, we'll think of something. It's getting chilly, are you ready to go back up to the room?"

"Yes, I'm starting to feel like a prune and it's too cold to be out of the water."

The newlyweds walked hand in hand back to their room and opened the door. Caleb's heart skipped a beat as Angie dropped her swimsuit onto the floor.

Caleb dropped his swim trunks as well, and the two found themselves in a passionate embrace.

Caleb looked out the big glass window and said, "Oh dang, maybe we should close the curtains!"

"Oh who cares, just get in bed!"

Angie reached for Caleb's hand as she laid back on the big king sized mattress and said "I was looking forward to the hot springs, but let's make this a night to remember!"

Chapter Thirteen

Angie was still fast asleep when the first rays of dawn awakened Caleb. He had noticed a small coffee pot the night before, and hoped he could find the packages of grounds to go with it. He carefully arose so as not to awaken the blonde beauty beside him, peacefully sleeping in the golden light of morning. He was relieved to find the complimentary packets of coffee, placed neatly in the drawer below the small carafe.

Soon the aromatic scent of percolating java wafted through the room, as Caleb relaxed in a chair while staring out the window at the light of a new day. It was still early, but the bright Colorado sun left no doubt that the ride home would be sunny and hot. As he poured his first cup of morning brew, Angie began to stir and moan quietly as she stretched her slender arms.

"Are you ready for a cup of coffee?" Caleb asked.

"Sure, did they give us any creamer?"

"Looks like we have a few."

"I'll take a cup with two creamers if you don't mind stirring it in."

"Coming right up!"

Angie slipped on a sheer nightie and joined Caleb at the table. The two sipped their morning coffee in silence for a few moments before Angie said, "Are we going to look around Glenwood for a day, or do you think we should head on back to Denver?"

"I'd say we should have one more day of honeymoon, but I kind of want to get this footage to the Denver news."

"Aren't you going to just publish it yourself?"

"Normally I would, but I think we'd probably be wiser to make this submission anonymously."

"Good point. No sense leading the feds right to us."

As they chatted, Caleb checked various news sites looking for information about the roundup. Finding nothing, he surmised that the feds had secretly gotten away with another brutal gather. He wondered how many mustangs had paid the price with life and limb.

Caleb commented, "Looks like I might be the first to provide the evidence of yesterday's travesty."

"Nobody is saying anything?"

"No, there's nothing at all in any of the news outlets this morning. Not even a word about our little adventure."

"They are probably hoping we'll be too scared to publish it."

"Yeah, well they are wrong."

Angie asked, "How long do you think it will take us to get to Denver from here?"

"The travel map is showing about 160 miles and two and a half hours."

"If we get going pretty soon, we'll get to Denver in plenty of time to show the footage on the evening news."

"Right, let's finish this coffee and grab some breakfast somewhere. I have a craving for some pancakes this morning."

"I think I'd like to have an omelet. Maybe I should have a Denver Omelet for good luck!"

Caleb laughed and said, "Whatever works!"

The morning and the miles flew by and soon the couple found themselves cruising past Idaho Springs with Mount Blue Sky towering over them to the south.

Caleb asked, "Can you set the GPS for the closest Denver news station?"

"Hold on, let me see what comes up."

"Okay."

"Looks like there's one downtown, not too far off of I25."

"Can you give them a call and ask where to deliver the footage? Tell them I have it on a thumb drive."

Caleb could hear the phone ringing and eventually Angie saying, "I have some anonymous footage of yesterday's roundup of the Sand Wash Mustangs. I was wondering if you would be interested in airing it."

"Let me connect you with our news director."

Caleb heard more ringing and then another answer, "Good morning, my name is Jennifer and I'm the news director. I understand you have some video for me."

"Yes, we have video footage of the wild horse roundup in the Sand Wash Basin yesterday."

"I wasn't aware they were having a roundup."

"Neither were we, until we found ourselves right in the middle of it."

"We are definitely interested in seeing what you have. Can you receive text messages on your phone?"

"Yes I can."

"Okay, I'm going to text you the address for the newsroom. What time do you think you will be here?"

"We are passing by Idaho Springs now, and will soon be coming down from the mountains into the Metro Area."

"Okay, I'll be waiting for you. Let me know if you get delayed for some reason."

"We will, see you in a few minutes."

Caleb drove down from the mountains along I70 to the I25 interchange, and then south toward downtown Denver while Angie kept track of their progress on the electronic map provided by her phone app. Soon she said, "Better get in the right lane so we can take the 6th Avenue exit eastbound into the downtown area."

Caleb made the all the required turns, and they soon found themselves in the parking lot of the television studio. The couple met the receptionist in the front lobby, and Caleb said "We have an appointment to see Jennifer."

"I'll see if she's available."

Soon the receptionist said, "Jennifer will see you now, first office on the right."

Jennifer greeted them at the door and invited them in.

"So you have some video of a mustang roundup, is that correct?"

"Yes," answered Caleb.

"Anything unusual about it?"

Caleb answered, "I don't know, I think it probably went about the way they usually go. Lots of injured horses, several deaths I imagine."

"Oh my," Jennifer responded. "Well this whole wild horse roundup thing is becoming a big news item lately. Lots of folks are really upset about it."

Caleb handed her the thumb drive and said, "Well here it is. You should be able to play it right off of the thumb drive, or easily copy it to your own devices."

"Do you need this back?"

"No, I have my own copy," answered Caleb. "You can keep it."

"Do you have a business card or something that I can use to make sure you get credit for this?"

"No, no need. I think we would like to remain anonymous this time."

"Are you sure?"

"Oh yes, we are sure. We just want this footage to get out to the public so they can see what is going on. That will be reward enough."

"No problem, but would you mind a short interview to get the details?"

"Okay, no problem," answered Caleb. "The roundup was yesterday."

"And you just happened to be there?"

"Yes, we were taking pictures of the horses when the helicopters and ATVs arrived."

"And the government just let you film it?"

"Well that's where it gets a little dicey," laughed Angie.

Caleb added, "But we did manage to get the footage, that's what matters."

Jennifer replied, "No problem, we'll watch the video and try to contact the government representative to see what we can learn. We should be able to get this on the evening news."

Angie replied, "That would be awesome. The more the public can see what is going on, the better for the animals."

"Well good luck you two! Hopefully we'll be able to work together on this sometime!"

Angie and Caleb departed the building and he steered the truck homeward.

"We should stop and eat somewhere," said Angie.

"Yeah, I'm starving. Do you want to go to a real restaurant, or how about the food court at the mall?"

"The mall sounds good, something quick. I just want to get home now."

"Yeah, me too. It's only been a few days, but it seems like forever."

The sun was low in the sky by the time Caleb and Angie pulled into their driveway.

"Looks just like it did when we left." Caleb commented.

"Thankfully the place didn't burn down or anything. I hope we have some wine in the refrigerator, I could really use a cold drink!"

"Well if we don't, I can run up to the liquor store in Franktown. What time does the evening news come on?"

"I think 6:00," answered Angie.

"Yeah, I think so too. I don't want to miss it."

Angie went into the kitchen to see what was available for an evening in front of the television and said, "Hey we're in luck, we have cold wine and beer in the fridge!"

"Fantastic, I really didn't want to go out again today."

Angie asked, "Is there anything we need to bring in from the truck right away?"

"Not really," answered Caleb. "I do want to bring in my camera bag though."

"Of course, do you want wine or beer?"

"I'll just take a beer. I can get it myself after I bring in my camera."

"Okay, I'll be in the living room when you are ready."

Caleb brought his camera in from outside and sat down with Angie on the couch. After a few sips of cold brew he said, "Maybe we'd better set an alarm for the news hour. I have a feeling I'm going to fall asleep in the middle of this drink."

As she finished her wine and leaned back on Caleb's chest she said, "Yeah, I'm pretty sleepy myself."

Caleb and Angie were rudely awakened by the sound of the phone alarm, and struggled to regain consciousness. "What time is it?" Angie asked.

"It's ten minutes to six."

"Oh, quick, switch on the television! Maybe they will show some previews prior to the news segment."

Caleb replied, "You got it," as he switched on the big screen and handed the remote to Angie, saying "Here you go, I'm going to grab another beer."

As Caleb was pouring his beer he heard Angie say, "Caleb hurry, it's coming on!"

Caleb dashed to the living room and sat down to watch.

"Caleb, this is really good filming! I didn't realize you could zoom in that much with your camera."

Caleb replied, "It looks a lot more dramatic on the big screen doesn't it?"

"Oh Caleb, this is awful. It looks much worse on television than it did in person."

"Yeah, the big screen makes it look like we are right in the middle of it."

Tears streamed down Angie's face as she saw the first horse go down, writhing in agony as it struggled to get up. However with a horribly mangled leg, the poor beast was left on the ground to suffer with no chance of escaping it's agonizing fate.

Caleb listened intently to the reporter, hoping to hear some shred of hope that the spectacle before them would result in a significant change of tactics by the government agency entrusted to humanely care for the majestic animals. Unfortunately none came and according to the news reporter, the government was offering only a terse, "No comment," in response.

Caleb sat stunned as the segment ended. Angie was still crying, and the two were unable to speak for several minutes.

When they had finally gathered their wits, Angie said "We need to do something."

"I wonder how many horses they captured this time?"

Angie replied, "I don't know, but we need to find out and do something about it. I like your idea of putting on fund raisers."

"Yeah, and maybe we can get a petition going for the governor. He seems reasonable, so maybe he can find a way to help. I know wild horse management is federal but without some major pressure from the state and the general population, they are never going change their tactics."

"Yeah, I imagine they have to justify owning all of those helicopters somehow. Someone should do an audit to see if the taxpayers are really getting their money's worth.

"Let's get started tomorrow," commented Angie.

"Agreed!"

The couple finished watching the news and silently got ready for bed.

After a restless night, Caleb was awakened by the gurgling of the coffee pot. With one eye open, he could see that Angie was already dressed and ready to go somewhere. As he slowly gained consciousness, it became apparent to him that she wasn't prepared for any ordinary day. She always looked like a million bucks, but today she was also wearing high heels and a long dress.

"Where are you going already, dressed like a runway model?" Caleb asked.

"I'm going to go in to the agency to talk to them about putting on a show to raise funds for the horses."

"I guess while you do that I'll give the running club a call and see if they might want to organize a 10K or something. Maybe they could do a trail run through the canyon over here. Do you want to sit out on the deck for a few minutes, and have a cup of coffee?"

"No, I'm going to take some along with me in my thermos cup. I just want to get going and get this over with."

"Okay, well good luck! I'll have my ringer turned up, so text me when you find out anything."

"I will, see you later."

Angie filled her cup and walked out the door.

Caleb poured a cup of wake up juice for himself, and wandered out onto the deck where he took in the magnificent view of the park to the west. After he had taken a couple of sips, the phone unexpectedly rang. He took a quick glance at the screen, expecting it to be Angie, thinking "*I wonder why she's calling already.*" However he soon discovered it wasn't Angie, instead it was Michelle calling from Gardiner.

"Hello Michelle, how are you?"

"I'm good, did I wake you?"

"No, I'm already up having coffee. Angie left early to talk to her modeling agency about putting on a fundraiser for the wild horses."

"Cool, I hope she's successful. Hey, I got to thinking seriously about your invitation for me to come to Colorado for a little while."

"What do you think, do you want to come out and see us?"

"I do, and I was wondering if this weekend is too soon?"

"No it's not too soon, and you can stay as long as you like! In addition to Angie's fashion fundraiser, I'm going to try to get a 10K or something organized for later in the summer. Maybe you could run in it."

"That would be awesome! Okay, I'll set up a flight to Denver. Do you think you could pick me up at the Denver airport?"

"No problem I can pick you up anytime, just let me know when!"

"Okay good, I'm going to go see our travel agent today then."

"Great, I'll send Angie a text to let her know the good news!"

Michelle was so eager to finalize her plans that she didn't even bother to say goodbye. Caleb chuckled to himself and sent off a text to Angie.

"Michelle called and it looks like she is going to be flying out next week."

Angie didn't respond immediately, but Caleb realized she was probably in traffic and unable to attend to her phone. With everything coming together so quickly, Caleb decided he'd better get started right away organizing the race. He searched the web for the running club's number and made the call.

As he expected, his call went straight to answering service, asking him to leave a message. He waited for the beep and left his name and number, along with a short message explaining his idea to the club. As he thought about the race and the canyon, a run through the trails along Cherry Creek seemed like a good way to start the day.

He laced up his running shoes and grabbed a water bottle before climbing down the steps and walking through the bramble to the flats bordering the east side of the canyon. He then turned south where he could take the trail down the steep embankment to the path along the creek bed. He had always loved that beautiful shady section of trail and jogged slowly to take in the fresh air while warming up his muscles, far from the brown cloud of pollution blanketing the city to the north.

His thoughts drifted away to the Sand Wash Basin, and he wondered how the mustangs were faring in the holding pen. He wondered if any injured animals might still be lying in the hot sun, suffering alone as they awaited death with nothing to ease the unbearable pain of broken and twisted legs.

He soon found himself running past the old dam and up the steep embankment on the west side. He looked forward to the moment when he would descend back to the road at the overlook to the waterfall, where he had stopped many times to photograph the beautiful cascading water. He thought to himself, "*Today it might be nice to just find a flat rock and watch the falls and collect my thoughts.*"

Just as he was getting comfortable, the phone rang. It was Michelle already calling back and he wondered, "*Could she already be calling back with flight information?*"

"I'm already set up to arrive on Saturday!" Michelle said breathlessly.

"That's great Michelle! Why don't you text me the flight number and time of arrival, and I'll be at the gate to meet you."

"That sounds perfect Caleb, I'm so excited! I've never been to Denver before."

"Well maybe instead of coming straight down to Franktown, I could take you on a little tour through the city. The airport is out on the plains to the east and there isn't much to see between there and Franktown, but you might like the city."

"That would be great Caleb, maybe we could get some lunch somewhere."

"Do you like Mexican food? I know a great place not far off 6th Avenue in the downtown area."

"I love Mexican food Caleb, I can't wait!"

"It will be great to see you again Michelle!"

The phone rang once again as Caleb was climbing the steps to the deck. This time it was the president of the running club saying, "I understand you are interested in hosting a race."

"Yes, as I mentioned I would like to raise funds to protect the wild horses in the Sand Wash Basin."

"Oh yes, I saw the news segment about last week's roundup. I think you would have a lot of support for that cause."

"I do too, so what do I need to do to get started?"

"Well, we are going to need a permit to run the race in your canyon. Can you make a preliminary inquiry with the park service to see if setting up a course there might be feasible?"

"Sure, I can do that."

"Great, give me a call back when you find out. In the meantime I'll text you my direct cell number so you can get right through."

"Perfect," responded Caleb.

Caleb set an appointment to talk to the permit department at the park service, and settled into his deck chair for a nap. He soon drifted off to sleep, with visions of majestic mustangs running free on the arid plains of the Rocky Mountain West.

The sound of the sliding door opening awakened Caleb, followed by the Angie's heels clomping on the wooden deck.

"How did it go at the agency?"

"It went great! They all saw the news segment and they want to do the show!"

"The president of the running club saw the report too, and he's also interested in contributing to the cause by organizing a race. I'm waiting for the park service to respond about a permit to do a trail run here in the canyon."

"That sound like fun! I wonder if we'll have to help with the aid stations, or if we'll be able to run the trail ourselves?"

"I don't know, I imagine the running club will be able to round up support staff like they do with every other race. Oh by the way, Michelle is coming in on Saturday morning. I told her I'd pick her up and take her on a short tour of downtown Denver. We are going to have lunch at the bar off 6th if you want to come."

"That's great Caleb, but I'm not sure what I'm doing on Saturday yet. I still need to stop in at the real estate office to see what's going on."

"Of course, I know you are busy. Just wanted to let you know in case you can make time."

On Saturday morning a faint glow appeared on the eastern horizon at sunrise, just as Caleb turned onto Highway 86 on his way to meet Michelle at the airport. Before the sun even had a chance to heat the eastern plains, it was obvious that it was going to be a very hot day along the Front Range. He thought to himself, "*I hope I'm already through the Tech Center before I hit any weekend traffic.*" Angie had a house to show later that morning, so Caleb cruised along by himself as he listened to the weekend morning show on the radio.

Fortunately it was a quiet morning on the roads in south Denver, and soon he was striding through the concourse to the gate where he would meet Michelle. The first passengers were strolling past the security check just as Caleb arrived, so he just stood off to the side and waited. Michelle must have been seated toward the front of the plane because it wasn't long before he saw her making her way through the crowd. She quickly spotted him as well, and both extended their arms for a long hug.

Caleb asked, "How was your flight?"

"It was fine. The time seemed to pass quickly."

"Right, it doesn't take very long to get to Denver from Montana. Do you have anything we need to pick up in baggage claim?"

"No, I just brought my carry on bags. I thought I would go shopping for new things in Denver. Maybe Angie and I could visit the mall together."

"I would think they might have something you like there. I hope you brought your checkbook!"

"Oh I did! Plus Mom gave me some money too."

"Are you hungry, or did you have a meal on the plane?"

"I'm definitely hungry! I am looking forward to the Mexican food place you were talking about."

"All right then, I figured we'd take a swing past downtown on Broadway so you can get a good look at the tall buildings. Then we can just turn on 6th Avenue and cruise over to the restaurant."

"Sounds good to me!"

Caleb navigated their way out of the airport area, and soon they were speeding along I70 out of Aurora and toward Denver. Caleb was well acquainted with the area, since he had recently done a fashion shoot near some old buildings just off Broadway. He took the southbound exit onto Brighton Boulevard, and soon they were cruising past the old downtown area. Michelle marveled at the towering structures of glass and steel as they negotiated their way through the city streets.

"I've never been to a big city like this before. This is amazing!"

"I guess it's not so different from LA and San Francisco, but it had been a long time since I encountered this kind of traffic when I first moved here. What do you think, would you like to live near a city like this?"

"I don't know, maybe. I'm getting kind of bored with my routine in Gardiner and Yellowstone."

"Yeah, I can see how that might happen when you see it everyday."

As Caleb and Michelle chatted, the miles passed by almost without notice. The restaurant drew near and Caleb found a good parking place along Kalamath Street, a couple blocks away. He knew that by this time there would be no parking spaces in the tiny lot beside the bar. They walked around to the front of the building and the massive wooden door was already open, beckoning them to enter.

"Wow, what a cool old place!" Michelle commented.

"Yeah, I think it's been here a really long time. I think there used to be a brewery in this area back in the 1800s."

"It does look old, but it adds to the atmosphere!"

There were no tables available, and the waitress asked if they would like to be seated at the end of the bar.

Caleb asked Michelle, "Is that okay with you?"

"The bar is fine."

The bartender came over and asked, "What can I get you to drink?"

Caleb responded, "I'll have a pint of dark from the tap."

"I'll have the same." Michelle replied.

Soon they were sipping ice cold beer from frosted glass mugs and Michelle said, "Wow, this tastes really good on a hot day like today!"

"Right, nothing better than a frosted mug on a hot Colorado afternoon!"

Soon the server arrived to take their food order, and Caleb ordered a smothered burrito with hot green chili.

Michelle asked the waitress, "How hot is the hot chili?"

"It's really hot. If you've never had it before, you might want to try the mild first."

"I'm feeling adventurous today, so I think I'll try the hot!"

The server laughed and said, "Name your poison!"

Caleb offered some advice, "I like to take my first bite and then wait a little bit. The chili will soon burn into your throat and your forehead will start to sweat. Then you will be ready for your second bite, and soon you will be able to taste the flavor. Best green chili in Denver!"

"Okay, sounds like good advice!"

Their glasses were soon empty, and the bartender brought them another in fresh frosted mugs.

"So are you really considering moving to Colorado?"

"I want to, but moving is so hard. And then there's my job, I really like being a ranger."

"Well we have Rocky Mountain National Park, which is a national park same as Yellowstone. Maybe they could give you a transfer. You also might be able to use your experience to get on with the state park service here in Colorado. We have a ton of really nice state parks, one right outside of our back door as a matter of fact."

"And then there is finding a place to live."

"I'm sure you can stay with us as long as you like, if it works out that you get a job close enough to be able to commute."

"You guys would do that for me?"

"I'll have to check with Angie for sure, but I don't see why not. Of course I don't want to get your mom mad at me."

"I've already talked it over with my mom. She understands that I need to make my own life."

They finished their meals and Caleb paid the bill. He commented as they walked out the front door, "I think it even feels hotter than before!"

"Yeah, it was so nice and cool inside the bar."

Caleb checked his phone and read a message from Angie.

"Angie says she's done with her showings for the day. What do you say we head for Franktown?"

"Sounds good to me. I can't wait to see Angie and your house. And I want to see Castlewood Canyon."

Caleb answered, "Maybe the three of us could take a little hike through there later when it starts to cool off."

"I'd like that!"

Angie was waiting in front of the house when Caleb and Michelle arrived in Franktown. Caleb pulled into the driveway and brought the vehicle to a stop. Michelle hopped out and rushed to greet Angie.

Angie said, "Hi sweetie, how was your trip?"

"It was great! The flight went smoothly and I'm just really glad to be here!"

"Caleb, would you grab Michelle's bags and put them in the extra bedroom? I'm going to show her around the house."

"No problem."

By the time Caleb had unloaded Michelle's carry on bags, she and Angie were sitting on the deck in the cool shade.

Michelle said, "It seems a lot cooler here than it was in Denver."

Angie replied, "Yes, I think it is usually a few degrees cooler here. Franktown is probably another thousand to fifteen hundred feet higher than Denver, so we are almost always five or ten degrees cooler."

Caleb brought out a pitcher of lemonade and three glasses.

"Oh, that looks so good!" Michelle exclaimed.

Angie asked, "So what are your plans for this visit?"

"I just want to look around, maybe do a little shopping."

Angie replied, "I bet I can help out in that department!"

"I would also like to check out the job situation while I'm here. Caleb said he would take me up to Rocky Mountain National Park to explore the possibilities with the National Park Service there."

"So you are seriously considering relocating to Colorado?"

"Yes, I am seriously considering it!"

Angie responded, "Well, you know you are welcome to stay with us as long as you need to!"

Caleb added, "That's what I told her too."

"I really appreciate that, you guys."

The afternoon temperature had already begun to cool by the time they finished their drinks, and Caleb said "I told Michelle we could take a little stroll through the canyon. What do you think, should we give it a try?"

Angie answered, "That sounds like fun, what do you think Michelle?"

"It sounds awesome! I'd really like to stretch my legs after the flight and the car ride."

The trio completed their walk and finished up the day in the living room watching a movie. Soon after, Michelle retired to her room and Caleb was the last to fall asleep listening to the sound of Angie's breathing as she snoozed beside him.

He was also the last to awaken in the morning, with Angie and Michelle already seated at the kitchen table sipping coffee. Angie was dressed in office clothes, and Michelle was relaxing in a loose sweatshirt with cutoff sleeves and jogging pants.

Angie commented, "I need to run in to the office for a showing this morning. What do you guys have planned?"

"I thought we might run up to Cherry Creek Reservoir to see if maybe Michelle could talk to the rangers about employment."

"That's an excellent idea."

Angie departed for her appointment, and Caleb said "Before that though, I'm going to relax on the deck and drink this coffee!"

"I need a little more waking up myself!" Michelle replied.

They each pulled up a chair on the deck and sipped their morning brew while gazing upon the beauty of the little mountain park behind them, on the outer edge of the Denver city limits.

Michelle asked, "How is your project to save the horses coming along?"

"Pretty well I guess. Angie's modeling agency and the local running club are both interested in hosting events to raise funds. The video of our little adventure made the evening news the day we got back, so hopefully the governor's office is being flooded with indignant calls."

"I hope I can be here for the events. I would love to participate!"

"Well I think we can make that happen. I would think your best chance for landing a job in Colorado might be a transfer with the U.S. Park service. Maybe we could run up to Rocky tomorrow and check it out."

"I'd like that."

"Okay, we'll check with Angie when she gets done with her showing and see what she thinks. She's always busy, so I don't know if she would be able to go along with us."

Michelle answered, "If she can't, I'm sure you and I can handle visiting the park while she's at work."

Just as Caleb and Michelle were ready to depart for Cherry Creek Reservoir, he received a text from Angie.

"Guess what?" Angie asked.

"What?"

"We have a date set for the fund raiser. It's going to be in August at the RSI store. We are going to model the latest outdoor fashions, and the proceeds are all going to go to wild horse foundations. Not only that, but the governor is on board with our efforts and is going to try to pressure the feds into stopping the round ups."

"That's great news Angie! Maybe we can make a difference after all. Are you done working for the day? Michelle and I were getting ready to go up to the reservoir for a while."

"I'm not too far from there now so why don't I just meet you there. Throw a couple of camping chairs and a towel in the back of your truck."

"Will do. We'll see you in a little while."

The three friends enjoyed a beautiful sunny Colorado afternoon while watching paddle boarders on the stunning blue waters of one of Denver's most popular swimming and boating spots.

Angie commented, "All we need now is for the race to come through, and I think we'll have a good chance at preventing the August round up."

"I hope so. I think they are talking about rounding up over 700 horses this time, almost the entire herd. It would be a terrible shame."

Michelle added, "Especially if they end up injuring or killing a bunch of them like they usually do."

After a long silence, Caleb said "I was thinking of taking Michelle up to Rocky Mountain National Park tomorrow. Do you think you might be able to come along?"

Angie replied, "No, I have a couple showings tomorrow. You guys go on ahead without me. That's a long trip for one day, so maybe you should think about camping out for a night. It would be neat if Michelle could see the elk herd at sunrise in Moraine Park."

Caleb asked, "What do you think about that Michelle?"

"That sounds awesome!"

"Okay, we'll head out early then. We can stop at the ranger headquarters on the way into the park to pick up employment brochures and applications."

Morning came early, and Caleb knocked on Michelle's door at sunrise to awaken her for the trip.

"I'm awake, I'll be right out."

"Okay, I'm not in a big hurry. I just want to get through Denver before the traffic gets too bad."

Michelle answered, "Good plan, I have a thermos if you want to brew a pot of coffee for the trip."

"Beat you to it! I have one ready to go, so I'm ready to go when you are. Maybe we can stop in Loveland to get some breakfast before heading up to Estes."

The bright Colorado sunshine was starting to warm the mountain air just as the pair exited the highway and turned toward Loveland, and eventually the park to the west.

Caleb asked, "Are you hungry yet, or would you rather just keep going all the way to Estes Park?"

"I'm not all that hungry. Let's just keep rolling if that's okay with you."

"Right, it's hard to stop when you get this close! We should probably fill up with gas though. Maybe we should grab a couple of muffins or something while we're here. How are we doing on coffee?"

"Looks like we're getting low. We can fill up a thermos at the station too."

Soon the red rock formations of western Loveland were in the rear view mirror, and the pair was cruising up the winding mountain road through Big Thompson Canyon toward Colorado's crown jewel just west of Estes Park.

Michelle was gazing at the rugged cliffs on both sides of the road when she exclaimed, "Look, bighorn sheep up there!"

"Yup, they love those high cliffs on both sides of the canyon."

Michelle asked, "What are all those ruins and fireplaces lining the creek?"

"Back in 1976 a terrible thunderstorm rolled in and dumped several inches of rain into the reservoir in just a couple hours. The big dam up at Estes eventually gave way, sending a massive wall of water downstream that took out the whole valley. It destroyed hundreds of homes, bridges and roads, and killed a bunch of people. Unfortunately that summer was Colorado's centennial celebration, so there were a lot of extra visitors and campers in the valley at the time."

"Wow, that's terrible. I had never heard that."

"Yeah, I think it was the state's costliest disaster at the time."

Soon the canyon was behind them, and they found themselves on the outskirts of the little mountain town of Estes Park.

"Caleb, it's beautiful! It looks like something that should be in the Swiss Alps or something. I just love this town! Hey look there's a pizza place, can we stop and get pizza?"

Caleb laughed and said, "Sure, that sounds like a great way to start off a camp out! Look, there's a liquor store right next door. Maybe we should pick up a bottle of brandy or something."

"That's a great idea. Nothing like a sip of brandy to stay warm on a cold mountain night!"

As they ate their lunch Caleb commented, "I think there is a ranger station on the way into the park. We can stop there and pick up some employment brochures. Maybe you can talk to somebody about transferring out here."

On their way through town Michelle marveled at the giant elk, nonchalantly hanging out in town amid the crowd of tourists.

Caleb commented, "They say the elk are totally used to the people and traffic here. Of course that doesn't mean I'd want to go up and start petting one!"

Michelle had a nice visit with a lady ranger at the visitor center, who seemed quite excited to see a young person with interest in joining their ranks. Before they departed, Michelle was lugging an armful of literature and an application for employment along with a Request for Transfer form.

"Wow, this is so much more than I expected! She sure was nice."

Caleb showed his season pass at the park gate, and soon they were on their way to the national park campground at Moraine Park.

"I guess we should go in and claim a campsite before messing around too much longer."

"That sounds good to me."

"When we get set up, maybe we can go hike around Bear Lake or something."
"I'd love to take a little hike and stretch our legs before we settle in for the night. What are all those people stopped for?" Michelle asked.

"There's probably an elk down there. That's how you find the animals here," Caleb chuckled. "Just look for a crowd of people along the road!"

"Yup, that's pretty much how it is out in the Lamar Valley too!"

Soon they were making the turn into the campground where they would find a place to spend the night.

"Caleb look, there's a nice spot right along the edge of the ridge. And it's not too far from the restrooms."

"That looks like a nice one. Let's see if we can register it."

They claimed the spot and dropped their reservation into the drop box. Soon they were slowly cruising up Bear Lake Road, eventually arriving at the main parking lot.

"Wow, what are those beautiful peaks?" Michelle exclaimed.

"I think those are Hallet and Otis, amazing aren't they? If you want, we could hike a few miles up the trail to Dream and Emerald Lakes to get a closer view. I guess you can actually climb all the way up there to the summit, but I don't think we're prepared for a serious trek like that today."

"No, but the lakes sound like a fun day hike."

They hiked up the steep trail back into the wilderness, and soon they were admiring the view from Emerald Lake, when Caleb said "I've wanted to hike up here since the first time I saw these peaks when I was first moving out here!"

Michelle laughed and commented, "Well I'm glad I could help you with your bucket list."

"Yeah," Caleb chuckled. "Thanks!"

As they made their way back down the rugged trail, Michelle said "It seems a bit chillier now than it did on the way up."

"True, we aren't working as hard but I also think the sun is also starting to lose some of it's strength. We should probably think about getting back to the campground."

As they drove past the low meadows elk were gathering for the night, and Michelle commented "Look, this reminds me of the elk coming down to the Lamar River at night for a drink."

"Right, the animal behavior in the two parks is very similar. You might feel right at home working here!"

Soon Caleb and Michelle were sitting beside a flickering campfire and Michelle said, "This place is beautiful! I think if I were working here, I might not even miss Yellowstone too much."

"I thought you would like it here."

The high elevation chill was starting to settle into the valley, and they snuggled closely to keep warm.

Michelle remembered a moment from Montana and said, "I still remember the first time you burst through the door of the cafe in Gardiner, wind blowing and snow flying into the entry. I thought you must be Grizzly Adams or something!"

"I remember that winter too, almost like it was yesterday. You know, I was basically homeless at the time, but I didn't even care. I was just so happy to be out of San Francisco and close to the wildlife that it didn't seem to matter. Your pretty young face was a sight for sore eyes as well!"

"Remember that one winter when you went out scaring the wolves away from the park boundary so the hunters couldn't shoot them?"

"How could I forget!"

"I honestly thought those guys were going to kill you."

"They tried! I was so lucky they didn't notice the knife on my belt. If I hadn't had those matches from the hollow handle I would have been in big trouble overnight. Speaking of wolves, have you heard about the Colorado wolf initiative?"

"No, what's that about?"

"Some people are trying to get a measure on the ballot that would mandate Colorado Parks and Wildlife Service to introduce wild wolves into the Colorado wilderness. Kind of like they did out in Yellowstone years ago. Maybe you could get involved with that."

"Cool, maybe we could get the team back together saving wolves and wild horses! It would be like old times out in Montana!"

"That would be amazing,"commented Caleb. "Perhaps it's all meant to be."

"Thank you for bringing me up here Caleb. I really appreciate you helping me out with this."

"It's no problem. You are like family to me and I would do anything for you."

Michelle replied, "Thanks Caleb, you feel like family to me too."

After a few seconds of silence Michelle said, "It's really getting cold, would you hand me that bottle? I need another sip to warm my bones! Maybe we should get in our sleeping bags to keep warm."

"Good idea. Hopefully we can wake up early and go over to the meadow to see the elk before they go back into the trees for the day. I hope they are bugling tomorrow. There's nothing like that sound early in the morning."

As the pair of wildlife activists huddled against the cold in the camper topper Michelle said "I love you Caleb."

"I love you too Michelle."

After a moment of silence Michelle added, "Good night Caleb."

"Good night to you too honey. Sweet dreams."

Caleb was awakened before first light by the bugling of a big bull elk. He glanced over at Michelle whose face and blond hair glowed softly by the light of the setting moon. She was still asleep, and to Caleb she looked positively angelic. He didn't want to disturb her, but really wanted to get out and stretch his legs. He quietly lowered the tailgate and stealthily slid to the ground. However by then she was already awake, and he heard her say "Don't shut the tailgate Caleb, I'm getting out too. Will you walk with me to the restrooms?"

"Let's just drive over there. When we're done we can head into town to fill our coffee thermos and get a snack for breakfast. By then it will be getting light and we can go see the elk, and maybe a moose over by Sheep Lake."

Just as they were walking into the station Caleb heard his phone chime. It was Angie asking, "How are you guys doing?"

"Great, we are getting coffee and then we are off to see the elk for a little bit. Later this morning we'll be returning home.

"Did Michelle get her applications and everything?"

"Yup, she's all set for now."

"That's good, I hope it all works out for her. I heard the governor has been getting a lot of calls about the footage we delivered from the Sand Wash. It sounds like he's going to try to do something."

"That's great Angie! I knew it would be worthwhile capturing that video."

"Okay, well I just wanted to see now your trip was going. I have a couple showings today so I need to get going."

"Okay, I'll let you know when we're on our way."

Michelle asked, "Was that Angie?"

"Yes, she says she hopes the applications work out for you. And she says it looks like the governor is on board to help out with saving the horses."

"That's sweet, and that's good news about the governor. I hope he can stop the September gather."

"Well Michelle, what do you think. Are you ready for a cruise through Moraine Park?"

"Let's go! Mostly I just want to get a good look at the river in the morning light. I have a feeling it's not going to be a whole lot different than the Lamar."

"You are probably right about that. Is that going to be your deciding factor on whether you want to transfer out?"

"No, I've already made up my mind to put in for the transfer. I just want to have a picture of it in my brain so I don't get scared and chicken out. The picture in my brain will remind me what I'm working toward!"

"That's sound thinking. I'm glad you are going to be moving to Colorado for sure. I've missed having you in my life!"

Chapter Fourteen

On a hot sunny August morning, Angie was the first to awake. Caleb, hearing the sound of coffee percolating was not far behind. He opened the sliding door to the deck and took a seat in the cool shade to wait for it to finish dripping. Angie walked out onto the deck as well, and sat down with the morning paper.

"Hey Caleb, check this out! I can't believe this, the feds are going ahead with the gather. Only they have pushed it back to September. They are still talking about removing 784 horses, but the governor is lobbying hard to reduce that number. They are going to allow observers this time though. Do you think we should go?"

"Oh I definitely think we should be there. Michelle will probably want to make the trip as well. Maybe we should go out a day or two ahead of time to get our usual camp site."

"Good idea," Angie responded. "We can bring the tent so there's room for all of us to sleep. I don't think the three of us would fit comfortably in your topper."

Caleb laughed and said, "Yeah, that might be a little cozy, especially after we haven't showered for a few days!"

"According to this article, the gather is going to start around the first of September and estimated to continue for about a week," Angie added.

"Are they going to be removing any of the sheep?"

"No, it doesn't say anything about the sheep."

"Seems to me if there isn't enough habitat, they should at least split the difference with sheep. After all it is called a horse management area, not a sheep management area."

"That's probably why they tried to sneak it in with their bogus emergency designation. The sneaky bastards somehow got that rule through, that if it's an emergency they can remove any animals they want with no public input."

Caleb answered, "We're lucky we are finding out about it at all. I wish the governor would send out the Colorado National Guard or something to stop them."

"Oh Caleb, that's not going to happen. You know what they say don't you?"

"What's that?"

"The pen is mightier than the sword. You know, you've gotten kind of lazy about writing since you have the book royalties from *Spirit of the Wolf* coming in. Remember back in Montana when you first moved to town and you wrote the park reports for the newspaper? We would sit for hours at the Tap discussing strategy for protecting wolves in the park."

"Yeah, I remember. I made a lot of trips down to the Lamar Valley to produce those reports. I guess I could run up to the newspaper office and see if they might be interested in publishing an article."

"Maybe you could get a regular column again. You need something to do."

"But this horse thing will be all over with in a couple of weeks."

"True, but at least you will have made some contacts at the paper. Plus there's the new wolf project. You are in favor of having Colorado restore wolves aren't you?"

"I'm not so sure. Colorado is a lot more densely populated, and what's to stop the pack from migrating to Wyoming where they will surely be shot?"

"It doesn't matter. The Denver people are probably going to vote for them anyway, and you could be the first to begin reporting on the subject. Besides, the predator animals need someone like you advocating for them."

"That's a good point. I guess I could take Michelle today and run up to the paper to see what they say."

"Oh no," laughed Angie. "You are on your own today. Michelle and I are going to do girl stuff. We are going up to the mall to do some shopping."

Caleb chuckled and said, "Yeah, I guess I have kind of monopolized her time since she arrived. You girls go have fun. I'll write a little sample article to take along as an example of my writing skills and the subjects I'm proposing to cover."

Michelle soon walked out onto the deck with a steaming cup of coffee, and took a seat facing Angie and Caleb.

"Coffee is done," she remarked.

"Thats sounds good," commented Caleb. "Would you like a cup Angie?"

"Sure, cream and sugar if you don't mind!"

Angie and Michelle were talking when he returned and Angie said, "I was telling Michelle about the horse round up next month. She says she wants to go with us."
"Good, the more eyes the better. You realize of course, next month is actually only a few days away."

Angie quipped, "Well, we'd better start packing then! That is of course after we go shopping today for new stuff. We girls need to look good for your camera. I assume you will be shooting video of the action again."

Caleb mused, "I hope they don't try to prevent reporting, and what about all your house showings next month?"

"No problem. I don't have any for a few days anyway, and then I'll just re-schedule any I do have into the next few weeks."

Caleb asked Michelle, "Are you free for a couple of weeks?"

"I am, my new job with the state park service doesn't start until the middle of September."

"Well if you want, you guys could stop at RSI for supplies later this morning. Maybe I could meet you for lunch at the food court in the mall."

Angie replied, "That sound like a good plan. We could also pick up some of those ready to eat meals."

"Get a few little propane bottles for the camp stove too," Caleb added.

They finished their coffee and went their separate ways. Angie and Michelle were off to the mall and Caleb sat down at his computer to bang out a few words on the keyboard.

As they walked through the front door at RSI, Michelle asked "How long are we going to be camping out?"

"I think we'd better plan for at least a week. Of course we can always run into Craig if we need supplies, but it will be less expensive to get as much as we can ahead of time. But if necessary, it's only about a forty minute drive one way from the Sand Wash."

"What are we going to eat out there?" Michelle asked.

"Well, we can get some stuff at the grocery store for the cooler, but we'll pick up a bunch of those dried meals here in case there's trouble. We'll also need some portable wipes and sunscreen. A new first aid kit might be a good idea too."

It was time for lunch by the time they had located and purchased all their supplies, and Angie asked "Does the food court sound okay to you, or do you have something else in mind?"

"No, the food court is perfect."

They made the drive down to the mall and just as they sat down to eat, Angie's phone rang.

"Hey Angie, it's Caleb. I got my sample article done and I'm on my way to the newspaper office. Have you guys already eaten?"

"We just sat down at the food court if you want to come on up."

"Sure, I'm just passing C470 now."

Caleb was soon seated at the table with Angie and Michelle, and he asked "Did you get a chance to stop by the sporting goods store?"

"Yup, we got the fuel and the meals. We picked up some clothes for the cold nights too, but we still need some groceries from the store."

Caleb asked, "Do you think we should leave this afternoon?"

Angie answered, "Maybe so, I imagine the good camp sites are gong to be filling up fast with activists and support crew."

"All right then, I'll see you at home after my pitch to the newspaper. You guys pick up some groceries and ice for the cooler, and I'll stop in Franktown to fill up the truck with gas and check the oil. I'll meet you at home right after that. Would you round up the tent and sleeping gear?"

"No problem, we'll have everything ready to go by the time you get here."

The rest of the afternoon was a blur, and soon the trio of wildlife crusaders were loaded up and on the road to the Sand Wash Basin.

Caleb commented, "I don't think the traffic should be bad on C470 yet. What do you say we swing around the west side to I70, and on over the mountains through the tunnel."

"That sounds like a good plan," responded Angie.

Michelle asked, "Where's the turnoff to the Sand Wash?"

Caleb answered, "We can hop on 9 at Silverthorne, and go north from there up to Steamboat. If it gets too late, we can get a room in town."

Michelle answered, "Works for me."

Once on the road, the three stared out the window and admired the scenery in silence. Silverthorne came and went, and it was already late afternoon by the time Steamboat Springs came into view.

Caleb said, "It's still early enough to do some more driving, and I'm pretty sure we could make the Sand Wash by dark. Should we get a room or press on?"

Angie answered, "If we stop for the night, we can all get in one more shower and still be at the Sand Wash by ten in the morning. Then we will also be able to pitch the tent in the light."

"I can't afford to get a room by myself," lamented Michelle.

"Don't worry honey," replied Angie. "We'll all fit in one room somehow."

They spotted a nice place right on the main drag in Steamboat, and went inside to see if a room was available.

They were greeted by the receptionist who cheerfully said, "Hello, may I help you this evening?"

"We would like a room with two queens."

"I'm sorry, but we have a race going on in town this weekend and most of our rooms are filled. I can get you in a room with one king if that's okay."

The three appeared startled by the idea, but then Angie commented "Well you know, that king sized bed is probably bigger than the tent we are all going to be sleeping in at the Sand Wash."

"Good point," added Caleb.

Michelle sealed the deal when she said, "Angie can sleep in the middle. It won't be any big deal."

Caleb responded, "Okay, we'll take it then."

He got out his credit card and signed for the room while Angie and Michelle went out to the truck to get their night bags.

Once settled, Caleb asked "Should we go out and get a beer or something?"

"Looks like they have a nice lounge right in the hotel. Should we go check it out?" Angie asked.

"Sounds good to me," responded Michelle.

After a few drinks to unwind, the trio decided to go to bed early.

Caleb awoke in the morning to the sound of the shower running. Michelle was seated at the little table sipping complimentary coffee, and Caleb arose to join her.
"Did you sleep well last night?" Caleb asked.

"I must have been really tired! I was asleep the second my head hit the pillow."
"Yeah, me too."

"I forgot to ask. How did your pitch go at the newspaper office?"

"Pretty well, they want me to bring in the report from this week. And they also want me to bring in s sample wolf article."

"That's awesome Caleb! Maybe the wolves will move into the park and we'll get to see them together sometime!"

Caleb answered, " That would be amazing wouldn't it? I'm actually starting to hope the ballot initiative passes."

After a few seconds of silence Caleb asked, "Have you showered yet?"

"Yes, I was the first to wake up, and I think I woke up Angie."

"I'm sure she didn't mind, we need to get an early start anyway. Maybe you and Angie can fill up the thermos in the lobby and pack up the truck while I get my shower. We should be in Craig in about an hour, and then it's only another thirty or forty minutes to the horse range."

"No problem."

They were soon on the road and in no time they were driving through the little town of Craig, less than an hour from the Sand Wash Basin. Traffic was still light, which bode well for getting a good campsite.

As they cruised through town Michelle commented, "I'm hungry, do you think we could stop somewhere for breakfast?"

"It's okay with me, how about you Angie?"

"Yeah, I'm a bit hungry myself. Our little cafe we usually stop at serves breakfast doesn't it?"

"I believe it does. I'm pretty sure I've had breakfast there before."

Caleb drove a few more blocks to the cafe and Angie commented, "There it is, and it looks like they are open for breakfast."

"Great, is this place okay with you Michelle?"

"Looks fine to me. Anyway I don't really care, I'm ready to eat!"

The three of them were met by the hostess who said, " Hi I'm Sandy, I'll be your server this morning. Three for breakfast?"

Angie answered, "Yes three of us for breakfast this morning."

"Can I bring you something to drink?"

Caleb answered, "Coffee for me, black will be fine."

Angie wanted coffee and Michelle was in the mood for orange juice. Sandy was soon back at the table with two cups of java with fresh cream and sugar on the side, and one glass of orange juice for Michelle.

She asked, "Are you all in town for the roundup?"

"Yes, we are staying all week to see the whole thing."

"Oh boy," replied Sandy.

"What?" Caleb asked.

"Well it turns out the government lied. They let on like people were going to get to observe the entire roundup, but they secretly started last week with no observers. They only ever intended on allowing wildlife advocates one day to watch, the last day."

Angie responded angrily, "How do they think they can get away with this?"

Caleb replied, "Arrogant bastards, they know they have the support of the ranchers and sheepherders, and they know damn well nobody has the clout to stop them. Heck, they don't even care what the governor thinks."

Michelle asked Sandy, "Do you think we still have time to see it?"

Sandy answered, "I think so. From what I've been hearing, they don't really care if they overheat the horses. They've been running them in the afternoons and loading them up at the end of the day, so you should still have plenty of time."

Caleb responded, "Okay then, I guess we'll just eat a quick breakfast and go. We can still camp tonight if it gets too late to drive back."

They quickly finished their food, paid their bill and hopped into the truck. Caleb turned onto the blacktop and soon they were speeding westward on Highway 40, hoping they hadn't completely missed the roundup. Soon Maybelle was in the rear view mirror, and the trio was on the home stretch to the Sand Wash. As they entered the refuge Angie exclaimed, "Caleb, there's our spot, and it looks like no one has claimed it."

"Hey look," observed Michelle. "There's a nice flat spot with a great 360 degree view of the entire area!"

Angie replied, "Yup, that's our regular site!"

Caleb added, "Let's get the tent set up, and then we can drive around and see what's going on. I'll put the pad down if you guys want to bring over the tent and stakes."

"Should we put the sleeping bags inside now or later?" Angie asked.

Caleb answered, "Well maybe we should at least open up the valves on the sleeping pads to let them inflate while we are out driving around."

"Good idea," Angie replied.

Once they were back in the truck Angie asked, "Should we just go straight in on Wildlife Loop like we usually do?"

"I think so, let's go to the high spot and see if we can see anything."

As they climbed the hill, a huge dust cloud to the west indicated that the roundup was already in progress.

Caleb said, "Let's cut through on 80 to the west side and take a look."

"Sounds good," said Angie. "Can somebody find the binoculars?"

"Michelle, I think they are under the seat. Can you dig them out?"

"I found them, here you go Angie."

Angie took the powerful glass and said, "I can see them now. There are two choppers chasing a big group in front of them. Let's get over there!"

Caleb stepped on the accelerator and said, "Hang on, it's going to get bumpy!"

Finally the mustangs were just ahead, and Caleb slowed to a stop.

The helicopters weren't flying quite as low on this day, and the ATVs weren't driving as fast as they had in the past.

Caleb commented, "I think the feds are taking it easy today, since they know they have a big crowd watching. Angie, can you see any fallen horses?"

"No, they aren't running very hard today. Why couldn't they do it like this all the time?"

Michelle answered, "You know, I think the ranchers actually hate wildlife. I think the more they hurt them, the happier they are."

"That was my experience in Montana. Not only that, they hate everyone who is involved with trying to protect wild animals," added Caleb.

Angie continued watching through the binoculars and suddenly exclaimed, "Oh no, one of the little foals just got separated from the herd. He will die out here on his own without his mother. The ATV riders don't even seem to care."

Michelle, who was watching through the lens of her little camera said excitedly, "What's that, what's going on? A big horse that already escaped the herd has turned around and gone after the foal."

Angie added, "It looks like a big stallion. He was free but he's herding the little foal back toward the gather."

Caleb asked, "Is he going to sacrifice his own freedom to save the foal?"

"I don't know," said Angie. "But it sure looks like it!"

"I didn't know a stallion had that kind of devotion to the little ones," commented Michelle.

"It's really quite astonishing," added Caleb.

Angie said, "Let's go up there and look at the pen."

"Okay, I'll pull on up. I'm dreading what we are going to see though."

"I know, but we have to get pictures of it for your story."

Michelle said, "Look, there's a bunch of cars and a crowd of people. Maybe that's where they are keeping the captured animals."

"Okay, I'll pull in and we can get out."

As the trio walked toward the holding pen, a big commotion broke out. Caleb noticed a bunch of people pointing and said, "Look, they are all pointing at something."

Michelle said, "They are, and it looks like one of the stallions is trying to jump out of the pen."

Angie exclaimed, "Isn't that Stormy's son? That's Swift Thunder isn't it?"

Caleb answered, "It sure looks like him. He would be about that age right now too."

Michelle who was watching the young stallion intently, exclaimed excitedly "Look, he's getting ready to jump! He's going to do it!"

Soon the powerful mustang was soaring over the fence and galloping to freedom. No one made any effort to stop him, and he was over the ridge and out of sight in seconds. Caleb tried desperately to capture an image of the fleeing animal, but could not get a good focus lock. They would never know for sure if it was Swift Thunder that had escaped his human tormentors.

Angie finally broke the silence saying, "I don't think I can bear to watch anymore. Do you have all the pictures you need Caleb?"

"I think so. There isn't much of a story to tell here, other than the government lied and did whatever the hell they wanted. There's nothing new about that. It's getting late anyway, maybe we should just go light a campfire and enjoy the rest of our day."

"Sounds good to me," replied Michelle.

"Okay then, let's go," said Angie.

The three wildlife lovers were soon back in the truck, and on the way to their campsite. Caleb reached under his seat and pulled out a bottle of brandy and said, "Anybody want to wash down the dust with a little fire water?"

Angie replied, "Give me that," and took a long swig from the bottle.

A few minutes later, they were back at the campsite and Caleb was retrieving a bundle of wood from the camper topper. As he lit the fire, Angie said "Here's the bottle if anyone needs a drink. Does anyone want a marshmallow to toast?"

Michelle laughed and said, "I'll have some of both!"

Soon Caleb had a beautiful fire crackling before them, and they passed the brandy around trying to numb the pain of what they had witnessed earlier in the day. For a long time, the three of them stared in silence as the fire flickered brightly before them. Michelle found a stick and was toasting a marshmallow over the flames, while Caleb and Angie watched her sugary treat puff up and begin to glow.

Michelle asked, "Do you think that was really Thunder that escaped?"

Angie replied, "I hope it was him. I hope there's at least one stallion left on the range to continue Winter Storm's legacy."

After a few seconds Caleb said, "So do you think all we have done all summer was for nothing?"

"I don't know," commented Angie. "At least the public will know how they are treating these animals now."

"True," responded Michelle. "But does it even matter? The government doesn't seem to care what anyone thinks."

"No they don't, but maybe someone with power will force change."

Angie added, "I heard that since the governor couldn't stop the feds outright, the state is considering purchasing sanctuary land for the horses."

Michelle responded, "But isn't that what the Sand Wash is supposed to be?"

"Yes, but this new idea is for the state to own the land outright. The feds would have no jurisdiction in determining how horses are managed on it."

"That's a brilliant idea," said Caleb. "Maybe I'll tailor my story to promote the idea. I wonder if we can direct any of the funds we raised this summer to purchasing land for a new mustang sanctuary?"

Angie answered, "I don't think the funds have been dispersed yet. I'll talk to my agency when we get back."

"I'll talk to the running club and see if they will transfer the funds we raised toward land for a new sanctuary."

After a few minutes of silence Michelle asked Caleb, "Have you heard any more about the Colorado wolf initiative?"

"No I haven't, but I know they are still gathering signatures to try to get a measure on the ballot. I guess I'll get involved with that when we return. I wonder if it would be possible to use the same methods for gathering signatures that we used for raising money for the wild horses? Perhaps we could arrange some kind of signature signing event to get a bunch of support all at once. Angie, maybe your modeling agency could put on some kind of show with faux fur or something."

"I'll ask them," replied Angie.

The sun slowly slipped below the horizon and stars began to twinkle in the clear western sky. Darkness descended upon the land like the sadness of a death in the family, and the lively conversation from earlier in the evening succumbed to the weight of the devastating loss of such a large part of the herd.

After a long silence Caleb looked around the campfire at his companions. Michelle and Angie had both fallen asleep in their camp chairs. The fire sputtered weakly, and he shuddered a bit as the inevitable chill of autumn descended upon them. He wondered how many horses were feeling cold and afraid on this night, with so many of their mates and offspring missing.

Even though his own companions were asleep, Caleb wasn't quite prepared to let go of the moment. He leaned over to slip the bottle of brandy from beneath Angie's arm, and pulled it in close his own body. Mesmerized by the dying glow of the camp fire, he reflected upon the events of the past few months. He shivered and took another big swig of brandy as he watched the last of the embers grow cold, along with the final vestiges of summer.

EPILOGUE

Ultimately, the Colorado governor's requests to spare the Sand Wash herd went unheeded by the Bureau of Land Management. According to this **article provided by the "In Defense of Animals"** organization, entitled **Sand Wash Basin Wild Horses Brutally Captured Despite Protests**, 683 of the 896 majestic wild horses were removed from the Sand Wash Basin. Due to Governor Polis' efforts to stop the gather only 100 horses were spared, just a few shy of the intended 783 animals slated to be removed.

According to the above mentioned article, "Young foals were being left behind, alone on the range, because they could not keep up with the fast pace over rough ground and sagebrush for an hour or more, sometimes over 15 miles because the panicked horses veer off course many times trying to escape the terrifying mechanical beast. Two times bachelor stallions sacrificed their own freedom to kindly escort lost foals to the trap site to try to reunite them with their mothers. Yet, wild horse haters still try to deny the obvious fact that these amazing animals have strong family and herd bonds."

In another article entitled, **Wild Horse and Burros Herds Decimated Using Drought as an Excuse** by the same organization, the BLM is allowed to remove wild horses from Horse Management Areas without public input using the "emergency" designation. Drought was the excuse for decimating the Sand Wash Basin herd, although it is important to note that no sheep were removed from the area designated for horses. Only wild animals were removed. "Using this outrageous and deceitful method, the BLM is systematically replacing wild animals belonging to the public with privately owned livestock on publicly owned land."

However, Governor Polis' efforts resulted in an important step in the right direction. "As a result of devastating 2021 gather, the Colorado General Assembly passed unprecedented and groundbreaking legislation known as the Colorado Wild Horse Project that was signed into law by Colorado Gov. Jared Polis during a special ceremony on May 20, 2023." You can read about the event in an article by "In Defense of Animals" entitled, **Victory: Historic New Law Passes to Protect Wild Horses in Colorado!**

The new **Wild Horse Sanctuary** has it's **own website,** where readers can find out about the animals, make donations, purchase additional land, and schedule tours for themselves, their friends and possible donors.

According to the website, "The Wild Horse Refuge is a private sanctuary that was created entirely for rescued Wild Mustangs that were taken from BLM Herd Management Areas (HMA) located within Colorado. The Wild Horses living on this special property are now protected and have regained the freedom and independence they had prior to government interference."

Much more is required before horse advocates are satisfied with the treatment of this valuable and iconic species. Groups such as **Wildlife Protection Management** and **Hanaeleh** are working hard to discover new ways to manage herds. Please consider contributing to these organizations.

Also please "Contact Your Representatives: Write, call and email your Congressmen and women WEEKLY. Urge them to stop the government's mismanagement of wild horses and burros. Let them know that you, a taxpayer and horse advocate, will not sit by and watch our Mustangs and burros be treated inhumanely. Take 15 minutes tonight and write to express your guarded outrage (no angry, hateful comments please – they fall on deaf ears)."

What does the author have planned for the main characters from this second installment in his series of wildlife advocacy books? Plans for a third sequel are in their infancy. The third in the series will include the new Colorado wolf reintroduction program. As of this writing, several wolves have been released into western Colorado and are currently struggling to survive.

Our one breeding pair has gotten into trouble with ranchers over the 2024 winter by killing a few sheep and cattle, but Colorado Parks and Wildlife denied any action against them until their pups were old enough to relocate. In the meantime, the new family was officially named the Copper Creek Pack, to the joy of many wolf advocates all around the state. However as of this writing, the family has been live trapped, and unfortunately the male was found in poor condition from a serious leg injury. Despite medical treatment he later succumbed to his injuries and infection, and the future of the pack is uncertain.

The Republicans lost control of the presidency in the 2020 election and in a final act of treachery against the wolves, the Department of Interior removed them from protection by the Endangered Species Act. As mentioned in the book, this wasn't entirely unexpected, but what was a surprise was the new Democrat administration going to court to defend the new rule. A federal judge later ruled that the decision was unwarranted, and returned wolves in most of the country to the endangered list. However a loophole was concocted by lawyers for the ranchers to keep gray wolves of the northern Rockies off the list, so their future is uncertain as well.

Also as one might imagine, not everyone is happy about the prospect of wild wolves on the land. Without the efforts of people like our main characters and wildlife advocacy organizations, Colorado's wolves will surely face a treacherous future. Hunters in surrounding states eagerly lie in wait for our animals to stray outside the Colorado border where they can be legally shot and killed. Colorado hunters are also eagerly searching for any excuse to kill every wolf they see. Little has changed since wolves were nearly driven to extinction in the 19th century.

As a result of livestock depredation over the winter, some of Colorado's ranchers are already demanding the right to employ lethal methods to protect their livestock. Non-lethal methods with a track record of success are meeting resistance from individuals unwilling to accept a new way of life.

The Colorado wolf reintroduction program is still in it's infancy. Please continue to follow the progress as the new animals donated by Oregon begin to expand their territory and thrive. Also urge your congressmen and women to provide habitat free of cattle for them to live on without harassment by ranchers and hunters.

Also please continue to support and follow the author through his website and blog, as he works to keep the public informed about the latest efforts to preserve our heritage of wild animals roaming free in America.

ACKNOWLEDGMENTS

A very special thank you to **J. Edward De Steiguer** for his book "**Wild Horses of the West**" and for his tireless dedication and meticulous attention to detail that provided valuable insight into the life and politics of wild horses in America.

Thank you to the **In Defense of Animals** oversight of the Sand Wash Herd during these difficult times, and for their detailed reporting of the herd round up efforts by the federal government.

Also many thanks to my friend Linda Stewart and **Wildlife Protection Management** for her work with modern herd management techniques.

Also special thanks to the organization **Hanaeleh** for their work in humane treatment of wildlife, and members of the two Facebook groups *Wild Horses of Sand Wash Basin Group* and *Sand Wash Basin Wild Horses* for their assistance in providing the names of some of some of the mustangs.

ABOUT THE AUTHOR

Mr. Krull is a widely published sports and wildlife photographer and author specializing in imagery of wildlife captured in the rugged Rocky Mountains of Colorado.

He also publishes a blog that concentrates on wildlife photography and the humane treatment of our wild birds and animals.

More of his work can be found on his official website at:

www.swkrullimaging.com

Steven W. Krull

BOOKS BY THIS AUTHOR

Spirit of the Wolf - Historical fiction novel about the main character and his fashion model girlfriend who work to save the wolves of Yellowstone National Park

Photographer's Guide to Rocky Mountain National Park - How to plan and execute a trip to Rocky Mountain National Park. Learn where and how to capture the iconic landscapes, weather and wildlife in the Crown Jewell of Colorado parks. Learn how to use the timed entry system, where to find lodging and how to make the most of your visit.

Winter Storm Warning: How to photograph the Rocky Mountain winter. Learn how to capture dramatic images of winter weather and wildlife in the beautiful frozen landscape of the Rocky Mountain Winter.

Wildlife Photography in the Colorado Rockies: Explore the great diversity of wildlife found in the Colorado Rocky Mountains. Learn where to find and how to photograph the birds and animals from the diminutive song sparrow to the mighty black bear.

Two Decades of Digital Photography: Twenty years of the author's favorite pictures and how they were made as camera technology has progressed through the years

Seasons of the Raptor: Four seasons of photography with Colorado's most beautiful raptors

Tunnel Quest - Learn how and where to get the best railway images along the Colorado front range rail system. Discover new tunnels and track access points to capture the most dramatic train images in the beautiful Rocky Mountains of Colorado..

www.ingramcontent.com/pod-product-compliance
Lightning Source LLC
Chambersburg PA
CBHW051131020726
47501CB00005B/1461